RIGHTS OF POWER

RIGHTS OF POWER

Michael Alan Claybourne

**LOCAL
AUTHOR**

To order additional copies of this book, contact:
Xlibris Corporation
1-888-795-4274
www.Xlibris.com
Orders@Xlibris.com
113944

DEDICATION:

To my parents and family, who put up with all the moods, flights of fancy and all of my second guessing. To S & V for reminding me it's possible just to have fun. Finally, to my wonderful teachers, Mrs. H, Mrs. T and Ms. N, who saw my potential and told me to reach it. Thank you for touching so many lives.

I am so glad to have all you amazing people in my life!

CHAPTER 1

Sheriff Fineas Tully shifted his car into park and sat with the engine idling, his hands still gripping the steering wheel. He looked down at the green digital clock display.

It was 12:34 AM; way too late for him to be out doing this kind of stuff.

He should have been home in bed next to Caroline, his wife of thirty three years. Instead he was parked on the shoulder of county Route 3 just past mile marker eight to deal with a pair of hooligans.

Ahead of him on the opposite shoulder sat his deputy, Jake Barry's cruiser, lights cycling red and blue, coloring the night.

Bordering the road were pines, currently just masses of gray and black shadows.

There was no moon tonight and even if there had been its glow would not have penetrated the evergreen's tightly woven boughs.

Tully sighed and shut off the engine, also killing the air conditioning, which, despite the hour, was still a requirement. He released his seatbelt and opened his door.

Immediately the heavy night air washed over him.

He climbed out of the Ford's sheltering confines and walked toward Barry's car.

His deputy wasn't alone.

Beyond the green and blue cruiser there was an idling ambulance and State Police patrol vehicle.

Three flares glowed on the blacktop but as he scanned the road ahead he didn't see much in the way of damage. Just then his foot brushed something in the road.

He pulled out a pocket sized LED flashlight and shone it at his feet.

He saw bits of red taillight.

He continued on, paying more attention to where he was stepping.

"Sheriff," Barry called from the shoulder making his way toward Tully. "Sorry about calling you out so late, but I figured…" Tully nodded.

"You did the right thing." He said.

Past Berry he saw the two cars involved, squinting into the dark he made out the second car, the lime green paint of Jeb Jefferson's Plymouth GTX was nearly glow-in-the-dark. The first car was instantly recognizable. It was the infernal Mercedes.

"Where is he?" Tully asked wearily.

"With the paramedic." Tully could only see one side of the two cars but neither showed any damage.

Apparently the thought was plain to see because Jake added.

"Just some busted lights and a couple scrapes, it was the beating afterwards."

"How bad?"

"He's not dead." Jake replied and sounded somewhat disappointed over that fact.

Tully withheld comment. He didn't know what to think, just made his way toward the ambulance, past the two cars.

Tully found Wesley Cobin in the back of the ambulance. The EMT, Rebecca Barnes, was still looking the kid over, shining a light in his eyes.

It wasn't as bad as Tully had expected.

A split lip, a cut along his cheek; it looked like his chin had been skinned along the blacktop. One eye was hidden behind a wrapped ice pack, covering most of the damage to the left side of his face.

"Evening Sheriff," Cobin said, trying not to move his lips. "You didn't need to come all the way out here yourself. I don't think Barry would mind dragging me to lockup." Tully didn't respond. He never knew how to deal with an un-convicted murderer. Especially one with which he had such history.

"What are you doing Cobin?" He asked and thought he saw the same flinch as always, but he refused to call him Wesley, he'd be Cobin till the day he died. If he kept up this behavior that day wouldn't be long in arriving. That thought didn't bring Tully the peace he thought it should. At least then this rollercoaster would be over.

"Well, I can't speak for the other guys but I was out street racing."

"That right?" Tully asked.

"Yep." Cobin tried turning to look at Tully which was annoying Rebecca. She firmly repositioned his chin with a glare.

"Sir, would you please look straight ahead." She said. Back when they'd been in school together she'd just called him Wes. More lost familiarity.

"I'm alright." Cobin said trying to brush Rebecca away. She didn't back down.

"Actually Becky, if we could have two minutes?" Tully suggested, summoning up his best appeasing smile.

Rebecca looked annoyed but climbed down from the ambulance.

"There's not much I can do anyway. He might have a cracked rib but I think at least the swelling around his eye shouldn't be too bad."

"Thank you." Tully said and fixed his gaze on Cobin. "So, you're admitting to a misdemeanor?"

"Am I? Huh." Playing dumb to the law didn't suit the former deputy.

"You know how fast you were going?" Tully asked, more out of obligation than interest.

"Not exactly, 140 for sure, probably more."

"You know what would happen at those speeds if a deer should cross the road."

"Considering I was there after Muldoon hit that buck at 90, yeah, I have a pretty good idea." Tully looked hard at Cobin, trying to read him, just like always.

Apparently thinking he was waiting for an answer Cobin added. "I'd die."

The words seemed to echo through the silence that followed as both men stared at one another. Tully made his face impassive, knowing the boy was looking for some sign to see if Tully wished he was dead.

"So, Sheriff, are you going to arrest me?" He asked, almost sounding hopeful.

The two men stared at each other for a moment but both remained inscrutable to the other.

Tully could no longer tell if it was a veneer of nonchalance or a tangible death wish on Cobin's part.

"You know the answer to that." Tully said eventually, sounding forlorn. Why had things worked out like this? Why did Cobin insist on putting him in this position?

"You want to talk about what happened here?" Tully asked, duty bound.

"Not really, little bit of a scrape I guess, I must have been wandering in my lane."

"It's a one lane road." Tully pointed out.

3

"Huh, must have been in the wrong lane then. Pulled over, traded insurance, called the cops I guess."

"And your face?"

"Same one I was born with."

Tully sighed.

"I take it you're not pressing charges?"

"We've been through that before," Cobin said and slid up the corner of his shirt, exposing a jagged scar across his stomach. "It's not the department's prerogative to help out the scum of this world." Cobin said. The lack of emotion in his voice had its own bite.

"A crime is a crime, regardless of the victim."

Cobin smiled hauntingly then. "And you've stuck by that." He sounded grateful.

"It's my job." Tully answered flatly. He stood for a moment, hands on hips. "Alright, you know the drill." Cobin stood up and made his way to the back of the ambulance, then climbed out the open doors.

Tully turned to Rebecca.

She shrugged, looking faintly disgusted. They'd been through this routine before.

Thus released into his custody, Tully led the man back across the scene. "Do you need anything out of the car?" He asked.

"No." Cobin answered flatly. His presence had been noticed; across the road two men shouted something, presumably uncomplimentary. Both Tully and Cobin ignored the jeering Jefferson brothers as they walked back to Tully's car and out of sight of the onlookers.

Tully paused at the passenger door to trip the rear door bypass. Unlocked, he walked to the rear door and pulled up on the handle. He looked back at Cobin watching him, standing in the light from the cruiser behind him he was just a silhouetted, but Tully imagined his blue eyes, sad and forlorn and hauntingly familiar.

Tully tightened his grip on the handle and slammed shut the rear door.

"Get up front." He said and made his way to the driver's side.

They climbed into the car and pulled on their belts.

Tully started the engine. Cool air blasted out of the vents.

The air came as a surprise. Tully realized he hadn't felt the heat and humidity outside, he was numb from the inside.

Neither man spoke as he put the car into gear and swung around on the road, heading back the way he had come.

He wasn't going to be locking Cobin up, not tonight at least. He couldn't.

They had a new enough station in town but all new detainees went into a general holding area and Cobin couldn't go into the general population, especially not if the Jefferson's ended up there, which they would make sure that they did. Even putting him in his own cell possessed its own dangers. Besides, there was no point to locking Cobin up, not for these petty crimes and scuffs that he got himself involved in.

Memories of the last time Cobin had been in the general population floated in the air in front of Tully along with the tang of blood. He might have thought that he didn't care if Cobin died, but he wasn't going to be responsible for it, not that way.

He glanced over to his passenger, who was sitting quietly staring out the side window.

Tully felt a mix of emotions, none of which he thought were healthy.

"New car?" Cobin asked suddenly. The scent of fresh plastic still clung about the interior.

Tully grunted in response, and then said yes.

He'd rather pretend Cobin didn't know him well enough to interpret his nonverbal responses. Even as he did it he felt a prick of guilt at denying what had been.

He tightened his grip on the wheel, annoyed that he should feel guilty when it was all Cobin's fault.

Silence lapsed again. Cobin stared out the window at the night.

"How's Loren..?" Cobin asked, then, catching himself added quickly. "I'm sorry."

Tully again wondered if the slips were intentional or legitimate missteps. He tried to decide if answering the unasked question would assuage his conscience, not that he had anything to feel bad over. Would it give Cobin some sense of control? Would it make Tully flinch at the thought of what had almost been?

"She's fine." He said curtly. It wasn't even gossip.

"I heard about..." Tully took his eyes off the road so he could turn and glare at Cobin, barely illuminated in the green wash from the instrument panel. He'd gotten the wrong idea, answering the unasked was not a license for free speech.

"I hope they're happy." Cobin risked in response and he sounded entirely genuine. But then why wouldn't he be? Cobin wasn't a psychopath, even if that gene flowed in his veins.

Gray faces, victims, flashed in Tully's mind.

The sins of the father.

So many victims in the family tragedy.

He turned away, back to the road and squinted into the night.

Silence hung heavy the rest of the ride to the house.

Tully slowed the car and turned off the county road.

As the car drifted between the brick pilasters Tully wondered if it was a testament to the town's self-control they hadn't burned this one down too.

The Cobin's had been the kind of money that had three residences in one sleepy town, the beach house, an apartment and this, the original family manor. The latter inherited, the rest bought with the cash from Wesley's father, Herod Cobin's software conglomerate, once the biggest on the east coast and an easy rival to many Silicon Valley firms. Since the double scandals the company had taken a hit but most reports still said that the younger orphaned Cobin would never have to work a day in his life. A good thing since he sure wasn't getting his accrued pension.

They had reached the end of the driveway and Tully whipped the Ford around the circular turn around, his headlights sweeping across the dark Victorian. Even in this gloomy setting the house refused to take on a haunting aspect. Decidedly odd, given the usual Gothic chill of grand old Victorian mansions. A testament to its architect he decided.

Tully brought the car to a stop at the porch steps and shifted into park. His hand hesitated over the key. Should he check the house?

Cobin opened his door and started to get out.

"Cobin," Tully said, looking over at Cobin, now illuminated by the overhead dome light. "Why don't you move away?" He asked softly. Then added more decisively, "Why do you stick around here where no one wants you?" He was careful with his emphasis to convey that he was included among those who wanted him gone.

Cobin sat for a moment, not out of contemplation but out of something else Tully couldn't quite place. He began to wonder if Cobin would give him an answer.

"Everyone seems to forget this is my hometown too." He said simply and got out, closing the door behind him. The cabin light dimmed and Tully was left to contemplate that in the dark. He found that he didn't know how to take it.

CHAPTER 2

Dawn came early for Tully. He was a man who liked to be in bed by 10 o' clock. He hadn't ended up there until after 1:30. It came with the job but was a blessedly irregular occurrence.

The annoying end result was that Tully was late as he pulled into the department parking lot. The source of his annoyance was parked opposite his assigned space in the hurricane fenced impound lot.

After he parked in his space he glared at the metallic black Mercedes. It looked sinister and brooding with aggressive flared wheel arches and double power bulges in the hood. It also represented more than his income for the year.

He shut off the engine and climbed out of the Ford, shutting the door harder than he had resolved to. It was a new issue; he'd had it less than a month, one of the last Crown Victoria's, purchased and mothballed until it could be used.

As such this one was dripping with advanced features like a remote key fob. He thought sarcastically and pressed the lock button on the key chain. Not that anyone in town was likely to steal the unmarked, yet obviously police issue, car.

Tully turned and walked towards the single story office complex, of which the department occupied most of the space.

He turned left at the small paved courtyard and pushed through the front door in the side of the building.

Marge Ulysses was behind her desk in the small reception area looking just as chipper as ever.

"Good morning sir, and a lovely morning it is, don't you think?" Tully found himself smiling despite his mood.

Marge's attitude was contagious.

"I think it just could be Marge. Anything new?"

"Nope, nice and quiet on the home front, sir, just Mr. Lewis." Tully sighed. Lewis, the local for whom the justice system was a revolving door, or, more accurately, for whom lockup was a B&B.

"He have his coffee yet?"

"Not yet, still sleepin'."

"Of course, why get up when everyone else has to. Well, make sure he gets his coffee so that he can sober up and get on his way."

"Leave his bed made up shall I?"

"Very good Marge, thank you." Tully started for his office, then doubled back.

"If Cobin calls about his car tell him he's free to take it but that he's not getting his license back."

Marge sighed. "He get into trouble again? Well, driving privileges revoked, that got his attention before."

"Yeah, when he was sixteen." Tully muttered.

"Maybe I should make him some cookies or something?"

Tully shook his head. "You say Lewis was the only one here, what about the Jefferson kids?"

Surprisingly Marge frowned, "Nope, James picked them up this morning. He let them stay the night I guess."

Tully checked his watch, making sure it wasn't later than he'd realized.

"He was here early."

"The man doesn't need sleep, he's a vampire." Marge said straight faced and meant it.

Tully shook his head and found himself smiling again.

He wondered how James Jefferson, viewed by the town as the only decent Jefferson boy, could get such a reaction from Marge, when the town pariah, Wesley Cobin, remained in her good cookie making graces.

Tully pondered Marge's reasoning while he waited for his computer to boot up and the fluttering Windows logo to disappear. He thought about earlier that morning up at the Cobin manor and the last thing Cobin had said to him.

He slapped the arm of his chair when he consciously caught himself.

He'd gone a full month without seriously thinking about Cobin and now he knew what process would take shape all over. He'd been through it enough in the past three years.

Around town the fervor had died down. Cobin had outlasted the mob mentality and now he was just a local black sheep. He'd get in bar brawls while stone cold sober and Tully didn't know how many windows and tires he'd replaced on all of his cars and he always accepted it, never pressing charges or encouraging any investigation. Like it was his penance. But last night…

Cobin had never denied that he was guilty, nor was he a sociopath, so how could he have essentially said he still had a right to this town? His right to life was questionable, unrestricted freedom was out of the question.

Sure, Cobin had paid on several levels. There was his army of lawyers which had to have cost him every penny he'd ever personally made for himself. Money well spent as they had swatted the D.A.'s case like an annoying insect. There was the cost of the apartment, though of course insurance had covered that. There was the total destruction of his name and a reported dip in company stocks, but what Tully hoped hurt the most was the loss of…

"Sir," Tully looked up from his desk top to find Lance Imahara in the doorway. He hadn't even heard the door opening.

"Yes Sergeant?"

"Sir, there's been a homicide."

In the modern world the word was hardly unheard of, but when the implication was local, a chill made Tully shiver. He stared at his Sergeant, wondering if it was a joke. He wouldn't have put it past Imahara, expect he didn't think he could ever be so deadpan in his delivery.

Then a new thought took hold.

"Cobin." Tully said quietly. Someone had finally done it. He wondered when the Jefferson's had been released. The thought of Cobin dead and gone suddenly left him feeling drained. He'd been preparing himself for this for the past three years, telling himself it wouldn't hurt, that it couldn't, but when confronted with it after the fact Tully realized he was wrong.

Evidently this realization was plain on Tully's face because Imahara looked at him confused.

"Uh, sir?"

"Cobin, it was… Wesley?"

"That's dead?" Tully stared at Imahara.

"Yes, Lance did someone kill Wesley Cobin?"

"No…" Imahara said, his look of confusion deepening. Tully tried not to choke with unexpected relief.

"Then who is it Sergeant?" he snapped, harsher than he was meaning to be.

"Oh, I get it now." Imahara said with a knowing nod. "Yes, sir it probably was Cobin."

Now it was Tully's turn to look confused.

"You just said it wasn't Cobin."

"That's dead?" Imahara asked.

Tully's attitude was quickly turning more to annoyance than anything else.

"Yes Lance, what do you think I meant if not, *is Cobin dead?*"

"Well sir, in twenty years there hasn't been a murder in this town that wasn't committed by a Cobin; I assumed you were asking if he was the killer."

Tully suddenly felt like he was standing too close to the edge of a cliff, a premonition of disaster ahead; the thought hadn't even crossed his mind.

"I see, Sergeant," he said cautiously. "I would appreciate it if you wouldn't voice that thought to anyone else, is that understood? I do not want any more incidents involving that man on my hands. Don't give anyone ideas."

Lance nodded, though they both knew it was a shallow promise.

"Now, would you please tell me who the victim is?" Tully asked.

"The team's just setting up but she didn't have a wallet or purse so no ID yet." Tully sighed, this wasn't sounding good.

"Anyone recognize her?"

"Apparently she was found face down on the beach." Tully paused in opening his desk drawer.

"The beach?" he asked wondering if someone had jumped to conclusions, hoping this might have been an unfortunate accident. "If the team's just setting up how do we know it's a homicide?"

"Alright," Imahara allowed, a smug smile settling on his lips. "The *apparent* COD is a GSW to the chest." Tully didn't appreciate the junior officer's tone or expression.

"Is there a reason Lance, that I'm the last to know?" Tully asked icily as he pulled out his badge and gun.

It was the sudden influx of light, that woke Wesley Cobin, rather than the noise the drapes being drawn back made. His left eye felt puffy and sore but at least it still opened.

"Is that really necessary?" He asked drowsily.

"Ah, good morning sir," Radburt said in his crisp and cheery sunny-morning-tone. It was also said as if there was not a direct correlation to the curtains being opened and Wesley picking that very moment to wake up.

Originally Wesley had been planning on getting up sometime around noon, but now that he was awake he decided he should make the most of it. He turned his head to look at the clock. It was 8:25. He groaned and reminded himself why he kept Radburt around. That was easy enough that he didn't need full brain capacity to work it out.

"I thought this ensemble might be the best," Radburt said and held up an outfit he'd chosen. It paired corduroy shorts with a polo shirt.

"Finally dropped the ascot have we?" Wesley asked.

"Well, I was thinking extremely casual today." Radburt admitted.

"What would I do without you?"

"I think I shall refrain from giving you an answer out of respect." His valet replied dryly.

"Possibly for the best." Wesley admitted, thinking about his life the past few years.

"I owe you a debt I can never repay." he said seriously.

Apparently much too seriously for before breakfast, because Radburt simply replied. "Just the usual rate will suffice for now, Master Wesley." Wesley smiled and slipped out of bed.

He winced when his feet touched the floor, not because of the cold, but because of the muscle spasm that raced up his leg.

"Speaking of causal," He carried on, covering his discomfort from Radburt. "I was thinking about not shaving today. Maybe even growing a goatee?"

Radburt's expression was one of barely restrained revulsion. "That, sir, would be a mistake." he said curtly.

"You sure? I thought a little face fuzz might liven up the old visage."

"Well, perhaps if you grew it strategically to cover the evidence of your shameless brawling..." Radburt suggested, eyeing Wesley with disapproval.

"It's only brawling if I fight back." Wesley made his way into the adjoining bathroom, trying to mask his limp. Once in the tiled room he experimentally pulled at his t-shirt, lifting it high enough to see the angry purple bruising.

"I see," Radburt said totally unconvinced. "Did we have a late night?"

Wesley considered, a shark smile on his lips. "I suppose you could say that." he answered and tried pulling his shirt off. He lacked the range of motion to do it.

Radburt followed him into the bathroom and helped him with the shirt. "On that note sir, just where is the Mercedes?"

Wesley hesitated as Radburt lifted the shirt free. He actually forgot for a split second. "Police impound," he said eventually.

"Ah."

"Thank you for reminding me, I'll call from the shower phone. Radburt pursed his lips as he handed over the clothes he'd selected.

"Are you sure that is entirely necessary?"

"What's wrong, I talk to you while I'm in the shower. King's used to hold privy councils after all."

"It's just rather... modern." he finished. For Radburt "modern" summarized most of what was wrong in the world.

"As you wish," Wesley said keying in the shower's memory mode. "Just don't let me forget." A chime sounded to announce that the desired water temperature had been reached.

Even Radburt had to admit modernity could have its perks.

Tully almost winced as he spotted the cluster of county vehicles that designated this, the likely crime scene.

The location was uncomfortably familiar, close to the site of two other homicides from year's back, a fact the press wouldn't likely fail to notice.

He pulled across the oncoming lane and parked on the widened shoulder of the road, next to the county forensics van. The spot was designed to provide parking in case someone wanted to go site seeing on the rocky beach. He was glad to see that the only vehicles currently parked there were police issue.

He left the car and was immediately buffeted by a stiff sea breeze, one that died quickly further inland. He checked his hat to make sure it wouldn't take flight and crossed the empty divide to the beach. Only a few stunted shrubs clustered around the upper slopes of the beach. Looking left and right trees were visible and the beach largely vanished, crowded out by cliffs.

It should have been a beautiful scene, now it was marred by the flash of yellow crime scene tape, doggedly clinging to stakes hastily driven into the sand.

Tully eyed the small forensics crew as they worked, mildly annoyed they'd started without him but he understood their wish to wrap up before the wind or the sea could contaminate the scene.

Tully looked down at the sand, pockmarked with footprints from the CSU team and his own people. Everything being relative he supposed.

At least the pounding surf was receding which meant they shouldn't be rushing to the point of making mistakes. He was grateful they were one of the fortunate few who didn't have to rely entirely on the FBI lab to get forensic testing done. In their jurisdiction there was a laboratory that was under contract with the state and the county, that, when the occasion called for it, provided them forensic analysis and crime scene processing. Somewhat ironically it had been originally funded by a grant from the Cobin Foundation.

Tully spotted Blaze Stark, one of his daytime deputies, easily by his explosion of orange hair. It looked like he'd been in a gale force wind, but Tully knew it was the kind of get up Blaze paid extra for.

Stark was standing just inside the crime scene border, hands on hips watching the CSU team work. Stark often watched people work, doing as little of it himself as possible. At least he'd learned to delegate Tully supposed but this was small consolation and made him wish for the good old days when he surrounded himself with real professionals.

Tully approached his deputy. "Good morning, Stark." he called over the wind. Stark startled and turned to look at the Sheriff. He grinned widely.

"Hey, boss!" he said and adjusted his aviator sunglasses. "Can you believe it, a real homicide?" His tone spoke of excitement. This was what he'd signed up for; this was like it was on TV.

"Frederickson say anything yet?" Tully asked referring to the county coroner who was crouched next to the body, CSU already having combed that area.

"Ha!" Stark laughed. "I figured I'd let you deal with Frederickson; he's a mite cranky and a bit scary, especially this early." Tully eyed his deputy. He noticed a stain on his white shirt just below his collar.

Blueberry jelly. Tully decided and turned away in quiet annoyance.

If Stark was unnerved by the occasionally temperamental, but mostly harmless M.E. he wondered how the deputy dealt with bad tempered old women.

His hair still wet Wesley settled into the dining room. As usual there was only one place set at the head of the table. It was a rare occasion that Radburt could be coaxed into eating at the dinner table. It was slightly more likely that Wesley could take his meal at the kitchen table with Radburt for company but even that usually bothered Radburt's sensibilities. At least he hadn't been lectured about sleeping in his clothes again.

The idea that Radburt was just an employee was ludicrous to anyone who knew the arrangement. Wesley might have inherited his valet from his father, along with the house, company and family name, but Radburt was now simply his friend. Wesley had no illusions that without Radburt he would have been dead and they both knew it. Wesley was more grateful than he could ever express, even though he'd resisted his friend's help at times, when death had been just what he was looking for.

That morning, included among the place setting was the cordless phone, its presence surprised him because Radburt generally did not allow electronic devices, especially the telephone in the dining room. It was an area reserved for face-to-face conversation and the enjoyment of food.

Still, Wesley picked up the phone and dialed the station, he waited and heard Marge Ulysses answer, he smiled.

It was good to hear her voice.

Tully crossed the sand to the kneeling medical examiner. He actually liked Frederickson, though the good doctor's personality was of the type he'd better not mind you.

Unfortunately most of the people Tully had working under him, deputies and officers, Frederickson didn't like.

Tully crouched down beside Frederickson, who was hunched over the cadaver.

"Have anything for me?" he asked casually.

"I don't know what you're expecting this early!" Frederickson snapped. "I've only taken her liver temperature and done the obvious examination. Judging from the relatively little blood loss it's a single GSW to the heart, no exit wound, but close range."

Tully didn't react to the M.E.'s outburst. "Would you happen to have a time of death doctor?"

"Yes, sometime early this morning, rigor is well advanced, still in the first twelve, I'd say around 1 AM."

"Are those defensive wounds?" Tully asked noticing the woman's hands.

Frederickson's shoulders slackened and he turned to face Tully. "Yes, I believe so. Her hands might have been bound as well." He pointed out some chafing around the wrists.

"And levidity?" Tully asked.

Fredrickson smiled slowly. "I was beginning to think no one asked sensible questions anymore. No insult on you meant, but your latest young recruits leave a lot to be desired when it comes to the creative process and observation skills. Working your scenes used to be enjoyable."

Tully nodded. "Deputy Stark there's afraid of you Doctor."

Frederickson turned to eye the deputy still hovering near the scene line.

"Hardly surprising I suppose, but he did irk me." He said contemplatively. Stark noticed him staring and took an inadvertent step backwards.

"Whatever you need to get your job done," Tully said sportingly. "Whipping boy included, he's got to be good for something, right?"

"Thank you, Fineas." Fredrickson said. "To answer your question, levidity is consistent, I'd say she was killed right here. I'll get her over to pathology and get the bullet to the lab." Tully nodded his approval.

"She doesn't look familiar to you does she?" Tully questioned, asking himself the same. He imagined her to be in her early thirties, blonde but with dark roots, a fair complexion, now rendered paler in death. She had been quite pretty. And hauntingly familiar, but Tully couldn't place her.

"No, but I almost forgot, detective dunderhead over there did make one observation, she's likely had mammary enhancement and I'd say she had some work done on her nose as well, likely cheekbones, too." Frederickson shook his head. "A waste based on what she must have looked like before. Still, it could make recognizing more difficult, identifying could be easier though; I'll check for serial numbers on the implants as a last resort."

Tully thanked him and stood up slowly, amazed at how difficult that simple action was becoming. Ah, the reminders of old age!

He looked toward the road and saw another reminder approaching on foot.

The silver Chrysler Sebring had been parked behind his car and the driver was heading across the beach toward them.

Tully walked over to Blaze and nodded back to the car. "Who called him?" he asked.

Blaze squinted. "Oh him, you didn't call him?"

Tully sighed, "No deputy Stark, hence my question."

"Maybe it was dispatch?" Blaze suggested lamely and left Tully to conclude that he must have heard it over the radio. He supposed he should have been satisfied it was just the assistant D.A. and not yet the paper or television station.

"Fineas!" Dillon Howard, A. D.A. called to him from behind the yellow police line. At least the man hadn't lost all sense of propriety.

Tully made his way back over to the line to converse with Howard. He had clearly been at work judging from the suit and tie. Aside from the wind it was still uncomfortably warm in the sun. Tully thought he would have removed his jacket were he in Howard's shoes since the A.D.A. wasn't exactly in an official capacity. Still, that was Howard.

"Dillon," Tully said once he was within ear shot, switching to first names since apparently they were to that level. "This is fast." he said, looking down at the shorter man.

"Murder is big news. Especially here and now, is it him?" Dillon rocked on his feet in his excitement.

"Him?" Tully asked, no one coming immediately to mind. "No, the victim is a woman, young, likely pretty. Those are the only details I have at the moment." he stated hollowly.

The deceased always imbued him with a great sadness regardless of who they had been. It wasn't fair a beautiful woman should have her life ended for the beauty she had to share; an ugly woman because of the hand she had already been dealt. The death of a young one was a tragedy because of the time they would never get; an older one just as much because of the experience they wouldn't get to share. Ultimately, death was not fair and Tully didn't believe it was natural.

"And what about Cobin?" Howard asked.

Tully blinked, returning to the present. His expression remained placid, his annoyance showed only in his eyes, too subtle a clue for Dillon Howard to pick up on.

"You want to explain to me how that makes sense this early on?"

"Well isn't it obvious? How many murderers do we have living within three miles? Then there's the location, you can't tell me you didn't notice that, Cobin's property's not even a half mile from here." Howard said pointing south, down the coastline to the remains of the beach house property.

"Sir," Tully turned to see Blaze hovering behind him. "The tech's just found some tire tracks down the beach; they're likely from a truck or SUV." Tully hid his annoyance again and thanked Stark stiffly, then turned back to Howard who had just jotted that detail down in a notepad.

"Cobin was involved in something else last night, I drove him home myself and his car is at the impound yard."

"What time?" Howard asked. Tully rolled his tongue around his mouth; he didn't like being questioned.

"I left at 1:04." He answered shortly.

"And what's the time of death here?"

"Doctor Frederickson hasn't released that information." Tully lied.

"Fineas, this is my job, and all I'm doing is trying to help by expediting yours. He got away once; justice will strike the second time. You have more than enough to look into Cobin for this. I'd of thought you of all people would appreciate that." Tully once again concealed his annoyance, and a sudden urge to pick Howard up by his collar and explain to him the course of events as they were supposed to be. He investigated and the D.A. built a case off of what he found, not the other way around. Still, he knew Howard had legitimate points.

"So you're theory is what? I left Cobin and he hiked down the beach to, what? Meet our mysterious woman, or was it an accident, a chance encounter, but since it was an odd numbered day he just decides he has to kill her?"

"Do killers like him need more of a motive? Besides, he didn't have to walk he has three cars, one of which," Howard flipped through his notepad toward the beginning, found a page and transferred the information to a blank page which he then tore off and handed to Tully. "One of which is an SUV." He pointed out the Jeep Grand Cherokee, complete with plate number. It was bracketed between the two Mercedes.

"And you have this why?" Tully asked.

Dillon looked at him, surprised. "Isn't that obvious, I want to know if he's out there, it's for our protection. You can't trust a man like that." Tully supposed to the average psychopath they might have made a tempting pair but that was one concern he'd never lost any sleep over.

"He's not going to come after Loren." Tully said, letting slip out some of his distain.

To be fair he supposed Cobin could come after Howard, after all the man had led the charge against him, but then it wouldn't serve any purpose and people always seemed to forget Cobin had only committed murder once and there was still a fine line between that, premeditated though it was, and some kind of unhinged serial killing.

"Look, you're going to check him out, right?" Howard asked, now he was sounding annoyed and Tully wondered, not the first time how they were supposed to become one big happy family.

Because we both love her. Was the answer he got every time, so he'd put up with Howard until then. He'd probably settle down with age, be less vigorous in his pursuits. At least that was Tully's hope.

"I'll check out *all* of our leads, but don't you think I should wait until I have some hard evidence before I do, what if he gets spooked?"

"I think we should try to catch him off guard."

"Fine, I'll wait till noon, see if we get an ID on the body and then I'll go pay a visit to Cobin, that satisfy you?"

"You'll take someone with you won't you?

"Why?"

"In case he should turn violent."

Tully smiled grimly. "I think I can handle that." He said, *because I taught him every move he'd make.*

After his delicious breakfast Wesley found himself wandering about the house.

The Victorian had originally been built in 1913 with no expenses spared, but simplicity had been valued in the design so that its lines were ageless and classically adorned without the gaudy excesses so many of the gingerbread style older Victorian's had. The house had been a family treasure up until 1929 and Black Friday when the Cobin family fortune vanished.

Eventually the house fell into receivership, was taken over by the bank, later bought back and again lost. Amazingly that cycle had repeated itself three times until Cobin Softworks had taken off and Herod Cobin had bought the house back, but with no plans to live in it. It was merely for form sake as he commissioned a great modern slab of a house built two miles out of town on beachfront property. Once the mob burned down the comfortable apartment he had grown up in Wesley had moved out to the manor, formerly the office.

It had been maintained well enough and his mother had taken an interest in its large garden but no improvements had been made to the house and as Wesley launched into the renovation process more and more casualties of time had been discovered. The result was that the house had been largely rebuilt from the basement up.

Light now played a large role in the layout and design of the house. Only the oak trim on ceilings, the wooden wainscoting, door frames and of course the floor had been kept. Most other surfaces and walls had been painted in shades of fall, cream replacing brooding dark wood and the period wallpaper had been removed. LED lighting had been fitted throughout the house, much of it recessed and a complete wired home network had been installed.

In the past year Wesley had been revisiting each room and making changes to get them just so. It had been something to do. Now he was running out of rooms.

"You're sure the cottage is fine?" He asked Radburt who was fastidiously polishing a brass statuette that had come with the house.

"Oh yes, it's quite up to my standards." Radburt assured him.

"Do you even have satellite hookup?"

"As you know I have no television, so I see little point of wiring the cottage for one." Wesley shrugged.

"You know I suspect you're a Luddite Radburt."

"Very good, sir." Radburt said throwing out his usual remark.

Wesley rubbed his hands distractedly and examined yet another bit of statuary standing on a display table.

"Do you have something on your mind?" Radburt asked.

"Why would you ask that?" Wesley asked.

"Because you've picked up and put down the same figurine for the third time just now."

"Oh," Wesley looked closer at the statuette. "I guess I have." He said though he honestly didn't remember picking it up before.

"About last night?"

"I suppose that could be..." Wesley said. "You never..." He trailed off, this hardly felt like the proper time to bring up this topic but it wasn't going to go away, he knew that from experience. "Do you ever wonder about it? Did you ever?"

"Sir?" Radburt asked, setting down the statuary and giving Wesley his full attention.

"If I did it?"

Radburt didn't sigh, but that was the sense that he gave off. Very slowly he said, "I've known you since you were a very small boy," he smiled in recollection, "and Margaret knew you and she liked you and her judgment never failed." he concluded matter-of-factly. Margaret had been Radburt's wife, theirs had been a touching love story that, ended devastatingly with cancer.

Wesley smiled sadly, thinking about the love Radburt had lost. "And that's all it took?"

"That was all." Radburt's voice trembled slightly, though he did his best to conceal it. They made a real great pair, two broken men.

"Now, if you will excuse me sir, I think I'll go wash the SL." Wesley nodded, though he was pretty sure he hadn't driven the roadster since Radburt has washed and detailed it last week, then again it was a nice shape to wash.

CHAPTER 3

Tully crept up the driveway to Cobin manor. He hadn't intended the slow crawl initially but now as he nosed over the edge of the ascending blacktop he saw a golden opportunity. Out in the courtyard sat the glittering blue Benz 230SL, beyond it was the three car garage, one of the doors open.

He parked the Crown Victoria and killed the engine, sitting in silence for a minute waiting to see if someone had spotted him. No one appeared. His eyes focused on the garage.

He'd been pretty defensive when Dillon Howard had been prodding him but he now found himself confronted with his own doubts. He decided not to pass up this chance.

He opened his door and strode across the brick courtyard purposefully. He refused to slink, if he was obvious and got caught because of it, so be it.

He reached the open garage without anyone stopping him.

Inside the garage the lights were on, one over each stall, the two on either end were empty but the maroon Jeep was parked in the middle stall, just like it had always been. The only thing that stopped the flashbacks was the fact this was a new Grand Cherokee, only a facsimile of the former.

Tully knelt and removed the flashlight from his belt and clicked it on. He ran the blue beam underneath the Jeep, looking for anything snagged in the undercarriage; then he checked the tires for obvious traces of sand. He didn't know if he was relieved or disappointed when he found none.

He straightened and looked inside the cabin; his eyes lingered on the navigation screen. He wondered if the Jeep logged all of its trips and how difficult it would be to find out. He looked behind him, self-conscious as he tried the handle.

The door opened.

Tully checked the driver's floor mat for sand.

The mat was in pristine condition, though it didn't look recently vacuumed. There were no obvious signs of sand.

Finally, he popped the cargo hatch, which powered itself up. He checked underneath the vinyl cargo cover. He wasn't sure what he was looking for, whatever it was he didn't find it.

He examined the leading edge of the hatch, looking for some way of closing it, finally he tried pulling it down. He winced as the Jeep emitted four long beeps, but the hatch powered gently shut and no one came running.

Without looking back he left the garage and made his way around to the front door. His knock was almost immediately answered by Cobin himself.

Cobin's eyebrow was cocked and his expression clearly questioning as he pulled open the door. "Sheriff Tully," he said by way of greeting. Only the threshold separated them, but the void between them was much greater. "Why don't you come in?" Cobin offered and Tully crossed the threshold without another thought.

It had been three years since Tully had been inside the house. He didn't know what he'd been expecting, maybe some obvious sign that Cobin had slipped off the rails, maybe just the disorder bred by despair. Whatever he'd been expecting there were no plaster chunks missing from the walls, no shredded paintings, no piles of laundry, not even dust. Then again... Radburt walked into the foyer from the right archway.

"Ah, Sheriff Tully," The valet said amiably enough. "How nice of you to finally drop in." The tone was accusatory, which confused Tully.

"Shall I bring something, tea?" Radburt suggested.

"I don't think this is a social call," Cobin remarked. "But of course if you'd like tea, Sheriff?" He raised his hand in question.

"No thank you, Radburt." Tully turned to Cobin. "We need to talk." he said and didn't wait to be invited through the archway to the left, into the sitting room.

"Sure thing, come on in." Cobin said to the vacant space where Tully had been, then followed the older man into the sitting room.

"There's been a murder." Tully said wasting no time. "Did you do it?"

Cobin was quiet, the seconds dragged on. "Oh, I'm sorry you actually wanted an answer? How about if I just ask for my lawyer and save you the time and expense of investigating?"

Tully glared at him. "Just answer the question." He said evenly.

"What do you think?" Cobin's response was bitter. "It was after 1 when I got home, I was tired I went to bed, besides the car was towed."

"You have three." Tully reminded him.

"And that road is the only way into town from Route 3 which means at some point the wrecker and the patrol cars would have been coming into town, you think I would have taken that kind of chance?"

Tully pursed his lips. "Never said it was in town," he said softly. "Or when it happened."

Cobin snorted, "Well that would be the obvious assumption, wouldn't it?"

"Was Radburt here when you got in?"

"No, I was alone all night, the best he can do is serve as a character witness, and we both know what good that does." Tully ignored the barb.

"Have you been drinking again?" he asked, surprised to see disappointment in Cobin's eyes.

"Not a drop since the day."

Tully wanted to believe him, but trust was something they didn't have anymore.

"Any more reason than my 'reputation' to check me out, Sheriff?"

"Some tire tracks, maybe from a Jeep. And the body was found about a quarter of a mile from your property on the beach, you still own it don't you?"

Cobin nodded.

"Bit obvious for me wouldn't you say?" And there was the snag. The fact Tully could never quite reconcile. If Cobin had wanted to murder someone, and he had the time to plot it out, he should never have been caught; at least not as easily as he was. Still, in the end he had used the rights that came with money and power to politely buy his way out of a conviction. Technically then, a skillful plan wouldn't have been necessary. It still felt out totally out of character.

"Thank you for your time, Mr. Cobin." Tully said and turned toward the foyer.

"Don't leave town?" Cobin asked from the sitting room.

"Not like you ever do." Tully replied, nodded goodbye to Radburt and shut the door.

When Tully got back to the station he spotted Dillon's car in the lot and inadvertently tightened his grip on the steering wheel.

If Dillon was going to marry his daughter he wished the man would try to be a little less annoying.

Dillon was waiting for him when he got inside.

"You went to see Cobin?" was the first thing he asked.

"Yes," Tully replied. "I don't think he knew anything."

Dillon raised his eyebrows.

"Well, you're going to want to hear this." he said and turned around to look at Blaze who was at his desk in the squad room actually eating a lollipop. Apparently Blaze had felt it alright to pass on information to the D.A.'s office before telling Tully about it. Blaze removed the candy from his mouth before speaking. At least he was learning.

"Hey boss, we got an ID on our Vic. Odette Boswell."

Tully straightened, he knew the name but it took a minute for the details to come back. He tried very carefully not to show what he was thinking.

By his behavior Tully knew Dillon had figured out the link but he wasn't going to give him any more ammunition until they had a better idea of the facts.

Odette Boswell had been a real piece of work who had managed to stay one step ahead of the police investigation against her. She'd been swindling people out of their life savings on a scam she was running. She'd gotten away in the end and everyone who'd worked the case had been left with a sour taste in their mouths.

"We've got her file from the last time she visited," Blaze said. "Also, doc said he popped the bullet, he's saying .32 revolver. Apparently there was some kind of fibers that the lab's working on, said a few days and they might have something."

Blaze held up the old case file but Tully didn't need it. He knew what the signatures would reveal: the officer working the case had been former Lieutenant Wesley Cobin.

After Fineas had left, Wesley went through his usual rollercoaster of emotions. He'd become more familiar with them over the years, so he ignored the stage that urged him to take a sledgehammer to one of the back bedrooms walls, knowing now that the anger would collapse into melancholy and that he needed to work now on fighting the despair to come. It was then he realized he hadn't actually given Fineas a direct answer to his question. He groaned but didn't slug the arm of the sofa.

"I really wonder about that man sometimes." Radburt remarked dryly as he entered the sitting room with a loaded tea tray.

Wesley sighed. He wasn't entirely sure if Radburt understood what had happened between him and Fineas. Comments like that made it seem as if they were friends only yesterday.

"Did you hear what he said?" Wesley asked.

"Not exactly, something about murder." Radburt's tone indicating he didn't much care and there was no falseness in his words.

"There's been a murder, last night apparently."

Radburt grimaced as he set the tray on an end table.

Any other day Wesley would have let the remark go as one of Radburt's peculiarities, but today he was restless and cranky, so he questioned him.

"You do know Fineas despises me now, right?"

Radburt didn't snort on principle, but if he did he would have.

"I hardly think so, sir."

"How do you figure that?" Wesley demanded.

"While I admit I haven't seen much in the way of interaction between the two of you, he tends towards treating you as a stranger but he still looks at you the same."

"He looks at me like I'm a monster." Wesley scoffed.

"No sir, he looks at you with concern and self-doubt, if I'm not mistaken. But there's also affection."

Wesley wanted to object, he didn't believe Radburt was right, but then he'd never actually known Radburt to be wrong, with the possible exception of clothes and hairstyles. If Radburt didn't know, he was smart and honest enough, to say. So, by saying something it likely meant it was true.

Even if he didn't believe it, Wesley felt better, more reasonable, curious even.

"Do I still get the paper?" Wesley asked.

"No sir, not since the *iPad*." Radburt spoke the name with subtle loathing.

Wesley nodded. It had been a while since he cared about what was going on locally.

"I think I'll take tea in the office, if you don't mind." Wesley said standing.

"Of course." Radburt said, tone clearly implying he was against the idea, but as he picked up the tray, after Wesley's back was to him, he smiled slightly.

Wesley was taking an interest...

"Right now we only have a coincidence." Tully argued with Dillon

Howard. They'd moved into the Sheriff's office but Tully knew their voices were carrying.

"We're talking about Wesley Cobin here Fineas, not a normal civilian caught up in an investigation. We are talking about a man who has killed before and in this case a man with a motive."

"He knew the victim, he worked a case against her; it's hardly cut and dried." Tully said. He was actually less inclined to think it was Wesley after seeing the preliminary report.

"Don't forget those tire tracks at the scene, the lab is working on identifying those too, but it looks like Boswell could have been dumped on the beach from an SUV, care to guess what the wheelbase is consistent with? A Jeep Grand Cherokee, and of course, Cobin happens to have a Jeep Grand Cherokee."

"That still doesn't prove this is anything more than coincidence. Strong coincidence? Perhaps. Proof of guilt? Not even close. Besides, none of this is like Cobin. The method, the scene, even the gun, Cobin doesn't like revolvers. If it makes you feel better I did a quick search of his Jeep. No signs of a struggle and no sand, it also wasn't recently cleaned."

Dillon didn't say anything for a full thirty seconds, considering.

"You're right Fineas. I jumped to conclusions." Dillon put his hands up to show he conceded the point. "I'll let you run your investigation. I just can't stand the thought of him getting away with something again."

"And if it is Cobin then we both have to cross our T's and dot our I's." Tully made the concession.

Dillon nodded.

"I suppose it is more wishful thinking than hard evidence."

"Completely, right now you could make a more convincing case with your boss as prime suspect. If I remember correctly his mother was one of the people Boswell cleaned out, the crime scene is a secluded location he'd know and he also drives a Grand Cherokee and has a .32 revolver." Both men eyed each other speculatively before Dillon smiled and gave a brief nod.

"Impressive, Fineas, very impressive."

"You've more than got the dedication, now you just need to work on playing things cooler." Tully suggested.

"Well, keep me informed," Dillon said turning towards the door. "And I guess in line as best you can." He said with a smile. "Are we still on for dinner Wednesday?"

Tully nodded, "So far as Caroline says, see you at six." Tully returned to his desk and sat down heavily. He shut his eyes for a minute to rebuild the

Boswell case in his mind, letting the particulars not mentioned in the case file come back to him.

Somewhat paradoxically, Cobin had been a Boy Scout type of cop, injustice had really bothered him and he'd done just about everything in his not inconsiderable power to end it.

Boswell had been smart and a professional, much more of a threat than would usually be expected in such a small county. She'd done it more to remain in practice as well as to add to her retirement fund.

Cobin had personally compensated most of the money they had been unable to recover, about sixty grand in all.

Boswell had been an arrogant woman and cold hearted but she hadn't deserved to be murdered and the Wesley Cobin he used to know wouldn't have killed her over it. For Cobin any satisfaction would have been in breaking her, getting her to confess to what she'd done.

Unless it went too far?

Regardless, Tully wondered if it was a judgment he could make. Last time he made that call, he'd been wrong.

Right now, it didn't matter.

Tully wobbled his computer mouse, bringing the screen back to life.

He typed in Odette Boswell's particulars and was soon perusing her police file; it had gained a few pages since their investigation in 2007.

Apparently, her luck had run out. She'd been arrested for a con she tried pulling in New York. Although, once again she managed to get by with no time served. The interesting part was that she'd apparently settled nearby, just one county over.

Tully considered, he could coordinate with the local police and handle everything over the phone but he didn't like leaving it to someone else if he could do his own investigation. Since Odette Boswell was now living with a roommate there was someone to question. He figured he could be back by seven that evening.

Marge had already coordinated with the locals to give them a heads up. Fortunately they hadn't seemed very enthusiastic to mount their own investigation. Still, Tully found the name and number of the detective who was supposed to have checked in on Boswell's roommate and collected a few personal effects.

Tully picked up his desk phone and dialed the detective's number.

"Jones, robbery homicide." The detective sounded bored.

"Hello detective Jones, this is Fineas Tully, Coolidge County Sheriff,"

There was a pause on the other end, when the detective came back he sounded a little more interested. If Tully were to guess the man had just taken his feet off his desk. Even though Coolidge was a small county the Sheriff's title could do that.

"Yes, sir, how can I help you?" Jones asked.

"I just wanted to give you a heads up that I would like to interview Odette Boswell's roommate this afternoon, if you don't have any objection?"

"Boswell, Boswell, right, no that's fine, we just grabbed a few of her things, didn't really talk to the roommate, don't really have the manpower for it. Sir." Jones added.

"So long as you don't mind I'd like to run with the investigation. I will, of course, have my department pass on any updates."

"Yeah, sure, that'd be fine... sir." Tully was relieved. Too often any jurisdictional issues were met with open hostility, Jones honestly sounded like he didn't care. Tully was glad he wasn't getting railroaded.

"I'd like to take a look at her personal effects if I could?"

"Sure, come on by, just the basics, laptop, some papers, whatever was lying around. Roommate didn't seem like a worry so we left most of it."

"Thank you so much detective Jones."

"Sure,"

"Good bye."

"Sir." Jones said and they hung up.

Tully sighed with relief. It looked like Boswell would remain his problem. As contrary as it seemed, that fact put him at ease.

Now it was just a matter of who to take with him. He considered the duty roster.

He could take Blaze with him but he had a feeling one of them wouldn't make it back, besides Blaze didn't have much to lend to the investigation so he decided to call Jake Barry in. He might be bigoted when it came to Cobin, but he was a competent detective.

Before he took further action though, Tully had another idea. He pulled up his computers second hard drive which was a clone of Cobin's, on which were his un-archived case notes. Because they were fastidiously organized it wasn't hard to find the Boswell case. Tully got a slight chill as the file opened and he found himself in Cobin's mind.

He clicked the print button and reached for his keys.

"Oh, not her again, surely, sir?" Wesley looked up from his computer screen. Turning, he saw Radburt reading over his shoulder.

"Not me this time," Wesley said nonplussed by Radburt's gaze. "She was found on the beach just outside town, dead."

"Oh, I see." Radburt said curtly. "Well, I can't say as the world will miss her unduly."

"She was a rotten fish." Wesley agreed then frowned. Radburt's phraseology was rubbing off on him. Maybe he did need to get out more?

"Strange she should be found dead here though wouldn't you say? I suppose, this is the homicide?"

"Oh, yes, according to the paper she was found this morning by a local jogging on the beach. She was shot." Wesley leaned to the side, allowing Radburt a full view of the screen.

"Quite a detailed report given it happened this morning." He mused.

Wesley nodded.

He wondered if Tully knew Blaze Stark was leaking most official police information to the gazette to supplement his income a little.

Radburt straightened up, finished reading the headline report. "Well, there are only a few motives for murder, correct?"

"Generally speaking yes, love, jealousy and money."

"Power, passion and pennies." Radburt reiterated.

"Basically."

"Why was she here the first time?"

Wesley thought back.

"Vacation, she said, wanted to get away from her big city life for a time and think about settling down. She ran her scams in her spare time. She never expected to get caught. I think it rather turned her off the thought of settling here."

"I daresay," Radburt mused. "Obviously anyone she wronged while in town would have a motive through money. If I recall sir, you were her most likely romantic interest." Wesley nodded with a wry smile.

"Unfortunately," he said then sat up straighter. "On the other hand there was something else." He mapped across the network to the secure server and opened a file that held his old case notes.

"Will you be wanting lunch at the usual time?" Radburt asked.

"Actually," Wesley said watching the pages of his report flash past in PDF format. "I was wondering if you needed to go into the city?"

"Need to go?" Radburt asked immediately sensing some ulterior motive.

"I may have temporarily misplaced my driver's license and I was hoping we could take a trip into the city, I have a… plant I wanted to pick up."

"A plant, sir?"

"Yes. A, uh, desk plant." Wesley said, squinting at the screen.

He found the list of people he wanted, people who had lost out to Boswell.

"Desk plant?" Radburt asked.

"Yes," Wesley straightened. "You know, to liven up this desk a little." Wesley pulled his iPad out of the desk drawer.

"I see, so this would have nothing to do with the late Miss Boswell living in the city would it Master Wesley?" Wesley looked up with his most innocent smile but found himself unable to lie to the man looking down at him.

"Well…" was all he managed.

CHAPTER 4

Before he left the station, Tully dialed the number of Odette Boswell's roommate, Lisa Cuthard. He made sure that she was planning on being at home the rest of the afternoon then met Jake Barry as the deputy pulled into the parking lot.

They climbed into Tully's car and headed for Route 3 and turned north.

They didn't speak until the car passed the turn off for the Cobin Manor.

Barry started to open his mouth.

"Not in the mood, Jake." Tully warned, giving him an entreating look that would, no doubt have baffled Blaze.

Barry nodded in understanding

"Trust me," Tully said. "I've heard all I want for the time being from Stark and Howard."

"It's a hard thing to get past." Barry said casually.

"And it's a backward way to run an investigation."

"Still, it has to be considered sooner or later."

"Then I've chosen later." Tully said firmly.

Barry shrugged in surrender. "Fair enough. So, Odette Boswell? I never expected to head another case file with her name. Why would she come back?"

"That's what I'd like to find out."

"I suppose we've got enough suspects, aside from the obvious one. How many people did she scam?"

"Twelve. Eight of them she took for over five thousand."

"She also managed to get all the power players. Didn't she even involve the District Attorney?"

"His mother."

"And the Mayor."

Tully nodded.

"Still, that was like five or six years ago, wasn't it? That's a long time to wait for revenge."

"Especially since most of them got their money back." Tully added.

Barry glanced out the window, not caring to dwell on *how* they'd been compensated. Then a thought occurred to him.

"So the one person who lost the most was still Cobin."

"He can't get sixty grand out of a dead woman." Tully interjected.

"It's not like he needs it."

"Then what's the motive?"

"Principle." Tully bit his lip, not pointing out that *murder* seemed rather unprincipled.

"We still don't know why she was killed on our beach. It could just as easily be someone else from her past trying to muddy the waters. The FBI's case file was a whole lot fatter than ours. She stole millions from very powerful people. The feds just couldn't find the money trail."

"So what are we hoping to get out of this little excursion?" Barry asked, changing the subject.

"I want to talk to her roommate." Tully pointed to the files he'd stacked on the center console.

Barry flipped through them.

"What do we know about Lisa Cuthard?" He asked.

"Nothing sticks out in our information. Detective Jones of Robbery Homicide didn't find anything suspicious. No questionable background that we could find. She pays her bills and she's willing to talk to us. Until further she's golden in my book."

Barry flipped to Fredrickson's preliminary report and glanced over it.

It looked like Boswell had been bound and gagged. There wasn't much in the way of defensive wounds, nothing under her manicured fingernails, not even dirt.

Her abduction must have been quick.

What appeared to be carpet fibers had been found on her clothing, they thought it might match the vehicle that it appeared she was hauled in. If so it could be a valuable lead, supposing they could match a supplier which was not impossible, but also not something to put too much hope in.

The trajectory of the bullet that killed her suggested someone close to six feet tall that was a fairly decent shot.

Evidence pointed towards a man, Barry decided.

"I suppose this rules out the D.A.'s mother?"

"I think she lacks the upper body strength and the height." Tully agreed.

"The Doc say if Boswell could have been kneeling?"

"If it makes you feel better you can add her name to the short list."

Barry shook his head. "So basically we're looking for anything and everything?"

"Pretty much." Tully didn't like the weight settling on him. It was up to him to figure out who had killed Odette Boswell and they were starting with a blank slate. It had been a while since he'd worked a case of this importance and the responsibility was coming back to him.

Barry sensed Tully's mood and decided quiet contemplation was called for. He turned his attention to making a mental list of questions to run past the roommate.

With just occasional remarks they finished the ride down Route 3.

Wesley decided that Radburt's sedate driving style was well matched to the Jeep as they wound their way up scenic Route 3. Had Wesley been driving, the Cherokee would likely have been heaving and rolling through the assorted corners that led gently up and out of the County through the trees.

As it was, Radburt seemed to know the exact speed at which to guide the SUV into corners to keep the ride flat and un-dramatic. Wesley had bought the Jeep more out of tradition than need or longing. The Cobin's had always had a Jeep since well before the term SUV was used and he hadn't seen a reason to change that, though this latest iteration was a nicer place to be a passenger than his AMG and since he was relegated to the passenger seat and the Benz was impounded he supposed that was a very good thing.

"Feel free to play with the radio." Wesley said taking his iPad from the door pocket where he'd stowed it earlier.

"Very good, sir." Radburt said and drove on.

Wesley powered on the iPad and opened his documents.

"Oh, sorry." he said catching Radburt's perusal of the center stack and discovering it was dominated by the ominous navigation screen. He reached for the power button but Radburt stopped him.

"It's quite alright, I doubt I could find a suitable station and I wouldn't dream of distracting you from your reading."

"Not a distraction, but really an aid. There's the satellite radio but I might suggest this," Wesley pressed the power button and tapped his way through menus. "Here, try this." He tapped a playlist suitably entitled *Radburt's Road Tunes*, moments later cool jazz was being circulated around the cabin.

Radburt brightened. "Oh, that is handy."

"Taken directly from your personal collection and ripped to the hard drive. You know it actually has... Never mind." Wesley amended seeing his friend begin to glaze over.

"Thank you, sir." Radburt said, though whether in reference to the music or not delving into technical explanations Wesley wasn't sure, with Radburt probably the latter.

He really should have bought him a nice simple Bentley with just a CD player, but then Radburt's duties didn't usually extend to chauffeuring.

For that matter they could have taken Radburt's Lexus, but Wesley wanted the Jeep's tech package as a backup. He returned to his reading and relaxed in the subdued atmosphere as they cruised their way to the city.

Wesley directed Radburt to an open air shopping market on 4th Street in the upper end Donnington Heights neighborhood.

Radburt pulled the Jeep to the curb and shut off the engine.

He looked over at Wesley.

"Will you be accompanying me in our quest for a desk plant?" He asked dryly.

"I trust your judgment completely. Whatever strikes you as working in the office by all means snatch it up."

"Shall I look for something for dinner as well?"

"They do sell fresh produce here. That would be wonderful."

"Are you waiting for me to stop asking questions and get out of the car?"

"Whenever you feel ready." Wesley pulled the iPad from the door pocket, not fooling Radburt with his nonchalance.

"Very good, sir, try and stay out of trouble." Radburt said and left the Jeep, soon disappearing into the market.

Wesley turned off the iPad and returned it to the door and pulled out his LabTech Memo smartphone. He flicked open his apps drawer, selected one and keyed in 2337 3rd Street. A couple of seconds later his download was complete.

The Memo was a clever phone, though not originally designed for use in the United States. One of its tricks was to use two separate, dedicated connections for voice and 4G data. By using the parallel technologies it sped up the phone and gave it a number of advantages, though the two phone bills at the end of the billing cycle was not one of them.

The app catalogue on Wesley's personal phone was entirely owner stocked and the majority of the cool ones were of questionable legality. It was one of those, not infrequent, times when it paid to have deep pockets.

On screen, six pages of blueprints appeared, one for each level of the building. Wesley scanned the basement sheet but soon discovered there were no large windows so he moved up to ground level. He flicked back to the web browser and checked the apartment vacancies page. #104 was currently unoccupied and the live-in management was in #101.

Wesley reached for his door handle, ready to launch his plan when he paused and returned to the apartment listings page and got the manager's name.

Lorenzo Washington, he tapped and held the name. The options menu appeared and he tapped *Search*, then the extension for one of his specialized apps. He chose to have the results e-mailed to him, then climbed out of the Jeep.

Tully parked the car and looked at the apartment building to his left. Boswell's building had been easy to find on 3rd Street, which was just off of a major road and in a modern enough area of the city so as to benefit from accurate signage and a working grid layout.

The building surprised Tully. It was in a swanky enough neighborhood, but the five story brick building was not exactly what he had been expecting.

In his imagination he'd pictured Boswell setting up in a lair of glass and steel. Making a home in something cold and full of sharp angles, just like Boswell herself. Instead, from outward appearances, the complex looked cozy. Around the right side of the building there was a verdant garden with tall trees dappling the grassy sections beneath their boughs.

He noticed a community garden in the back. He doubted Boswell had anything to do with that. Then movement caught his eye as he climbed from the cruiser. He did a double take and squinted.

"Jake, is that?" The man walking in the park disappeared into the garden after throwing a quick look over his shoulder. At that distance he had looked remarkably like Wesley Cobin.

"What?" Barry asked, looking toward the park, trying to follow Tully's gaze.

"Nothing." Cobin was on his mind, he supposed it wasn't surprising he was starting to see him in the faces of strangers. He'd need to stop doing that.

Tully leaned back into the car and picked up his voice recorder then headed for the apartment. Barry followed him to the front door of the secured building. He pressed the corresponding apartment buzzer and waited.

He was also surprised that Boswell had taken in a roommate. She certainly didn't seem the chummy type and he would have thought she had the cash to fund her lifestyle.

"Hello?" A timid voice rasped through the cheap intercom speaker.

"Miss Cuthard, I'm Sheriff Fineas Tully with my deputy Jake Barry, we spoke on the phone."

"Oh, yes… uh, one minute please." They waited in the chill of the shade, the sun having cleared the roof of the building and leaving them in its shadow. Barry opened his mouth to remark on something when Lisa Cuthard spoke again.

"Please, come on up now." The door lock buzzed. Tully pulled at the handle and held the door for Barry, then followed after him. They headed for the stairs and made their way up to the fourth floor where they knocked on the apartment door. The sound of locks and chains being opened and drawn back reached them and then a short woman with frizzy brown hair and a red nose peeked out at them.

Tully already had his ID out and showed it to Miss Cuthard who squinted at it but didn't really read any of the details there in.

"I'm Sheriff Tully this is my Deputy, Barry." He said again.

"I'm pleased to meet, you, come in," She said opening the door for them. "Please excuse my mess." She suddenly sneezed violently into a tissue kept in the sleeve of the turquoise robe she was wearing. "You'll have to excuse me as well but I'm just coming off of a cold." She squeaked out and sneezed again. Tully excused her.

They were in a small kind of hallway that opened directly onto a long main room. Cuthard led them into the great room and towards the windows set in the sitting room area.

"Please have a seat anywhere." She said and dabbed at her nose, stopping to pick up and stuff a few used tissues into deep pockets on her robe. There was a couch and two chairs. Cuthard retreated to the far chair. It faced the couch with the windows to its back.

Tully perched on the couch and Barry sat down next to him.

"So I suppose you'll be wanting to hear about Odette?" Cuthard asked.

"Of course the local police were here already but I quite understand your coming here and will be glad to help in any way I can." As she spoke she drew up her legs underneath her.

"Thank you, Miss Cuthard." Tully said, genuinely appreciative of her cooperation.

"Not at all, and, please, you can call me Lisa. No, aside from the clearly regrettable circumstances I find this rather intriguing. I've read about this process so many times, to get to experience it is... well..." She blushed, pale cheeks taking on the color of her nose. "I don't mean to sound ghoulish or anything." She trailed off then seemed to give up explaining herself with a sigh and shrug.

"Do you mind if I record our conversation?" Tully asked starting the recorder.

"Oh, no, go right ahead." Tully placed the recorder on the coffee table in front of him.

"Were you close to Miss Boswell?" Tully asked and Barry removed his notepad.

"Oh, no, not very; I mean, aside from the obvious, we shared this apartment, but on a personal level no."

"So you don't know what she was doing last night?" Lisa looked thoughtful.

"Well, not directly I suppose, I mean, I know she said she was meeting someone, I assumed a man."

"Any reason why?"

"Oh, none really, I mean that was just Odette's way, she was always out meeting men. It was one of the only reasons this arrangement worked out, she was rarely here."

"So, she didn't say anything specific about last night?"

"She seemed excited," Lisa broke off to sneeze. "I'm sorry, I haven't offered you anything to..." another sneeze. "to drink?"

"No, no, we're fine, would you like us to come back later?" Tully offered, concern evident on his face.

"I'm really quite alright, just a sniffle." Tully hesitated.

Barry took the opportunity to ask. "Do you remember when exactly she left?"

"Uh, a little after four-thirty, maybe as late as ten-to-five." Jake noted the times at the top of his page and Tully took back the conversation.

"Were you aware of Miss Boswell's criminal charges?"

"Only because the police just told me, I didn't know how to go about getting a background check when Odette moved in."

"So this apartment is in your name?" Tully asked. He'd been assuming it was the other way around.

"Yes and I think I'm going to be much more careful in the future about my roommates."

"Do you know anything about Miss Boswell's financial state?" Tully asked.

Lisa looked momentarily confused but answered nonetheless. "Aren't you able to get her financial records, I'm sure they could tell you more than I can."

"Miss Boswell wasn't the type to put her money where someone could make records."

"Oh, I see." Lisa said a catch of excitement in her voice. "In that case, she was never late with her rent payment. As I said it wasn't as if we were friends or did things together but she always had nice clothes and her hair and nails were done very regularly, never a hair out of place and often a different color." Lisa looked thoughtful. "You know, I can't even tell you what her hair color was the day she left." She sounded very disappointed. "I always imagined myself to be a good eyewitness and I can't even tell you about my roommate."

"Don't worry you've been most helpful." Tully said soothingly but he was beginning to realize this was a dead end. "Did you ever meet any of the men Miss Boswell was seeing?"

"Maybe two or three, she didn't bring them around which was the way I pretty much wanted it. One of them I think she called Bill. Another could have been... Fred I believe."

"Bill and Fred?" Barry asked skeptically.

"I know what you're thinking and you're probably right. Either her taste in men ran to generic or she was making it up as she went."

"Could have been marks?" Barry turned to Tully.

"Or even johns." Lisa chimed in. Barry looked confused.

"No, not as in, named Mark, but..."

"I think Miss Cuthard knows what you meant." Tully said dryly.

"Oh." Barry said as he figured out what Lisa had been implying.

"Do you think they could have been?" Tully asked.

"I don't know. I would tend to doubt it. Odette thought too highly of herself, if that's the right word... You said marks, what was Odette involved in before?"

"Running cons."

"A con artist? I really should screen my roommates better! Was she any good?"

Tully nodded. "I was one of the people who tried to bring her down. She got away."

Lisa arched an eyebrow. "So I suppose there could have been any number of people after her, especially if she was still at it." Tully was noncommittal but he'd been thinking the exact same thing. They had her real name and a few aliases but who knew how many identities Boswell had assumed in the course of her career. She'd gone after powerful people to get a bigger score and that kind of behavior was exactly the kind that got one face down in the sand.

"Did your roommate have a car?" Barry asked, looking up from his notepad.

"No, well, at least not that I knew of. From what you've told me though I don't know that my word holds much weight anymore, maybe she conned me out of mine."

Barry and Tully exchanged glances.

"I had to run to the store this morning," Lisa said quickly, my car isn't missing.

"Would it be alright if we looked around Miss Boswell's room?" Tully asked. Maybe they would find some kind of memento that would give someone with greater motive away.

"By all means," Lisa got to her feet. She motioned for them to follow her. "I haven't done anything with it. I'm thinking I may just turn it into a sitting room or something quiet, I don't really need a roommate. I thought it might be nice for the company. I'm beginning to doubt that ever really works out." She led them across the long great room to a door on the left and pushed it open. Tully looked inside.

The disorder surprised him. He'd been expecting some stark and impersonal room with just a few things fastidiously arranged. The room wasn't messy so much as it was cluttered, mostly with papers arranged on top of bureau, a low bookcase and the night stand. There were also pictures on the bookcase which was on the same wall as the door, so Tully couldn't see what they held. He stepped into the room and looked back at them. There were about twelve framed photos, over half of Boswell in various poses alone, their presence screamed narcissist. But about four were Boswell and different men. One, unframed and tucked to the side, featured Wesley Cobin.

The live-in manager had an apartment on the ground floor as well as an office. It was to the latter Wesley let himself in after using an unlocked window in vacant apartment 104 to gain access.

He hadn't expected to be able to walk right into the manager's office so he had a background story to go along with his plan.

It was with surprise that he twisted the door knob to the office and found the room unlocked, greater surprise when he opened the door and found the room empty.

There appeared to be nothing more than just a large closet with a desk and computer, some filing cabinets and a stack of video recorders plus a fax machine.

Wesley first made his way to the DVRs. They were hooked up to a small monitor, next to which was a stack of blank DVDs.

Wesley turned his attention to the cabinets next to the recorders and pulled out drawers. Archived footage, burned onto rewriteable DVDs filled the drawers.

He found the newest dates and then found the appropriate disc for when Boswell went missing. He pulled out the disc and slipped it into his pocket.

Next he found the DVR remote and pulled up the menu, then navigated to the internal hard drive.

He found the block of time that Boswell would have left her apartment and deleted the backed up footage with only a small twinge of guilt.

As the progress bar inched across the screen he turned his attention to the small room.

There were stacks of paper on any available surface along with full page printed pictures.

He perused through the papers on the desk, they all seemed to be rental applications and the usual stuff one would expect an apartment manager to be in possession of.

The pictures, on the other hand, were weird contorted images, clearly Photoshopped into some strange facsimile of the original. One of a dog he found particularly unsettling, but he couldn't place his finger on the reason. They all seemed to run toward disturbing.

He turned his attention to a stack of folders on a corner of the desk.

The top folder read *Cuthard, Lisa.* It seemed to be a very thick file.

Wesley picked it up and flipped through it.

On top was a background check, followed by a detailed financial report, followed by a few black and white photos, followed by a list of investment assets, followed by a list of phone numbers. A few pages later, Wesley began to have an idea of what he was looking at.

He pulled out his phone and snapped pictures of the pages, then replaced the folder like he had found it.

Next he thumbed through the rolodex and checked the desk drawers, the top two of which were locked. He decided not to pick them and checked the DVR.

Video Deleted displayed on the screen.

Wesley turned to leave when he heard the sound.

"What do you think?" Barry asked when they were on the sidewalk outside the apartment building.

"About Miss Cuthard?" Tully shrugged. "She seemed genuine to me. So far as we know she doesn't stand to gain anything. It's her apartment and by her own admission and in our findings so far there's no other connection between Cuthard and Boswell."

"Do you think she's telling the truth?"

"Any particular point you were wondering about?"

"No," Barry said, "Just in general."

"I agree she looks clean."

"You notice anything about the building?" Tully asked shifting the conversation.

Barry turned back to survey the building's façade.

"Five floors plus a basement, build out of brick, probably about a grand a month based on the wood floors and granite counters."

"It has a security door…" Tully prompted.

"So anyone who goes into the building has to be buzzed in…" Barry glanced at Tully, trying to see what the older man wanted.

He didn't like the look he saw and knew he needed to up his game.

He turned back to the building and examined it. Just above the door he caught site of a red flash.

"And a security camera." Barry said.

Tully nodded. "Go find out if the building management keeps an archive."

"And get the tape that has our girl on it." Barry said heading for the door of the building.

Tully eyed the camera, hidden up under the eaves, and tried to work out if it would cover the street.

If it did, and if Boswell had been picked up they could ID the car and then they might have a solid lead.

While he waited for Jake return Tully looked across the street. There was a cozy looking café advertising fresh artisan sandwiches. Actually they sounded kind of good.

He studied the café for a minute, looking over the brick and glass building, then back at the apartment. Soon he had an idea.

It was the apartment intercom, Wesley realized a second after hearing the shrill screech. Someone was paging the manager.

He listened carefully.

The noise was coming from behind him, from the desk, but he could also hear it through the wall of the office, the wall shared with the manager's apartment. He tried to decide if he should use the opportunity to run. He stayed.

"What?" he heard a gruff voice say from the other side of the wall.

"This is Jake Barry with the Sheriff's office. I'd like to talk to you about your security footage."

"I already told that other guy about it!" came the snapped reply.

"Yes, you spoke with the local police officers. I'm from the sheriff's department. We are the ones handling the murder investigation, so I need to see the footage for the security camera out here."

"Dude, I don't even know if I have it, why don't you ask that detective Jones guy or whatever!"

"This is a separate matter, I have spoken to detective Jones but this is not his investigation, it's mine, so buzz me in and let's go take a look at the surveillance footage." Jake ordered.

"Whatever," the building manager said, "But this buzzer doesn't work, I'll come let you in."

Wesley heard the manager's apartment door open and shut, then foot steps down the hall.

He waited a moment, then left the office and walked straight down the hall.

He heard the outer door opening and Jake's voice as they started toward him.

Wesley put his head down and ran to 104. He twisted the knob and slipped in just as the manager rounded the corner.

Wesley wasted no time. He bolted for the high set window and climbed through. He closed the frosted pane behind him and replaced the screen. Through the glass he just made out the door opening. Apparently he'd been seen, but he doubted much would come of it.

He turned and hurried for the Jeep.

It hadn't gone as smoothly as he'd hoped, there had been two near misses, starting with that moment in the garden when he thought Fineas had noticed him. But, as Wesley unlocked the Jeep and climbed into the passenger seat, his heart rate was back down to a steady pulse and he felt a faint thrill.

Radburt was still out shopping in the market and probably wouldn't be back for a few minutes, which was just the way Wesley wanted it.

He leaned across the console and pressed the starter once, not enough to start the engine but sufficient to power the accessories.

Then he removed the DVD from his jacket pocket and slid the disc into the slot in the center stack. The DVD drive hummed away, on screen the Jeep logo faded and Wesley selected the option to play the disc.

An onscreen menu appeared, offering a variety of chapters arranged by dates. He picked the one he wanted and watched security footage fill the screen. It was fairly good quality, better than most convenience store's footage at least. It would be enough to clearly identify someone but the camera didn't cover much of the street out front.

It was enough for someone who knew cars to make an identification but it wouldn't be possible to get more than a make and model, even color was tricky since the footage was black and white.

He advanced the disc forwards starting at 12 noon the day of. He'd thought about calling Lisa Cuthard and asking her what time Boswell had left but that would have been too easy for Tully to find out. He set the fast forward to 2x but quickly realized that wouldn't fit his time frame. He tried bumping the speed up to 6x but the compressed video started to pixelate too much to follow. Then he remembered Boswell's punctuality. She was fastidious in her planning and always left on the hour if she could. He skipped to 1 o' clock, then progressed covering 2 and 3 in just a few minutes, he skipped to 4 and at 4:03 he got her.

It looked like she was wearing a black dress with a white jacket, though that could have just been the footage. Her hair was down and her face was never turned toward the screen but Wesley knew it was her by her proud, swaying walk. He watched as she left the building and walked down the sidewalk. At the edge of the screen a vehicle was parked, only visible from the wheel hubs down but obviously an SUV. Wesley watched as Boswell walked to it, opened the rear door out of shot and climbed in.

He backed up the video and paused it was as clear a shot of the car as he could get. He took out his phone and flicked over to the camera, engaged one of the filters and snapped a picture of the in-dash screen. The wide aperture camera lens and digital enhancement compensated for the screen's backlight and the 12 megapixel shot looked crisp.

Wesley ejected the disc and returned it to his jacket pocket and opened the directory app on his phone.

He found the local police department number and copied it to his contacts. He launched an app that let him spoof the phone's outgoing caller ID information and loaded the appropriate outgoing data. In a couple of seconds he was talking to the receptionist at the local precinct and soon thereafter a Detective Jones.

"This is Jones." The detective said.

"Afternoon Detective, this is Blaze Miles from the Coolidge County Sheriff's department. First of all Sheriff Tully wanted me to send you his thanks for faxing us your files on the Boswell case. Very quick work, it was invaluable and he wanted me to make a special point of saying how much he appreciated the detail notes. We just had a small problem getting the evidence inventory list and the list of contacts you had for Boswell. There's something wrong with our fax machine, is there any way you might be able to send at least some of that information in an e-mail?"

"Oh, um, right, okay." The detective sounded confused, likely because he may not have faxed over any files. But so long as he was being commended for a job well done he saw no reason to cause trouble.

"Right, Boswell?" Jones asked. "I just talked to your boss he said he was going to stop by. I can make sure he gets duplicates." Wesley swallowed. Of course Tully had already called!

"Yes, he was going to interview Lisa Cuthard, the victim's roommate." Wesley said, wondering if he should push the e-mail or let it slide. "He also wanted to make sure he could get the surveillance DVD, if that would be alright with you?"

There was silence on the other end of the line.

"Uh, you said surveillance DVD?"

"Yes, I believe he said it was referred to in the notes, apparently it had the victim on it leaving her apartment building?"

"Oh, right *that* DVD." Jones said, clearly having no idea what Wesley was talking about.

"If it's alright?"

"Sure thing, I'll let the front desk know he's coming. Any idea on how long?"

"Oh, no more than fifteen minutes I would say." Wesley spied Radburt making his way through the marketplace shoppers.

"OK, tell your boss to have the front desk call me when he gets there, I can meet him at the evidence cage."

"Excellent, thank you so very much detective. Keep up the excellent work now."

"Uh huh. Good bye."

Wesley hit the end button. It was good to be back in the game.

Tully was back in the car when Barry returned from talking to the building manager. Tully noticed that he was empty handed.

"The manager checked but he said the disc we're looking for is missing," Barry explained as he pulled on his seat belt. "He thinks the locals must have taken it with them."

"He thinks?" Tully asked.

"Yeah, not the most organized guy, the room where they keep the surveillance equipment is a mess. I don't know how he'd ever find anything! Very into Photoshop too, I suspect that's his one skill since he couldn't stop talking about it."

"Call Detective Jones at the precinct. Ask if they'd be good enough to let us take a look at that DVD."

CHAPTER 5

Wesley directed Radburt to East 22nd Street and a little bistro.

"If you wouldn't mind ordering for me, there's just one little thing I have to do first." Wesley said. Radburt eyed him hard and clearly didn't like it, but acquiesced nonetheless.

As Radburt entered the Bistro Wesley crossed the street to the precinct station.

At the front desk Wesley gave his name as Carlos Vaughn and showed her his credentials.

"I'm with Sheriff Tully, I think detective Jones was going to mention that we would be stopping by?" The woman at the front desk consulted her computer and then nodded.

"Yes, he did, just a moment." She picked up her phone.

"Oh, you don't need to bother him right now, the Sheriff isn't here yet. I was just going to see if I could make some copies before he got here, I think they're in the evidence locker.

The woman nodded and slid a sign-in sheet across the desk along with a visitor's tag.

"Thanks." Wesley said and clipped the badge on, then headed down the side hallway.

From past experience Wesley knew where the evidence locker was, he was just glad he'd managed to bluff his way back and now hoped he didn't run into anyone who recognized him.

He reached the evidence counter without incident.

"You the guy from the Sheriff's?" The officer behind the glass partition asked.

"That'd be me." Wesley said and pulled a clear plastic bag with a red evidence label around the top from under his jacket.

"Sheriff Tully is definitely going to want this." he said.

The officer handed him a pen and he initialed the bag, which already had several initials on it, then passed it across the counter. The officer did the same.

"Which bin?"

"Boswell, Odette." Wesley answered. He was then handed a corresponding clip board that listed the items in the locker. Wesley checked the contents and added one surveillance DVD.

He held his breath as he handed the clip board back across the desk. If the officer checked he'd notice Wesley had back dated the DVD as being entered that morning.

The man simply said "Thank you" and returned the clip board to the rack.

Wesley nodded his thanks and hurried for the exit.

Tully nosed the car into an unmarked parking space in front of the precinct building and killed the engine. He eyed the dashboard clock and hoped he'd be making it home in time to grab dinner then unbuckled his belt and climbed out of his car.

He was immediately reminded why he didn't like the city, there was the inescapable background noise of traffic and other ambient noises that, even if you ignored them played in your subconscious.

He closed his door and walked away, pressing the lock button on the key fob from his pocket. Barry followed him up the six steps to the precinct's front door and into the dated lobby.

Tully was also reminded how nice their new offices were when he eyed the drab green vinyl flooring and bad fluorescent lighting. They'd lived with something similar for years, finally though they'd been approved to occupy the municipal building where they were now.

Tully walked up to the front desk and gave his name to the receptionist. She said that Detective Jones was expecting them and that he'd meet them at the evidence locker. She handed over visitors passes and pointed them down the hallway.

Tully was relieved Jones was willing to share his evidence.

They found him, true to his word, outside the evidence locker going over a clipboard, a puzzled expression on his face.

"Detective Jones?" Tully asked. Jones looked up and nodded.

"Sheriff Tully," he extended his hand, "Deputy Barry," he added and shook Barry's hand.

"Thank you for letting us take a look at what you've got."

"Well it's your case," Jones said. "She's your problem now."

"I take it you are aware of Miss Boswell's career?" Tully wondered.

"Not from personal experience but she was a person of interest to a couple of the boys here." Jones said. "And from her file I see she'd given you a pack of trouble too." Tully nodded.

"What I was really hoping you had was a DVD of some surveillance from her apartment building."

"Yes, the DVD." Jones was shaking his head as if puzzled, he sounded strange.

"Is there something wrong?" Tully asked.

"No, not at all, it's logged." Jones said quickly. Tully wondered what his underlying reluctance was a sign of.

"And we can take a look at it?" Tully pressed.

"Of course, there's a player in locker, we can also run you off a copy."

"A copy would be great." he said with a nod.

Jones tapped the clipboard absently. In his mind he was straining to remember anything to do with a DVD. According to the sheet he'd logged it in yesterday, along with the rest of the evidence but he didn't have the slightest memory of it, nor did he remember where the financial records would have come from that had been signed in earlier that same day. He wondered if he needed a vacation. Fast.

Wesley wasn't lurking. Outside a police building one didn't lurk. Hence the bistro with its table by the window.

He didn't fool himself into thinking that Radburt hadn't noticed where he'd returned from and he was betting Radburt would notice when he excused himself that he would head in the opposite direction as the restroom. It was one of their unspoken agreements. He wouldn't lie to Radburt and Radburt wouldn't ask. It simplified life a great deal.

As soon as Wesley spotted the familiar Crown Victoria he'd slipped from the bench with a soft apology then walked past the maître d', who eyed him strangely, and back outside.

Now he was taking his biggest risk, he crossed to road and headed straight for the parked Ford. Tully opened his door and Wesley tried his best to look inconspicuous.

Tully didn't look behind him, nor did Barry. They both got out of the car and headed for the precinct steps.

Now came Wesley's gamble.

He pulled out his phone and pressed the soft key labeled "burst".

Tully continued up the steps and entered the precinct.

Wesley crossed to the car and squinted at the driver's door panel. The door lock was raised above the edge. He let out a breath he hadn't noticed holding.

He didn't have the ability to snatch the radio frequency door lock code for the Crown Victoria out of the air. He couldn't enter the VIN number into a clever app and instantly be granted access to the car, but he could sufficiently jam the key fob's lock transmit code thus preventing it from reaching the car and locking the doors.

He tugged on the handle and slipped inside.

He didn't waste time combing through the interior. He grabbed the pocket recorder from its place on the bolt-in center console and popped the back off of it.

He pulled the micro SD card and slipped it into his phone, then navigated to the card reader and copied the audio files across to the phone's internal storage. The transfer took twenty seconds. During which Wesley watched nervously through the windshield.

The phone vibrated once to let him know the transfer was complete and he replaced the card in the recorder and put the cover back on.

He climbed from the driver's seat; hit the lock button on the door and slammed it shut. He slipped the phone, now containing the recorded interview with Odette Boswell's roommate, into his jacket pocket and crossed the street.

After dinner Wesley and Radburt left the city and began the drive back home. Wesley had connected his headset to the Memo and was playing back Tully's interview with Lisa Cuthard. He couldn't say it was especially interesting or enlightening, but it was reassuring to a certain degree. At least *she* wasn't pointing the finger of suspicion at him, which made for a pleasant change.

Route 3 was quiet, free of commuters and any other traffic to speak of, but there wasn't much to see on the forty minute drive home.

That was why the sudden appearance of a sage green police issue Crown Victoria was such a brilliantly bad stroke of luck. As they passed the side road on the outskirts of town Wesley looked automatically away, then was riveted to the side mirror waiting to see which way the car turned. Of course it turned towards them because it was Fineas and Jake on their way home as well.

Tully got caught on a one way street that took him in the wrong direction, then he missed the turn off for the interstate junction and ended up lost in suburbia. He drove according to his sense of direction and eventually the houses ended and they were in undeveloped land on the edge of town. Throughout the ordeal Barry had wisely chosen to remain silent and Tully didn't voice any of his acerbic remarks about the city planners and their apparent loathing of street signs.

Eventually they found Route 3 and Tully nosed out behind a red SUV. A couple of seconds later it dawned on him that it was a newer red Grand Cherokee exactly like the one Wesley Cobin owned.

Tully added a little power so that he could easily read the license plate but he could only manage the first string of numbers and if they were both identical Jeeps bought at similar times they could have nearly sequential license numbers. It was not enough to confirm his suspicion.

Barry hadn't noticed the significance of the Jeep, but then nor had he spotted Cobin back at the apartment complex.

Or at least Tully had imagined it was Cobin.

To be fair Cobin didn't have many distinguishing features from across a garden and he didn't have a motive for him to be there.

Actually that wasn't true. During their original investigation Boswell had expressed interest in Cobin, an interest he had rejected both personally and professionally in no uncertain terms. Boswell was supposed to be meeting someone she was excited about. It was possible Cobin had called her, invited her over, met her on the beach, shot her and drove off. That was motive for him being at the apartment, but not for shooting her in the first place.

Tully ran through the possible motives but he could find nothing realistic, allowing that Cobin wasn't a sociopath who killed just for the thrill.

He thought about that.

No, he'd known Cobin too long for that to be the case. The kid wasn't that good an actor, or at least Tully knew how to read him. The only motive he had was revenge, but that left the question of why now?

Cobin had become somewhat more reckless but that was self-destruction, anyone he'd hurt would be unintentional collateral damage.

So, he didn't have a good motive, but Cobin also lacked a good alibi. If he had been at the apartment earlier then something else was going on and it was something Tully fully intended to get to the bottom of. The picture, tucked inside his jacket pocket also raised questions of its own. He needed to know.

He turned to Barry and told him his plan.

Wesley continued watching the side view mirror intently.

The Crown Victoria was still filling most of it.

Radburt wasn't worried, but then, he didn't think there was a reason to worry. They were going exactly 55 miles per hour with the cruise control set, he was a licensed driver and the vehicle had full insurance coverage.

Radburt wasn't entirely privy to the fact Wesley was a person of interest in an ongoing murder investigation and that Fineas Tully was after him. Wesley had been sure to keep him in the dark during the trial, deciding ignorance was bliss, though he doubted Radburt would have agreed if he'd known the entire preceding.

Wesley wondered what Fineas was up to. It only took him half a mile to come up with an answer. As soon as they crossed the line from county to county Wesley had a sinking feeling that Fineas was going to pull them over.

Of course there was no reason why he and Radburt couldn't be out for a drive, except for the part where he was pretty sure Fineas had seen him, or thought he had, at Odette Boswell's apartment building.

Wesley's presence in the Jeep would likely confirm Fineas' suspicion and who knew what wrong assumptions that could lead to.

No, it was best if Fineas didn't find him at all. Not to mention Jake Barry, slumped in the passenger seat. The deputy already had it out for Wesley and there was no reason to give him any more ammunition.

In order to evade detection it would require a little cunning and a team effort. He turned to Radburt.

"I need you to do something a little odd." He said and then filled his valet in on the plan.

Ahead of them, the Jeep passed the Coolidge County border sign, crossing back into Tully's jurisdiction. He reached for the lights, just waiting for the cruiser to cross the imaginary line.

"What's he doing?" Barry asked suddenly. The deputy had been sitting tensely, ready for action the last half mile, now he twitched as the Jeep's turn signal flashed on. Tully stared, then checked his dashboard display just to make certain he hadn't accidentally turned on the lights. They were still off, yet the Jeep's brake lights flashed red.

Tully applied his brakes and returned his hand to the wheel. The Jeep pulled off of the road, onto the shoulder and across a shallow ditch before stopping, angled back towards the road.

"Apparently he saw us." Tully muttered, also following the Jeep off the edge of the road, though not attempting to straddle the ditch. They both reached for their door handles and got out of the car.

Tully caught Barry's eye and shook his head when he saw his deputy's hand drifting toward the butt of his gun.

They approached the Jeep, Tully on the driver's side, Barry on the passengers. The idling engine was shut off and Tully heard the window powering down.

"Good evening Radburt." Tully said amiably.

"Good evening Sheriff Tully," Radburt said. "Forgive me for my presumptuousness but it looked like there was something you wanted?"

Tully raised an eyebrow.

"Your boss around?" Radburt eyed him strangely, then looked around the cabin which was obviously empty. Tully looked across the roof at Barry, who had already peered discreetly into the back seat. He shook his head.

"Are you asking if Mr. Cobin in this vehicle?" Radburt continued to look at Tully as if he might be batty.

"Well?" Tully supposed he might as well ask since he already looked like a fool.

"Absolutely not!" Radburt sounded insulted, which was probably fair enough. "Have a look." Reaching over he pressed the button to activate the power rear hatch. Motors hummed as the tailgate rose on automated hydraulics.

Barry discreetly walked around the Jeep and peered into the cargo hold, then continued around and stood next to Tully.

He shook his head.

"Just a house plant and some groceries." he muttered.

"Desk plant actually," Radburt corrected.

"A desk plant?" Tully echoed.

"Of course, brightens up a desk and is supposed to improve productivity."

"Cobin sent you into the city to pick up a plant?"

"No, I mailed some letters, had a spot of lunch then picked up the plant. He's very particular, the last plant had mites, ate the roots, nasty business! Are you, um?" Radburt gestured to the rear hatch control.

"Oh, yes." Tully nodded and Radburt pressed the button. "Well, thank you for your time."

"Not at all Sheriff!" Radburt called and powered up his window.

The tailgate latched as Barry reached the back of the Jeep.

"Tie your shoe." Tully ordered.

"What?"

"Tie your shoe."

Barry leaned over and in that moment understood what Tully had meant. He checked underneath the Jeep.

"Nope." he said straightening. Tully breathed a sigh of relief, feeling foolish. "Alright, let's head home." He headed back to his car. Behind him Radburt started the Jeep and pulled back onto the road.

As soon as Radburt angled the Jeep back towards the highway Wesley pulled the door handle inching open the door. As soon as the Jeep settled back on its suspension he dropped out of the truck to the ground, then he rolled into the ditch under the Jeep.

Immediately he started sweating, partly out of nerves, mostly because of the heat wafting off of the silent Hemi.

He made a mental note to avoid the tail pipes.

He was on his back with his head towards the rear of the Jeep so he could look straight back to see the tires of Tully's Crown Vic. He heard the doors open and saw four feet approaching. Slowly, he started inching towards the rear of the Jeep. He heard Radburt powering down his window, exchanging good evenings with Tully. He watched Barry pacing along the passenger side, leaning in to see past the tinted glass.

Wesley hoped that either Tully or Barry would suggest opening the hatch but Radburt played offense admirably. The motors whined as the tailgate was leveraged up and Wesley readied himself to move. Barry moved from his position next to the driver's door and approached the rear of the Jeep. His boots stopped at the open hatch, less than three feet away from Wesley's nose. Wesley tried very hard not to sneeze. After a few seconds spent searching the cargo area Barry continued around to the driver's side of the Jeep and stood next to Tully.

The coast was a clear as it was likely to get.

Wesley inched farther back until his head was even with the rear bumper. He looked up at the nose of Tully's Crown Victoria parked about eight feet away. The engine was silent and he hadn't turned on the lights.

Wesley breathed a gentle sight of relief. That meant the in-car camera really shouldn't be recording as it was tied into the lights. He had to move quickly now, time was almost up. He reached above his head and grabbed the bumper, then leveraged himself as gradually as possible over the bumper and into the cargo hold. The vinyl cover was thankfully still covering the area, blocking it from view of the windows. There was a heart stopping moment when the Jeep started to sag with his weight and he worried something would creak, but the air suspension didn't let him down and he rolled into the cargo area and lay still.

Ultimately, none of these antics were necessary and if he was caught at them they would be more damaging than if he'd just stayed in the passenger seat. But if at all possible he wanted Tully thinking himself slightly paranoid in imagining him places he wasn't. That and he didn't trust Jake Barry in the slightest, even under Tully's watchful eye.

Now there was only one thing that could go wrong. Wesley listened to Radburt explaining his alleged day, which was all true if not entirely inclusive of everything Radburt had done in the city. Then he delivered his line about the plant dutifully and casually mentioned the hatch. Wesley held his breath.

"Oh, yes." Tully said in reply and the tailgate motor's whirred away, shutting the hatch to the outside air. Wesley caught a flash of Barry's shoes and then he was sealed off in the dark confines of the cargo area. Mutedly he heard Tully telling Barry to tie his shoe, a not so subtle checking beneath the Jeep.

You're too late. Wesley thought.

Then the starter whirred and the engine rumbled to life, the exhaust magnified as it was exiting somewhere just below Wesley's ear, then they jolted forwards, crossed the ditch and rejoined the smooth county road leaving the Sheriff and his Deputy safely in their wake.

Tully dropped Barry off at the station before continuing on his way home. It was after seven now, he'd told Caroline not to wait up for him since he hadn't know exactly how late he'd be getting back. As it turned out he might be able to get his dinner while it was still warm.

He slowed down as he approached his house and surveyed it as he always did with satisfaction. It was a modest two story built in the late nineteen forties just before craftsmanship and pride in home design seemed to begin dying out, leading inexorably to the sorry state of prefabricated cookie-cutters that had been popping up daily for a time on the outskirts of town.

His was a home with character and it had been their home since Loren was three, as such it was packed full of memories, most of which seemed to have converted themselves into detritus stuffed into the attic and back shed.

Tully pulled into the driveway and parked behind Caroline's 1967 Mustang Fastback. It had been her father's passed on through Uncles and two cousins until she'd laid claim to the baby blue GT. Loren's Mazda was also in the driveway and, Tully was happy to find Dillon's car was nowhere to be seen.

He didn't know if he could have handled him this evening.

He climbed up to the back porch and entered the house through the kitchen door.

Caroline was at the sink rinsing dishes. She automatically turned her cheek for him to kiss as he crossed the kitchen to her.

"Hi," he said and wrapped his arms around her from behind as she shut off the sink.

"Hi, back." she said and leaned back into his embrace. "Long day." she said, as a statement rather than a question.

"But not as long as I was afraid of."

"Dinner's still on the table."

"I can smell that," he sniffed in illustration. "Jambalaya." Tully's wasn't a question either.

"Eat up and I might give you some dessert."

"What would I do without you?" Caroline turned to look at him.

"Honey, I don't think you really want an answer to that." she said with a smile.

"I love you." he kissed her smile then made his way to the hallway and into the cozy dining room.

Loren was still at the dinner table reading through a novel. When Tully entered the room she smiled, attention still on the book, then reached a stopping point and gave him her full attention.

"Hi Daddy," she said, still smiling and Tully felt his heart begin its nightly liquefaction process.

Loren could still catch him off guard. He'd glance at her and see her doing something she'd done as a little girl, that smile she'd given him since she was tiny for instance. The way she'd kept reading, the light in her eyes and then he'd be shaken by the realization that she was all grown up, a baby no longer. But she still owned his heart.

Tully had vowed to himself that he wasn't going to be a smothering father. That he wouldn't meddle in his daughter's affairs when he wasn't wanted. He'd taken great pains to acknowledge the subtle shift in role from instructor to advisor and thought he'd managed it reasonably well. He was proud of her and put trust that he and Caroline had done a good job during her impressionable years and now he lived for the moments she asked for his advice and was always ready to talk with her about anything.

It hadn't been easy, he hadn't been perfect and he'd overstepped before.

As he sat down at the table such times came drifting back to him in quick flashes.

He'd learned from those early mistakes and so had kept his mouth shut when Dillon had proposed to Loren without first asking his permission. In fact he'd kept his mouth shut on Dillon as a whole. He knew Dillon wasn't a bad man, wasn't likely to hurt his daughter any more than any man could. He knew what Dillon could be like, sometimes overly dedicated to his job, extremely impassioned in the pursuit of justice. But he had to be fair, as Caroline had pointed out, he had the same tendencies. She'd grinned and said she'd been "happy enough" in their thirty three years together.

"Dad, you alright?" Loren asked and pulled him back to the present.

He smiled automatically.

"Fine sweetheart."

"Long day?" she asked, this time it was a question.

"Yes," he said not wanting to go into any details and knowing that Loren wouldn't probe for more information. She nodded.

"So how are the plans?" Tully asked as he dished the Jambalaya into his bowl.

"Oh, *that* kind of bad day?" Loren joked. "It would have to be to get you interested in wedding plans."

"I'm always interested in my only daughter's wedding plans, especially as I'm expected to pay for them." Tully rejoined.

"Ho, ho." Loren said in mock amusement. "And, no nothing new, Dillon said he was busy so we didn't do lunch, something about a new case. He said we could talk about it Wednesday." Tully picked up on the note of disappointment easily but didn't know what to say.

In a flash Tully imagined Loren gone, moved out after the wedding. It wouldn't be the first time, not as hard perhaps, but that memory haunted him.

Yet more incentive to keep his mouth shut.

His mind slipped back to the murder that morning and felt the connection.

The time Tully hadn't kept his mouth shut had been because of Cobin.

Loren hadn't believed he was guilty, probably still didn't. Instead of letting her find out for herself he'd stomped his foot down and made her decisions for her. For nearly six terrible months Loren had moved out and largely broken off communication with him. During the time they'd needed each other, the time she needed her dad the most they'd had that awful rift between them.

Eventually she'd returned, the tears were gone and she was as much at peace as could have been expected. Tully pretended he didn't know what had happened to change her mind. He pretended that he hadn't interfered one last time. But through his pretending he suspected Loren knew the truth and yet, his wonderful baby girl had forgiven him.

He still carried the burden of unspoken words and any time Dillon let her down as he evidently had today he had the option of using them. He could end it.

He could tell Loren what the trial had been like. To give her a glimpse of the man Dillon could become when he was on a tirade; a peek at what happened when her past and future collided.

He picked up his fork.

CHAPTER 6

Wesley sat at his desk in a good mood.

He'd even acquiesced to Radburt's plea he eat in the dining room, now he was digitizing the documents that he'd taken pictures of in the apartment manager's office.

Once the documents were formatted correctly he sent them to the laser printer and turned his attention to a timeline.

If he was going to stay ahead of Tully, he'd need to know everything Tully had on the investigation, which would mean running his own investigation simultaneously.

According to the *Gazette*, Boswell's time of death was sometime around 1 AM. According to the building footage, she left at 4:03 PM. There were 9 hours unaccounted for. Factor in a drive time of approximately two and a half hours and she could have spent a total of six and a half hours in the county. Wesley swallowed.

With that wide a window in such a small county someone was bound to have seen her, especially if she'd stopped to eat.

The last page dropped into the printer tray and Wesley picked up the documents.

Next he opened his e-mail and skimmed the computer generated report on Lorenzo Washington, or at least the eleven months of history his search had turned up.

It was a very through report that spanned banking, tax history, property ownership as well as the usual sources. Normally it was enough to bind together for a coffee table book.

These search results might fill a pocket sized note pad.

On a piece of paper he drew a line to connect two names.

L. Washington and *O. Boswell*.

Partners, he wrote underneath.

He glanced at his stack of information, at Lisa Cuthard's phone number and wondered if he should tell her she was in danger.

He had a gnawing feeling that things were far from over.

Tully was dower after dinner as he ran the facts and feelings of the day through his mind. The interview with Lisa Cuthard hadn't been especially productive. She had shed light on Boswell's goings on, which could lay a motive for someone else to want her dead but they'd already known that based on her record. Miss Cuthard herself didn't seem like a likely candidate as the murderer, so far as they knew she only gained an empty apartment, not that people hadn't killed over much less. But the murder seemed too complicated for a casual dislike to turn deadly.

Then of course there was the picture.

Tully made sure that Barry hadn't seen it.

It was the first time he'd ignored evidence as glaring as that in an investigation and his conscience was not going to let him off lightly about it.

On the other hand he hadn't destroyed the evidence. He'd just quietly tucked the picture in to his jacket pocket.

He looked at it now.

They were in a poorly lit bar and the picture had been taken with a very bright flash, washing out both Boswell and Cobin, but they were still recognizable. Cobin was grinning ear to ear and Boswell, Tully thought, looked like a wild animal about to strike. Her apparent glee was more of a snarl than a smile.

Tully wondered when the picture had been taken, if it was after Loren, while simultaneously thinking there was something not right about the picture.

He was shaken out of further contemplation by the ringing of the telephone. He hurried out of his chair in the living room and crossed to the phone on the far wall. He answered it on the second trill.

"It's Jake," Barry said over the line. "We've got another body."

This time Tully wasn't the last to the scene. The CSU team was just arriving, the van awaiting unpacking parked level with Barry's cruiser, leaving a goodly distance between the evident crime scene and themselves. Because the CSU wasn't in motion yet no lights had been set up, but then they didn't need any since the crime scene was in a well illuminated parking lot.

Tully left his car next to Barry's and made his way over to his deputy standing sentry next to the lot's single parked car. Never had a white and characterless Toyota looked so foreboding.

Barry watched his boss approach without saying anything, not that there was anything to be said but Tully had no problem imagining Blaze calling out to him or even waving his arms to attract Tully's attention. He much appreciated Barry's sober attitude in light of the scene that awaited him.

The driver's door was open and the interior dome light dispelled shadows inside the car otherwise untouched by the sodium vapor overhead lights. The annoying warning chime was dinging away, forever to go unheeded by the driver.

Barry's expression was blank, again differentiating him from Blaze in whom the prospect of the previous murder had excited. Tully made a mental note to see if he could discreetly acquire an alibi from his junior officer.

"Sorry to call you out so late." Barry said apologetically, meeting him before he reached the car.

"Well unless you're the killer I'll forgive you; what do we have?" Tully asked clearing his mind.

"Another one," Barry said. "White, female, thirties, plainer than Boswell, no makeup."

"Recognize her?"

"Ran the plates, it checks out clean." Tully noticed Jake hadn't answered his question directly. Then he noticed his deputy was looking past him and Tully turned around to see Dillon fast approaching. He sighed and turned back to Barry.

"Check for ID yet?"

"Just made sure she was really dead." Another difference between Barry and Blaze; Tully knew Barry wouldn't have contaminated the scene, he'd check for a pulse, make sure everything was secure but he wouldn't go through her pockets or purse until after CSU or Tully cleared him to do so.

"Have CSU check it out and get someone to pull those keys out." Tully said as the bonging continued. He turned toward Dillon and met him before he could get close enough to see the interior of the car.

Dillon didn't say anything but his slightly self-satisfied expression was enough to make Tully exert much self-control in not snapping at the A.D.A.

"I just heard on the radio. Another one huh?"

"Another homicide? That's what it looks like but we don't know anything yet." Tully said carefully.

"Except another woman's dead within five miles of the last one, what was the cause of death?"

Tully looked around expressively. "You see the M.E. yet?"

"No, but you are the County Coroner in his absence."

"And you Mister Howard are the Assistant District Attorney, all pertinent information on this case will be presented to you through your office in due time." They both locked eyes for a few moments. Dillon's gaze was hard to begin with but quickly softened and he nodded his acceptance.

"Can you at least tell me if it fits the same pattern?"

"What pattern is that?" Tully asked. "There has been one homicide and one suspicious death, no one's ruled on this one yet."

"I mean a pattern from the other homicides." Tully stared, knowing what Dillon was referring to but shocked at the leap it was implying.

"Those deaths are totally unrelated to this." he said flatly. He'd had about enough of Dillon's amateur investigating and wild speculation. The A.D.A. didn't seem to understand just how hard Tully took every one of his jibs, how personal the mere suggestion of this latest thread was.

"I know, I know," Dillon said, his tone making it plain that he didn't know. "But let's suppose those earlier crimes might not have been committed by the father. I know he was just a teenager at the time but what if the Cobin that really needed to be under investigation..." Tully caught himself unconsciously resting his hand on the butt of his gun and toying with the strap release.

"Dillon," he said coldly, cutting the other man off. "You're young and you don't know better so I'm not going to make a big deal over this. You're driven and you're passionate. You don't like to lose. I respect that, but believe me when I tell you; drop that line of reasoning and don't you ever go back there because you don't have one single clue what you're talking about." Tully concluded softly enough but his tone was cutting.

Dillon's mouth wasn't exactly hanging open but the expression was ultimately the same. He knew he'd just crossed a line but he was surprised to have found it there. He cleared his throat.

"So you're saying it couldn't possibly have been Wesley Cobin who killed those seven other women?"

"Yes," Tully said in a low voice. "That is exactly what I'm saying. Are we clear?" He could tell by the flash in Dillon's eyes that they weren't clear but he also knew the younger man wouldn't be voicing that hypothesis to him again anytime soon.

"Now what I'm going to recommend," Tully said in a lighter and cheerier tone of voice. "Is that you go on home, maybe watch a little TV, get an good night's sleep and read my preliminary report when it's finished tomorrow." He made it clear that it wasn't a suggestion and thought that even if his position and demeanor weren't enough to get Dillon to follow his advice the fact that Dillon was dating his daughter should. Whichever motivation it was, it worked because Dillon nodded stiffly and turned on his heel, heading for his car. Tully allowed himself a grim smile and turned back to Barry.

"So, how bad is it?" he asked his deputy. By his earlier aversion when Dillon had been within earshot Tully assumed that it was bad.

"Remember Marana Epcot?" Tully looked at Berry in disbelief.

"No," he said flatly. "No, it can't be!" Barry didn't look as thrilled as Tully would have expected him to.

After all, Wesley Cobin now had a passable motive to kill both victims.

CHAPTER 7

Fineas felt like he was dragging himself into the dining room the next morning. Thought he'd actually gotten to bed at a reasonable time, the events of last night, and the previous day, were clearly taking their toll. Solving murders was not a walk in the park, especially since he was relatively unaccustomed to it.

When he seated himself at the table he found Caroline skimming the paper and Loren reading off some printed pages in front of her, probably something to do with one of her jobs.

He reached for the cereal box in front of him and poured it into the bowl already at his place.

As Fineas poured the milk he caught the headline.

Murder Epidemic Continues!

He felt his blood pressure rise. This was exactly the kind of press he didn't need!

The only good news was that their reporters were too uninspired to follow him around town, the same with the TV news. Small towns had their advantages, but eventually bigger groups would get involved and he needed some headway to show.

His mind just felt so scrambled at the moment he was worrying he would miss something vital. He decided he would call Deanna and see if she could help him work through some of the confusion.

He took a bite of cereal.

Caroline folded the paper and set it aside, she fixed him with her gaze.

"Do you want to talk about it?" she asked.

"Talk about what?" He wasn't normally evasive with Caroline but he didn't like the darker sides of his job being highlighted.

"Marana Epcot." Caroline said simply.

Loren looked up from her paperwork.

"Marana Epcot, that awful crime reporter?"

Caroline and Fineas both looked at Loren.

Caroline slid the paper, front page up, toward her daughter, who skimmed the headline.

"She's dead?" she said in surprise. "That's what last night was about?"

Fineas nodded.

"So there were two murders in twenty-four hours?" her eyes returned to the paper. "This isn't nearly as detailed as yesterday's write up they posted online." she commented, almost absently, her stare was vacant, thinking about something. She seemed unsettled, but then, she probably should have given the fact they were discussing murder over the breakfast table. Only Loren was more likely to instigate that conversation than back away from it.

"So, do you have any leads?" She asked, sounding a little more like herself.

Fineas debated if he really wanted to talk about this here and now, then again, it wasn't like he had much to say.

"The CSU is processing the evidence at the scene, odds are it's connected to the earlier murder but I wouldn't exactly call it an epidemic."

Loren nodded. "You haven't really had a lot of time to work on the case. Do you know what she was doing here, the reporter that is?"

Fineas shook his head.

Loren nodded. "Well I guess it's job security."

Fineas and Caroline both stared at her, surprised by her glib remark.

"Yeah, I know, still, it's not like she was that great a person, not that I'm saying she deserved to end up this way, but it could have been worse, more tragic at least. Did she have family?"

"No one turned up immediately, I'll find out more today. Are you alright?"

Loren nodded quickly. "Yeah, it's just a surprise, that's all." She gathered up her printouts and stood up. "Well, I think I'll try and get an early start." She left with her papers and bowl.

Caroline and Fineas exchanged glances but decided there was nothing they needed to do. Loren would be alright.

Fineas then turned his attention back to Marana Epcot, the one he'd had run-ins with three years ago.

"Marana Epcot was an up and coming crime reporter back then." Tully said, leaning back slightly in his office chair, phone pressed to his ear.

It was an hour and a half since breakfast and he had just composed and submitted his latest report. The Mayor was taking an expected uncomfortable interest in the whole thing and was demanding regular updates on the investigation. Not that Tully was presently talking to the mayor or to anyone in his office.

He was on the phone with Deanna Casale, the only other woman besides Caroline he truly felt comfortable confiding in.

They'd been partners for a few years back when he was still sir-ing everyone and their paths crossed again four or five years ago.

In the first relatively brief time they were together they formed a symbiotic relationship and in his entire career Tully had only once worked with someone else that could read him as well as Deanna.

From there they'd kept in touch.

Tully had climbed the ladder to become Sheriff, Casale on the other hand had switched career tracks to move up the ranks of the FBI, then ATF, where she'd eventually contented herself with becoming a squad leader of some kind. It was in this capacity that they had met up again on the job and the dynamic duo had bagged another public enemy.

It had been a struggle, Tully knew, for Deanna as a woman, both as a cop and in the FBI and he freely admitted she was a good deal tougher than he was.

Whenever either of them needed to talk out their troubles with someone other than their team members or family, they'd call.

Now Tully was bringing Dee up to speed on the two murders.

"Funny thing was," he continued in his Epcot explanation. "She usually was anti law enforcement, always investigating claims of police brutality and rallying the public to her causes; even when she was dead wrong. She managed to get five officers thrown off the force in Raleigh under charges of brutality. Seven months later the story was proved to be a thin fabrication but Epcot was ruled an unknowing participant. Either way none of the cops got their jobs, or pensions back and two ended up losing their homes because of the layoff and bad press."

"Epcot huh? Can't say as I recall the name." Casale said thoughtfully and Tully could imagine her twirling a pencil in her fingers as she reclined slightly in her office chair in D.C. surrounded by drab beige walls and grey carpet. To be fair though, he'd never seen her office.

"She wasn't really on the national level yet, though it was only a matter of time I'd say."

"A once and future 60 minutes reporter?" Dee suggested.

"Something like that. For some reason though, she took a strong dislike to Cobin and decided we were the good guys for once."

"That's a shock," Casale said, a thin smile in her voice. "Kind of reminds me of a serial changing his favorite M.O."

"Maybe 'good guys' was too strong. The lesser of evils? She tried bringing the whole thing back to my office but it was a thin accusation even for Epcot. Basically she concentrated on Cobin and the trial. I'd say she's largely responsible for working the public into such fervor as to burn down his apartment complex."

"I'd imagine that would have made jury selection difficult."

"Not like it ever got that far."

"True," Dee admitted. "So, you're faced with two murdered women who both tie back to Cobin. The one who got away and the one who ruined him."

"He ruined himself, she just told the world about it in the most bigoted way possible." Tully corrected automatically. "And like I said, in her reports she did a number on law enforcement as a whole, trying to get his behavior to sum up all officers of the law."

"So, I'm guessing Cobin isn't the only suspect since I've just heard about her and she already makes me look for ways to write her up."

"No one here is mourning the loss of her that's for sure."

"And you said Boswell was equally disliked?"

"I suppose you could say so, a con artist with a knack for slipping through loopholes."

"Remind you of anyone?"

"No, I have to admit she used talent. Cobin just used money." Casale's sigh crackled the phone line and Tully creased his brow wondering what she'd meant by it.

"And what are your initial impressions?" Casale asked, apparently moving on.

Tully grinned. "Perhaps you're not remembering some of my former first impressions?"

"You mean you haven't grown better with age?" She asked feigning surprise.

"I'm Sheriff now; I have lackeys for that sort of thing."

"From what I remember about your lackeys, that's a truly terrifying thought. You had that moody guy and the way-too-into-himself-to-look-where-he's-walking desk sergeant but the only real detective type you had was, well…"

"Yeah," Tully muttered. It was a fact and circumstance he was all too familiar with. "But then that's what I call you for."

"I should start charging per call, I accomplish more than those 900 numbers." Tully withheld any comment. "Have you noticed that so far both murders took out people who had beaten the system? I'd say cop or wannabe cop."

"How like a fed," Tully remarked. "Blame it on the local LEO's."

"If the profile fits…"

"Since when did you become a psych player?"

"Since I started putting away bad guys full time, maybe you should try it."

"Ouch." Tully still smiled.

"But really, do you think Cobin's your guy?" Tully didn't respond right away despite the fact he'd already given this exact question considerable thought. "I know what you want but I'm not in a position to give it to you." Casale said after his silence had stretched on. "Two and a half weeks four and a half years ago is not enough time to get an accurate read."

"Dee." Tully said.

"Fineas." She replied sternly.

"I'm perfectly capable of knowing my own mind." Tully remarked.

"But you don't always listen to it. Besides, you already know what I think, thought, guessed, I don't know, whatever you want to say."

"Cobin didn't do it?"

"But clearly he did, you had the evidence."

"Good evidence, eye witness testimony both reliable and otherwise, all saying similar things…" Tully said slowly. A silence followed but he knew Deanna well enough that she was building to something, probably something profound and by her reluctance to voice it, something he wouldn't like.

"I have to ask, that original case. As diplomatic as I can here, no phone taps, I promise. Did you find stronger evidence than was presented to the D.A.?" This time it was Tully's sigh that crackled the phone line.

"You're asking if I tampered with the evidence to leave Cobin enough leverage to get out of his noose." Since it was out in the open Dee wasted no time.

"Yep, pretty much my question."

Silence hung for a few seconds, neither even breathing.

"No." Tully said with heavy finality.

"Well that answers one thing." Tully resisted the urge to give the handset a questioning glance.

"What?" he asked.

"Its early days, if you ask me these cases are connected but the Cobin link is way too obvious. The kid I met would never leave such an obvious trail. How is he?" The segue caught Tully off guard.

"What?"

"Cobin. The only reason I can think that he'd shoot two people with which he had an obvious tie would be if he wanted you to bring him down, not impossible but it takes some serious mental screwy-ness, so, how's the kid?" Tully didn't know how to respond, he considered the number of times he'd hauled him in over the past year.

"Out of control I suppose. Self-destructive."

"Implosive or explosive?"

"Honestly? I don't know for sure. I'd like to say implosive. I'd really like to say implosive." he added.

"Well, that's not good. You want my professional opinion on him then?"

"I think that's what this whole conversation was for, Casale." Tully said in a playfully gruff tone.

"Cobin's not your guy. But either way he's going to end up dead and as much as you think you're alright with that you're not, so Fin, make sure you're square with him as best you can be." This time Tully did stare at the handset.

"Where's this coming from?" He asked and thought back to her question about him tampering with evidence; it hadn't had a bearing on the present facts. "Why'd you ask if I withheld evidence?"

"Cause I wanted to know where you stood with him, really."

"So, what's it prove?"

"Fineas, you gave them everything, all the evidence, and from the second that you did, up until now you've been wishing you hadn't." He wanted to make a hasty reply but he found he couldn't. "We're going to say good bye now and you're going to hang up and figure out these cases. I know you will. But you're going to have to square yourself with Cobin whichever way this falls."

"He shot and killed his partner in cold blood." Tully said flatly.

"And since he lost his parents you raised him like a son. That is not something you can just ignore." The silence lasted only a second or two. "OK pal, I've got to get back to work, take care." she said and mechanically Tully said good bye. They both hung up. Tully sat in his chair and gazed vacantly at the opposite wall.

Was Casale right? Did he regret handing over everything he had on Cobin?

It hadn't mattered in the end and, truthfully, he'd never expected Cobin to get much of a sentence. Even when the D.A.'s office threw their best resources and their brightest young attorney at the case Tully had known Cobin's gaggle of lawyers wouldn't settle for anything more than a couple of years in a designer prison. But it hadn't been guaranteed.

He'd liked Mike, he'd wanted justice for him, but they were dealing with a legal system. There was also the fact that he'd liked Mike but he'd loved Cobin, Wesley, he missed Wesley even now.

Of course Deanna was right. She was always right, or at least near enough. Among the feelings he'd done his best to bury, was guilt.

Simple acknowledgement brought some small amount of peace.

Though they had no relationship now Tully decided that this time he wasn't going to abandon Cobin. If he turned out to have committed the murders he would bring him in, he would prosecute, but he was going to make damn sure he knew the whole story before he did anything drastic.

Some inner-turmoil resolved Tully actually felt like he could devote the proper attention to the case right up until the phone call from the Mayor's office.

CHAPTER 8

An hour later found Tully outside Mayor Brett Slane's office and in a much worse disposition. He'd basically been ordered down to city hall for a sit-down with the Mayor who wanted to be "apprised of all the facts" in his current investigation and that annoyed him. Slane never took an interest in the workings of the Sheriff's Department unless he felt he had something to add to skew an investigation his own way.

"He'll see you now." Slane's young secretary said with a flash of her whiter than white teeth.

Tully nodded thanks to her and walked through the door.

"Ah, Sheriff Tully, come in." Slane called out from behind his giant generations old oak desk in the depth of his dark office. The office was oppressively decorated with dark woods and oil paintings that hid most of the dark red wall papering. All-in-all it was not a pleasant room aside from the four floor-to-ceiling windows that over looked the cupola and gave a view of town square beyond.

Dillon Howard sat in one of the two wingback chairs facing the mayor's desk. He was looking back at Tully, looking ill at ease and therefore immediately Tully had his guard up.

"Please take a seat." Slane said and gestured to one of the chairs. The Mayor himself wouldn't have seemed to quite fit the office aside from the fact that Tully knew he was plagued with a chronic illness; the inability to change. He was also tight fisted which would explain away any of the antiques present, like the Persian rug under the desk, which was beginning to wear thin.

The Slane family had always owned most of the county and therefore had been in a position to buy the best and their miserly dispositions made them hang on to everything for as long as possible.

Indeed Brett had merely assumed his role as Mayor hardly considering the possibility people wouldn't vote him in. The astonishing thing was that people did because, evidently, the familiarity made them comfortable. It was also why the new station headquarters had been constructed largely from donated monies and not out of the regular county budget.

Tully sat down and immediately began to chafe. The thing he most hated about being Sheriff was that he was an elected official. He didn't mind the process and that the people had a say, it was that he had to work closely with men like Slane in order to keep his candidacy open.

It was nice on paper.

You couldn't sketch in corruption and good-ole-boy networks out there in the open.

"I've just been talking with Mr. Howard here about these two horrible, horrible murders." Each time he said horrible the Mayor shook his head and squinted, apparently feeling this best conveyed his expressed horror.

"Yes, I know," Tully looked over at Dillon who seemed to withdraw from his gaze. "Mr. Howard here seems to be taking them very personal."

"Well, yes, yes, of course, every concerned citizen is and it's my job to give them something to comfort them with."

Really? Tully thought sarcastically.

"Now I understand a bit about police work," Tully resisted the urge to snort. He knew what was coming, as he'd heard it before. "You know my great-granddad was Sheriff and he taught me a lot about the law, made me the man I am today." Tully tried not to take that as the unintended insult it was and almost choked on a laugh remembering one previous time Slane had used the same turn of phrase. That was back when Tully had a partner worth running inside commentary with.

They'd talked over the mayor's head throughout the whole interview.

And of course you have a law degree, was the next line.

Of course, that too. Slane had said happily, missing the joke that he'd never actually been allowed to practice law and the fact that everybody knew.

Tully turned his attention back to the Mayor.

"I know how these things work and I know I can't ask you to work any faster." Translation: Work Faster. "But, I also need these killings to stop because they are starting to make my people nervous as is well understood, I mean, they're making me nervous, too!"

"I don't think you have anything to worry about." Tully put in helpfully.

There isn't that much justice in the world.

"Oh, I'm sure of that Sheriff, I know where your priorities are and if you thought I was in danger you'd be sure to keep me safe."

"Thank you for your trust."

Misguided though it is.

"But as I said the citizenry needs reassuring and these murders aren't good for tourism."

Or the victims.

"So, Mr. Howard here tells me you have a prime suspect." Tully shot a look of annoyance at Dillon.

"Oh, does Mr. Howard really?" he asked.

"Oh, yes, not that it's a surprise really, there hasn't been a murder in this town that wasn't committed by a Cobin since my granddad took office." *A woeful overstatement everyone seemed to keep making.*

"Your honor, if Mr. Howard led you to believe that I have a lead suspect, Wesley Cobin or otherwise then I'm afraid there's been a… misunderstanding." Tully said employing his best self-control not to call Dillon a liar to his face.

Slane showed that he clearly didn't believe Tully by giving him what Slane probably thought was a knowing smile.

"I know, innocent until proven otherwise and all of that, but as I said we need to lock this down."

"What are you suggesting?" Tully was running out of patience.

"It's very simple," Slane paused, possibly for praise, which he didn't get. "What you need to do is keep an eye on Cobin at all times." *Simple?*

"Sir, I don't have that kind of manpower."

"And I don't have enough citizens to let someone keep killing them off." *Actually neither have been locals.* "You don't have to be watching him twenty-four hours a day Tully, just enough to make sure he's not out killing people, most have occurred at night correct?"

Tully tried to figure out what he could say to serve as damage control. "Yes, of the *two* homicides Dr. Fredrickson has concluded both times of death were between 12 and 4 AM."

"There you see! All you need is someone to watch Cobin at night."

"The Cobin estate is six acres of trees and the house is on a hill in the middle of that."

"So use some of those heat seeking port things."

"Sir?" Tully asked, clueless as to what Slane was getting at.

"Like they have in helicopters to find people at night, really Sheriff, you should be up on the latest advancements in policing." Tully bit back his retort and asked calmly.

"Do you mean infrared cameras?"

"Yes, that's the thing." Tully counted to five before he allowed himself to speak. "A good idea," he lied. "But, I'm afraid we've never been given a budget sufficient to buy any." he hoped Slane picked up on the implication there but doubted it.

"That's too bad," Slane said regretfully, but his regret was in Tully not the budged he and the commissioners had signed off on. "Still, you are a resourceful man with high approval ratings; I'm sure you'll manage to come up with something." Tully started to open his mouth and probably watch his approval rating plummet but thankfully Slane cut him off. "Well, now that's all taken care of, if you'll excuse me gentlemen I have some other people to see. Keep up the good work!" Tully nodded and rose from his chair followed by Dillon. He walked briskly to the door and back into the anteroom, which was curiously empty for Slane to be meeting with other people. Tully nodded to the secretary on his way out and left the courthouse as quickly as possible.

"Fineas I need you to know that was not my idea." Dillon had waited to speak until they were descending the stairs out front. Tully was still leading, briskly and didn't look back to see Dillon.

"Really?" he asked.

"Yes, I didn't even go in there to make him think you had a lead suspect or anything, he got it on his own and wouldn't be dissuaded." Dillon said. It was a plausible story knowing Slane.

"But you like the outcome." Tully pointed out.

"Well, you have to admit it's convenient, maybe you can find something if you're looking in one place." They reached the bottom of the stairs and Tully whirled to face Dillon who took a hesitant step back.

"And maybe he's totally innocent of these two murders." Tully said evenly.

Dillon straightened himself. "Well then, maybe you can prove that, either way you have to admit it's a win."

"And what if while we're concentrating on one man who may, or may not be the killer, another murder is committed, one that if I'd stepped up patrols, or was using resources in a more general way, could have been prevented?" Dillon was silent, rocking on his feet. "Oh, and another thing, how is it that

Slane knows so much about an ongoing investigation? The last time I checked I wasn't reporting case details to his office." Dillon looked away.

"I didn't mean to get you in trouble."

Tully stared at him. "What?"

"I mean, I wasn't trying to leak any details or anything, besides the gazette already seems to publish any sensitive case details in their morning edition."

Tully grimaced. Howard had a point. "Alright, fair enough. Obviously I have some leaks to find internally. We aren't used to having cases of this import and security needs to be tightened. Let's just agree that this never happens again." Dillon was quick to nod his agreement.

"I'll see you this evening." Dillon said and Tully nodded, then the two men turned and went their separate ways.

Tully called Lance Imahara from the car. He told him to take the cruiser and set up on route 3. He told him he was checking for speeders but added that he was to be informed if one of the Cobin vehicles was spotted coming into town. He ignored most of Imahara's comments and hung up a short time later and drove home for lunch.

He needed to talk a few things over with Caroline.

He didn't discuss ongoing investigations for the most part, but he would involve his wife in abstract discussions where he thought the feminine point of view could be enlightening. Or if the case involved her directly which he was beginning to worry it would.

If Slane and Howard wanted him keeping an eye on Cobin he had an idea how to go about it and the bonus was that neither of them would like it.

Caroline had known something was up as soon as Fineas walked in the door but she'd let it go, waiting for him to make the first move. They'd eaten lunch in a companionable silence with just a few causal remarks passing between them. Then Fineas had picked up their plates and glasses had taken them into the kitchen, which was commonly the room for discussions in the Tully household. Caroline was rinsing the dishes when Fineas came down to it and wasted no time with preamble.

"What do you think about having Cobin over to dinner?" he asked Caroline. She took a minute in turning around to look at him closely. She knew he was serious because of his manner previously, but nevertheless she waited for his real explanation. None was forth coming. Her hard look served as her *What!*

"You can't do that," she said severely. "That would not be fair!" She sounded firmly determined in her reply.

"Look, I've always been able to outdraw him if he gets it in his head to do something crazy..."

"That is not what I meant Fineas!" Caroline cried, clearly scandalized by his attempt to lighten the mood. Her glare was surprisingly fierce. "I meant it wouldn't be fair to Wesley and Loren. You can't just go throwing the two of them back together, especially not if Dillon's going to be here."

"Actually, it was kind of Dillon's idea." Caroline arched a brow to show she wasn't buying that one. She turned off the tap and put her back to the sink so that she could give him the full benefit of her searching eyes.

"Dillon suggested that you invite Wesley over to the family dinner we've been planning for two weeks?" Fineas considered his options since a flat out lie wasn't on the table.

"Not in those words so much but the implication was there."

Caroline crossed her arms. "I think you've been doing some first rate reading between the lines here, even if Wesley and Loren had only dated casually I still wouldn't believe you." There followed a brief silence as they reflected on the "what *had* been".

Fineas shrugged as nonchalant as possible. "But you personally have no issues with it?"

Caroline looked mildly exasperated. "No, I would personally sit through a dinner with Wesley Cobin, but Fineas that's not the point. This is about your daughter."

"Well then why don't we let Loren make that decision?" Fineas said as Loren stepped through the back door.

"Hi, Daddy," She said and kissed him on the cheek. "What decision is this?" Fineas hesitated, seeing his daughter before him, imagining the possible negative outcomes, the risk of upsetting her, he almost backed out, but then he said it.

"What would you say to Cobin coming over to dinner?"

"Wesley? Dinner?" Loren asked, clearly taken completely off guard. "He wouldn't." She quickly looked to her mother. "Would he?" back to her father, "Have you asked him?"

"No," Fineas said slowly.

"What's the occasion?" Loren sounded excited, hopeful almost.

78

"No occasion, just, uh…" He shrugged, just the commissioner and your fiancé insisting, he thought.

"Think about it." Caroline suggested. "Your father doesn't need an answer right now." She said her eyes locked with her husbands, almost daring him.

Loren nodded, started to turn away and then rubbed her forehead. "If he'd come, I'm okay with it." She said unconvincingly, then nodded twice each time with greater conviction, then she smiled. Her decision made.

"Alright," Fineas said brightly. "That settles that." Caroline's quick glance let him know that the matter was *not* settled and they *would* be discussing it later.

For the second time Tully found himself on Cobin's porch ringing the bell and marshaling his thoughts. Truth be told he hadn't given this much consideration, on an impulse it had seemed a good idea but now he was seeing all of the snags.

Still, it wasn't really like Cobin would agree.

It was Cobin himself who opened the door. Apparently he sat close by because Tully hadn't had any time to change his mind.

"Uh, hi." Tully said and for a second couldn't remember where to go with the conversation.

"Hello." Cobin said but left out his usual cutting opening remarks forcing Tully to go on. He was annoying even when he wasn't doing anything!

"Do you have plans tonight?" Tully asked.

Cobin put his wrists together and held them out to Tully, awaiting cuffs.

"No, no, not like that." Tully snapped and found himself back in stride. "I wanted to see if you would be able to join us for dinner?" Tully thought he was doing an admirable job of masking his emotions while actually grimacing a little.

"Dinner? At your house?" Cobin's smile was wry and an eyebrow lifted slightly. "The occasion would be?"

"Do I need an occasion to be neighborly?"

"No but you also don't need much of an occasion to shoot me."

"Really?" Tully asked with a trace of humor, his grimace was replaced by a look of mild annoyance which gave way to surprise. Cobin was serious. "I'm not going to shoot you."

Cobin opened his mouth to ask a question but Tully headed him off.

"Without cause," he added. "Caroline is cooking a big meal and we have an extra seat."

"Is this an apology for accusing me of killing Boswell and Epcot?" Tully frowned and Cobin knew he was on thinning ice.

"Alright, would that be just the three of us?" Cobin asked. Tully's slight hesitation was easy to see, he was still making up his mind about this, or at least including Loren and Dillon.

"The four of us?" Cobin asked, his interest noticeably peaked.

"Five, actually," Tully said quickly just to watch the smile fade, then feeling bad about his glee when it did.

"Dillon Howard." Cobin said flatly and Tully readied himself for the objections, he admitted they would be deserved. For most men spending an evening with their, say, mortal enemy would put a damper on things. "Alright."

"Alright?"

"I'll come." Tully hesitated on the verge of saying more, of warning Cobin to be on his best behavior, of threatening him if he wasn't and a small part of him even wanted to tell him the real reason so as not to foster any false hopes in Cobin. This was not an olive branch, an invitation to reconciliation. Actually, Tully realized it was almost more like a trap.

"Okay." Cobin said, waiting for something more.

"Fine."

"Radburt has the night off and I can't drive."

"I'll pick you up." Tully said.

Both men nodded at each other.

"Five o' clock." Tully said and without further ado he left the porch.

Wesley closed the door behind him and wondered. What was Fineas up to? That this invitation surprised him was a huge understatement. He hadn't reasonably expected to ever see the inside of the Tully's cozy house again, much less have dinner there.

He thought back to past stomach splitting dinners. Caroline was a first rate cook, she'd trained to be a chef and had a knack for creating her own dishes and an archive of old family recipes. His mouth was already watering.

It certainly beat something run on the defrost cycle in the microwave. Of course his own home cooked meal wouldn't include dining with the Assistant District Attorney and that made up for a lot of culinary lack.

Again, what was Fineas' motive?

Sure, Fineas could be trying to trap him in something, catch him in a lie, to start the prosecution over again. Dillon could grill him over coffee.

But that wasn't the way Fineas worked.

Besides Caroline would never stand for it, the dining table was sacred ground. Then again, maybe they'd eat on the deck... and then he figured it out.

He couldn't square the dinnertime plot with Fineas' M.O. because it wasn't Fineas idea. Wesley would have bet the Manor that the mayor had something to do with the impromptu invite, if he was putting pressure on Fineas that could explain the evening. It also meant Dillon was siding with the Slane. Furthermore, it meant that Fineas didn't actually think he'd committed these last two murders. That was reassuring to some degree.

Confident he'd worked it out Wesley went upstairs to pick out something to wear.

When Tully walked through the office door, Marge was waiting. She pushed a typed transcript of his interview with Lisa Cuthard across the counter to him.

"Thanks Marge," Tully said as he glanced through the neatly spaced text, maybe he would find something useful by reading their exchanges, but he doubted it.

"You've got more stuff in your office, courier from the crime lab dropped in."

Tully nodded. "Thank you." he said and headed for his office.

Tully dropped the transcript next to a department branded external hard drive on his desk with a rough index of the contents presumably included in a packet of papers next to it.

The hard drive should be a dump from Boswell's laptop. The papers were other requested materials, phone records and banking information as well as the latest pathology report from Fredrickson.

He started with the papers.

Boswell had certainly had an active social life, judging from her cell phone records. Tully concentrated on any local numbers but he didn't come across any in the ten pages he skimmed from the most recent working back. He'd already requested a report to see if any of Wesley Cobin's numbers appeared, they didn't cross.

He moved onto pathology which confirmed the cause of death as a single gunshot wound to the chest. The bullet, a .32 caliber had been recovered; good news if they ever found the gun.

Boswell had also been bound, hands behind her back.

The fibers Fredrickson had found were still in line to be analyzed, maybe by tomorrow they would have something since they got priority use of the lab, but it could potentially be more like a week.

At this rate that was six more women.

Tully realized he too was beginning to assume a pattern.

It was a good thing Cobin would be under surveillance for most of the night.

As he skimmed the reports it felt more and more improbable to Tully that Cobin was the killer.

The gun was too low a caliber, the single shot and the bound wrists; it was all out of character with what he darkly thought of as a probable Cobin murder.

Mike had been shot twice with Cobin's .45, there had been defensive wounds and they'd found Mike's gun, kicked to the side, the CSU had suspected after he was dead. It had been one of the slip-ups Cobin had made, training overruling his conscious mind at the time.

Tully blinked as he looked down at the report and saw Mike's face staring up at him. His imagination had overlaid that report with Boswell's. He shut his eyes, hoping to clear the image.

Unbidden, the morgue headshots of Herod Cobin's six original victims appeared behind his eyes.

Father like Son... He shook the crazy thought, planted by Dillon, from his head.

He set aside the pathology report and concentrated on the hard drive index, sticking to intelligible sections.

Fortunately, Boswell had used an e-mail client and they had been able to gain access to her electronic correspondents.

Tully skimmed spam and advertisements, concentrating on the addresses that made sense. Evidently Boswell also hadn't been big on cleaning out her inbox. There were six pages just of the headers and those appeared to just be the last few days' worth. On the second to last page Tully's eyes skimmed across an address that made him do a double take.

mepcot@tndpaper.com

The subject line held his attention too: *Talk about WC now?*

He plugged in the external hard drive and navigated to the folder the index said contained transcripts of Boswell's e-mails.

He found the one he wanted and opened it.

It was indeed from Marana Epcot but it seemed to be a continuation of some earlier conversation because the body of the message was short, just four words:

Contact me when ready

He re-read the subject heading.

WC? *Possibly.*

But it wasn't anything to build a case on.

The correspondents did mean one thing though; he had another thread to connect his victims; unfortunately it was again through Wesley Cobin.

CHAPTER 9

Tully was having serious doubts about his plan when he pulled his car around in front of the Cobin Manor.

He was slowly realizing this had been a knee jerk reaction over his annoyance at Slane for butting in on his investigation.

Despite the connection he'd found in Boswell's e-mail he was still largely unconvinced that Cobin had anything to do with the ongoing investigations, directly at least. Maybe it was a coincidence, or maybe someone was using the obvious connection to overshadow one less conspicuous and the real reason for the killings.

For the first time the thought that Cobin might have hired someone to commit the murders crossed his mind. He summarily dismissed the idea. It would have been much easier to kill them where they lived, the connection might have gone completely missed, not to mention it was too sloppy for the kind of hit-man Cobin could have afforded to hire.

The only reason Cobin had to kill either woman was revenge or for something they could say. Tully thought back to the picture on his phone.

Depending on what Boswell was going to talk about with Epcot there could be a motive, but it was unlikely to be strong enough to prompt a murder to silence them.

It wasn't like Cobin had a reputation to worry about; blackmail seemed unlikely for the same reason and thanks to double jeopardy he couldn't be retried for Mike's murder.

Maybe he was dismissing valid possibilities. Maybe there was a trace of sentimentality clouding his judgment. Tully thought that it was more a knowledge of Cobin's character.

For five years after his parent's deaths Cobin, Wes or Wesley then, had lived with the Tully's. From age fourteen to nineteen he'd lived in what was now

Fineas' office. For the six years following that he'd been at the house almost once every day he'd been in town. After he graduated from the academy he'd worked cases with Tully day in and out. Their history meant Tully was pretty sure he knew who he was dealing with, though Mike's murder had knocked him for a loop.

Enough time combing the past he decided and honked the horn. He was startled when Cobin opened the passenger door seconds later. Apparently he'd already been coming down the steps.

"Evening." Cobin said and Tully realized for the evening to work he'd have to stop his automatic tensing every time Cobin spoke.

"Hard day?" Cobin asked when Tully didn't immediately reply.

"Very long." Tully replied. *And getting longer* he thought.

"Slane leaning on you again?" Tully glanced sharply towards Cobin, then caught himself. The thing about their history was that it went both ways. Apparently the question was rhetorical because before he could reply Cobin moved on. "Just so I don't make a complete fool out of myself, what's the mood that I'm walking into?" Cobin asked. "I know this isn't a good will gesture and I know it doesn't mean anything's settled or that we're friends again but I think I deserve to know what I'm getting into."

"Fair enough. Slane wants you watched, I figured short of putting you in lockup this was the best way to keep an eye on you."

"You think there's going to be another murder?"

"I don't know, but so far we've been getting one every night."

"Thanks." Cobin said, catching Tully off guard.

"For what?"

"I know this isn't going to be easy and I know this probably wasn't your best option and you've realized that but you stuck by it and I appreciate that."

"I didn't do it for you."

"I know, nonetheless, thanks." Tully shifted into drive and wondered why the since of guilt he'd ditched earlier that day was coming back.

Wesley found that his heart was racing as he stood in the driveway looking up at the familiar old house. He wasn't struck by a flood of memories like he had imagined he would be. Instead he was filled with longing and felt an unexpected calm at the heart of him, unexpected given just how anxious he was. He followed Fineas over to the back steps, climbed then right after him and without consciously realizing it he found himself back in Caroline's cozy kitchen.

The room didn't look like it had changed at all in the intervening years. But then, why would it have? That last year they had gone through and updated everything getting Caroline appliances that would maximize her cooking abilities which had taken it beyond the realm of mere mortals.

Right now the kitchen was empty, though wonderful smells permeated the space. Wesley brought his gaze from the kitchen around to the archway leading to the hall and the dining room. Caroline stood there watching him and Wesley was relieved to see a smile on her lips. It was infectious and he returned the smile. Fineas hugged her and asked about her day but Wesley wasn't able to focus on the conversation, he was too tightly gripped by emotion. Then Caroline was in front of him, looking up at him.

"Wesley. It's good to see you." She reached her arms around his neck. Wesley stooped into her embrace and felt his tension dissolving. He forgot how good this felt and suddenly the intervening years all seemed so stupid, everything he'd been trying to prove, the confrontations, the provocation, all an utter waste. In a flash of clarity he knew what he wanted.

"Well," Caroline said after pulling out of the embrace. "I hope you brought your usual appetite." She looked him up and down. "And it looks like you could use some extra helpings." Wesley smiled and started towards the small kitchen table then caught Fineas' eye upon him and read the message therein contained. He diverted toward the archway and past Fineas standing what felt like sentry. He glanced back and saw a conversation of looks being exchanged between husband and wife and worried he was going to cause an argument. It was the last thing he wanted to do. Still, it wasn't like he'd invited himself.

Wesley made his way through the heart of the house to the living room, which he was assuming was the safe neutral ground. He took off his jacket and hung it on the coat rack, then turned back to the room.

Furniture had been moved and the bulky old TV had vanished entirely but it was still recognizable and therefore another comfort. It was as if the whole house was a mental salve to his abused brain.

He made his way to the fireplace on the far wall and peered at the pictures on the mantle. It turned out to be a good test in self-control because the first one he focused on was one of Dillon Howard and Loren the former looking entirely too smug, his arms wrapped possessively around Loren. Wesley let it go and moved on.

The next thing he noticed was his conspicuous absence.

Admittedly, he hadn't expected to be included but a part of him had hoped at least the adolescent Wesley Cobin might get some kind of mention. Instead the pictures seemed carefully arranged for the express purpose of excluding him. Again he let it go.

At least he hadn't been cut from any of the pictures on display.

"Wes?"

She caught him off guard and Wesley almost knocked over a row of family photos. He turned slowly and there she was.

Loren Tully smiled across the room and Wesley didn't care about a single picture.

She'd always run more towards girlish with curly chestnut hair and big, expressive eyes, but standing in the light coming through the big front windows Wesley was struck by the woman before him. Maybe it had been the tricks of time that had made him think of her as the girl he'd grown up with instead of the woman she'd become, but now he saw it and was awed anew.

"Loren." he said and, if possible, her name tasted good on his tongue. For a few seconds they were kids again and they both dashed forwards to hug each other.

Entire conversations ran through in both their minds, things that could be said but neither knowing where to begin or even where they stood, instead settling for a silence that conveyed this all to each other.

"Hi," Loren said when they stood apart.

"Good afternoon." he replied. They had fallen into old patterns instantly, but the greeting over they suddenly lapsed into a disconcerting silence. Where did they go next?

Wesley looked up to find Fineas watching from the doorway, his expression was inscrutable but made Wesley slightly uncomfortable.

"So," Loren said. "How's business?"

"Business? The company? Oh, um, fine I guess." She gave him a surprised look. "I don't really do much with it, I have people for that kind of thing but I guess I keep getting checks so it can't be too bad."

"Oh right, I just thought maybe you took on more since," She trailed off. "Since you have more time."

"No, no, not really." Wesley thought hard. "I've done some remodeling; I think you'd like it. Which reminds me Radburt said to tell you hello." Loren smiled.

"Radburt, how is he?"

"He's well, just as against technology encroaching on his life as ever."

"That doesn't surprise me." Radburt had always approached technology with extreme skepticism. He'd been one of the ones who said the personal computer would never last. It had also been his firm belief that technology would never simplify life and on that count he might have been largely proved correct.

Wesley found that the sudden tension was leaving again as they talked of inconsequential things. It would have proceeded nicely onto weightier matters, if, at that moment, the doorbell hadn't chimed.

Instantly his stomach knotted as he guessed for whom the bell was tolling.

Fineas moved quickly for the front door and slipped through it without a word.

So Dillon doesn't know? Wesley thought, he wondered how that would play out and expected to hear shouting from the front porch.

Loren's smile was now apologetic and they stood awkwardly, though not because of each other but in anticipation for what would come next. Wesley suddenly wondered how much she knew about the trial. He'd done his best to keep her out of it and he knew Fineas had done the same though each for different reasons.

He'd been surprised, yet relieved, when Loren had kept out of it but if he'd know she'd end up with Howard he would have seriously considered doing things differently.

The front door opened and Fineas appeared, wearing a forced smile and leading Dillon who looked considerably the worse for wear. His skin was blotchy, his hair mussed and his lips were hardly visible clamped as tightly as they were.

Wesley waved to him from across the room and thought he got a facial tick in response.

Maybe the evening would be fun after all.

They ate on the patio, the temperature was perfect on the shaded deck and that way they played fair, no one had their back in a corner.

Things had maintained a more civil keel than Wesley had expected and he had to begrudgingly give Dillon some small credit; he managed to just treat Wesley like the ex-boyfriend rather than a suspected murderer.

For Dillon Howard the evening was worse than he was expecting. He hadn't considered that, in their conversations, Wesley, despite his year's long absence, still possessed the home court advantage. Wesley knew who Uncle

Pat had been and could make a suitable reference when the relative was mentioned. He knew too about past family pets and something about the living room drapes that Loren found very amusing. Basically things were not going as they were supposed to.

Fineas had explained the situation briefly out on the front porch and had brought up Dillon's own involvement in the affairs that led up to dinner for five. Dillon hadn't imagined it as being this chummy but at least the women of the household seemed to be enjoying the company of a cold blooded murderer.

For the time he held his tongue and had to remind himself that in some circles Cobin would have been considered a gentleman, given his station, and that he was more than capable of earning out that reputation. For some reason Dillon always expected someone brutish, loud and with terrible table manners. Instead Cobin was perfectly behaved which only made him all the more annoying to Dillon.

It was when Loren was laughing, though obviously guiltily, at something that Cobin had said that Dillon decided it was time to interject.

"So, Wesley," he said, making a point to draw out the name. He liked the flash of annoyance in the man's eyes. "Do you have any plans for your lovely beachfront property?" Dillon peered over his wine glass.

Wesley eyed Dillon and could just imagine the smirk concealed by the Château du Magmacore. He tried his best to not let it get to him, but Dillon addressing him as Wesley grated against his nerves. He longed for Fineas to call him by his first name because of the familiarity and normality it held, hearing it from Dillon was to make a mockery of what it represented.

Still, he tried to let it go and to just view this as polite dinner time conversation and, most importantly to avoid getting into any childish confrontations with Dillon.

If the ADA wanted to make himself look petty and brutish in front of his prospective bride, for Wesley couldn't bring himself to think of Loren as his Fiancée, that was all well and good but Wesley was not about to go down with him. His relationship with Loren and the Tully's as a whole might have been shot but it could always get worse.

So, when Dillon asked him about the property, Wesley just smiled.

"No, I haven't given it a great deal of thought. There are too many memories there for me to rebuild. At the same time those same memories keep me from selling it." He answered honestly. Dillon quite visibly rolled his eyes.

Wesley was pleased to see Loren notice Dillon's reaction. She was not impressed.

"So what exactly is it that you do?" Dillon asked next.

Wesley smiled, later he would marvel at how quickly his will power faded as he made his reply. "Actually I'm glad you brought that up," he said. "I was thinking about stopping by your offices, I think your boss was just saying something about always looking for fresh blood. I actually have the foundation for a law degree, I figure two years, maybe?"

"I think you would make a better defense attorney, Wes, you have the skill set and the status most of the… shall we say "individuals" looking to fight a state run trial are looking for. It takes a certain lack of conscience, but isn't that what you're used to?"

Wesley just smiled. "Defense you said? They're the ones that have the six to seven figure incomes right?"

"Well, it's a sacrifice in other areas." Dillon retorted and took a savage bite of chicken.

"Ah, no soul I suppose?" Wesley said bemused. He glanced at Loren and saw her disapproval of them both this time and Wesley had to admit he was baiting Dillon and degrading the dinner time chit-chat as a whole.

"I saw you got the Mustang touched-up." Wesley said, turning to Caroline.

"Oh, that." She said with a smile turned toward Fineas. "My anniversary present. A reward for putting up with my darling husband another year. Only 263 days until the next one." She grinned.

"One day I don't have to worry about forgetting." Fineas remarked wryly.

Wesley's smile concealed the sudden pain in his heart and he knew Loren saw it from across the table, he supposed it showed in his eyes.

Once-upon-a-time he had imagined he and Loren would be just like Fineas and Caroline, happy and comfortable with each other; looking forwards to their next anniversary. They hadn't expected perfection; he'd thought they were realistic in their expectations. For the first time in his life he wondered if they would have made it.

He was now acutely aware of all of his shortcomings and back then there had been more. The last three years had changed him and this was the first time he realized that he liked himself more for most of the changes. Sitting here with his former friends he realized that this was what he had been missing.

91

"Excuse me, please." Wesley said and slid away from the table and headed inside.

As he left he heard Caroline say something about dessert and dishes were collected together.

Wesley let himself in the house through the side door and stood in the back hall, he was safe here as the kitchen had its own patio access.

He leaned against the wall and tried to just breathe, to fight off the rising panic while his life of the past three years flashed before him. Before he could reach any conclusions the door opened and Dillon entered the hallway.

Wesley straightened and composed himself, pretending to look at the pictures on the wall but not seeing a thing.

Dillon approached and stood next to him.

"My grandfather was a magician, you know." The ADA said offhandedly.

"No, I did not know that." Wesley said, steeling himself against the unknown.

"Yeah, he taught me a few tricks, a lot with mirrors and deception."

"Magician, lawyer, I see the connection. Those must have been very useful lessons for you."

Dillon smiled, and Wesley was annoyed to admit it was unnerving at the edges.

"It's made me good at spotting certain activities. I know what you're trying to do here and it's not going to work."

"Hey, for your information this was not my idea." Wesley said, deciding to be painfully honest with Dillon, for once he wasn't in a mood to fight. "You think I'm enjoying this?"

"The ingratiation?"

"Oh, please! You honestly think I'm trying to work some kind of angle here or something? Do you think I enjoy watching you live my life?"

"Excuse me?" Dillon asked and Wesley could tell the man was dreaming up all kinds of hidden threats in his words.

"You're still trying to fight me, but you've already won!" he snapped.

While he had enjoyed the evening to a certain extent he knew that it was going to end. For Dillon this was a day in the rest of his life, and dwelling on that too long was more than Wesley could bear at present. "You've got them." he finished quietly.

He could tell that Dillon hadn't been expecting this admission of sorrow, he hoped it gave the ADA something to think about, but then he saw the hooded look return as Dillon tried to puzzle this statement into place with the Wesley Cobin he'd constructed in his mind.

They'd never work out their differences, and Wesley didn't really care to try. Only one person could have made him and in just a few months he'd lose her absolutely.

He turned and left Dillon in the hallway staring after him.

In the living room Wesley composed himself, he didn't want to spend whatever minutes were left of the evening on grief and self-pity. He'd devoted three years to that already.

At the same time he was realizing that he might be able to again some amount of reconciliation.

He knew what Fineas had said about dinner, that it was simply the more effective solution to his problem, but was that really all it was?

True, things would never be the same. Even if he was somehow exonerated of all wrongs it wouldn't change the three years of alienation, it wouldn't change the things they both hadn't said. He could live with that. But he was beginning to think that he couldn't live without the Tully's.

Over dessert Caroline apologized in her usual way that she had only made an Apple-Cranberry pie and, in the way that used to be their custom, Fineas, Loren and Wesley rolled their eyes and praised her singular culinary abilities.

Dillon smiled along but Wesley noticed that he didn't really get it. He surprised himself by feeling slightly sorry for Dillon. He wasn't at ease and Wesley didn't think it was entirely his presence. He realized to someone like Dillon, Fineas was a reasonably imposing figure, even if they did somewhat work together.

His sympathy was short lived as he remembered the exchange in the hallway and as the evening wore on, and they migrated inside to the living room, coffee mugs in hand, Wesley couldn't care less about Dillon's fitting in.

The phone rang a few minutes after nine, as they were all sitting lazily around.

Fineas grunted, a sound of protestation, so Loren, somehow always light of limb, hopped up from the loveseat and headed toward the phone by the stairs.

"Tully residence," she answered. "Daddy, the phone's for you."

Fineas groaned again and boosted himself off of the couch.

"Who?" He asked as Loren handed over the receiver.

"Lance."

"Good evening deputy." Tully answered into the handset.

"Maybe for you and me but not for the stiff we just found." The deputy reported.

"What?" Fineas asked, involuntarily glancing at Cobin.

"We have another dead guy."

"How long?" Fineas asked fighting back his relief.

"Still warm, called the doctor and CSU." Fineas noticed he was the last to know once again but didn't remark on it yet.

"Where are you?"

"South side, on Benjamin Avenue."

It was a residential area, somewhere people out of the ordinary might stand out.

"I'll be right there." He said and hung up. More of him than he would have admitted was relieved. If the murder was recent then he could provide Cobin with an alibi, better still Dillon could and that should get the mayor off his case. Now there was just the issue of what to do with Cobin for the present.

"I just got called out, I have to go." Fineas announced to the room.

"What happened?" Dillon demanded, in a tone that Fineas didn't appreciate. He rolled his eyes toward Loren but Dillon didn't take the hint, Loren on the other hand was to his back and she did.

"It's alright, I'm not six. I can handle it." she said and by her inflection Fineas could tell she already knew what he was going to say.

"They've found another body."

"Oh, no!" Caroline cried in dismay.

Dillon immediately got off of the couch and picked his coat off of the rack.

"Where do you think you're going?" Fineas asked.

"To the scene with you, photographs simply can't capture it, I need living color." Tully bit off his sigh. Dillon started for the door, then remembered Loren, glanced at Cobin, then walked back across the living room and made a show of kissing her. Tully noticed Loren was frowning when Dillon pushed through the door. She turned on her heel and walked toward the kitchen. Cobin's expression on the other hand was blank except for his eyes and a slight furrow to his brow that Tully found himself fully approving of.

"I'll come, too." Cobin said after a moment's silence.

"No, you will not." Tully said firmly. Cobin got up from the chair and stretched. Tully walked to the short hall between living room and kitchen when he kept his stuff in a drawer. Cobin followed him.

"Well, I can't drive home beside the fact I don't have a car."

"Call Radburt."

"Can't, I told you, it's his night off and he doesn't have a cell phone."

"Then enjoy the walk."

"Hah! In this town, after dark, really Sheriff? Look, either I go with you or I stay with Caroline and Loren. I guess Loren could take me home." Cobin said considering.

"You don't get out of the car." Tully said and noticed the flash of pain in Cobin's eyes. It was something he was seeing a lot of lately.

"Fair's fair." Cobin said and led the march to the living room.

"Thank you so much for dinner it was even better than I remembered." He was saying to Caroline when Tully caught up with him, having grabbed his badge and gun.

"Loren, it was great to see you and congratulations."

"Come on, let's go." Tully said gruffly and kissed Caroline of the cheek. Cobin tailed him out to the car.

CHAPTER 10

"So, I suppose this wipes me off the murder board?" Cobin asked as Tully drove through town. It was the first thing either of them had said since getting in the car. In the dark Tully made an unconvinced face.

"Of course, I suppose I could have rigged something to fake the time of death but Frederickson is good, he's a big city man and he knows how to process a corpse. I doubt there's very little he hasn't seen." There was a pause and then Cobin started in again. "I have been meaning to ask you since when did we switch to a 'guilty until proven innocent' credo?"

"What exactly are you implying with the 'we'." Tully asked.

"We, as in 'we the people'. So who's the victim anyway, anyone else I'm connected to?" Cobin asked and tried to lean around the console mounted laptop to read the report screen. Tully canted the screen away from him but answered the question.

"Earnest Kitman."

"What?" Cobin's disbelief sounded genuine. "Who would possibly want to kill sweet old Mr. Kitman. We aren't going to the store so we have to be going to his house..." Kitman had run the last independent grocery store in town, managing to compete with the big chain stores by offering that small town personal touch.

"I suppose I bought groceries there so I'm sure you can find a motive somewhere... he once refused to sell me a bottle of scotch. There you go, just gave myself away, sure, it was four years ago but that just shows how premeditated the whole thing was."

"You know you never used to be this annoying."

"Well actually I was. Flippant sarcasm has long been a personal trademark of mine I was just nicer to you seeing as how I hoped to marry your daughter and you were responsible for my upbringing from age fourteen onwards."

Tully bit his tongue and just drove on. Wesley regretted his retort but couldn't very well take it back.

This time it was just the coroner's van and one cruiser parked at the curb in front of the Kitman Bungalow. As Tully brought the car to a halt across the street from the van he felt Cobin's eyes on him, he turned to look at his passenger and was disquieted at how naturally he could still read the look.

"I know." he said. This was unlike the two previous crime scenes.

"Which I suppose means I'm still on the hook?"

"You don't need to put it quite that way." Tully said.

"Because tonight was Dillon's idea?" Tully laughed but it was a little too forced. "Oh, he's in on it too is he, our dear honorable mayor?" Cobin asked. Now Tully was spooked.

"Am I still staying put?" Cobin asked, knowing that with Tully it was better to ask than to just get out of the car.

"I don't see any reason for you to come in." Tully said and opened his door, leaving Cobin behind.

Tully crossed the street and climbed the three steps up to the wide front porch of the small Bungalow. It was a cozy place and did not lend itself well to the murder tableau. The front door was open and he made his way inside the house. He heard some muttering and a camera flashed from beyond the archway to the kitchen. In the small kitchen he found Fredrickson and his assistant around the prostrate form of Earnest Kitman.

Fredrickson turned as Tully approached, a puzzled expression on his face, one that faded into annoyance quickly.

"Sheriff, don't tell me he called you all the way out here?" Frederickson asked.

"Yes doctor, I like to be kept informed of the murders in my county." Tully replied, not understanding the surprise or annoyance, he didn't think he'd done anything to elicit them.

"Fineas, that's just my point," Fredrickson said acerbically. "There is no murder here."

"But Imahara said they found a body."

"Well, yes they did but it was a heart attack." That explained the doctor's behavior. "At least I'm ninety percent certain of it, willing to stake my reputation on it. I will of course be doing a thorough examination in light of recent circumstances to make sure that it's... Wesley." It took Tully a second to realize the Medical Examiner was looking past him at Cobin, who stood staring down at them.

"Good evening, doctor."

"Good evening to you." Frederickson said, then glanced to Tully not entirely sure what was going on. Tully turned to Cobin.

"I thought I told you to stay in the car?"

"You said that originally but then said I didn't have a reason to come in."

"And?"

"I have a reason." Cobin held out a box of shoe covers, his own feet already covered by the blue booties. "You left these in the car." Cobin said simply.

"So, doctor, it was natural causes?" Cobin asked.

"It appears that way yes; at least he wasn't shot or bludgeoned." Cobin nodded and leaned past Tully for a better look.

"We can also rule out strangulation, no ligature marks and it doesn't look like there's any petechial hemorrhaging." Cobin commented.

"I see you haven't lost your edge."

"Just his right to be here, come on." Tully said.

"Actually, seeing as he's attired better he has more of a right to be here than you."

"Very cute, come on Cobin." Tully pulled Cobin back across the kitchen threshold.

Not satisfied Cobin kept talking. "Do you have a time of death?"

"I would say not any longer than two hours."

"Very good doctor, thank you." Cobin said then retreated back to the hall.

"Keep me informed." Tully said and followed Cobin out.

"What were you thinking?" Tully asked as they crossed the threshold onto the porch.

"I didn't want you contaminating a crime scene. With these homicides the press is already in a frenzy they don't need to hear the Sheriff contaminated his own crime scene."

"Very thoughtful." Tully said dryly. "Don't do it again." But internally he was berating himself. Cobin was exactly right about the press and what he'd done was extremely stupid.

"Whatever you say." Cobin said, flashing his palms in submission.

"Where's Lance?" Tully asked, wondering how Cobin had gotten past him but then realizing he hadn't seen him at all.

"Around back looking for any signs of an intruder." They were outside in the front yard now. Tully stopped and stared at Cobin.

"How could you possibly know that?"

"You know Fineas you used to like that about me." Cobin said trying his best to sound hurt.

"Would you go back to the car now and stay put?"

"Alright if you think that's the best place for me I'll go back, well, short of spontaneous combustion, a drive-by, or if I get hungry." Cobin broke off and Tully went in search of his deputy and let off some steam.

When he got back Dillon's car was parked against the curb. His first reaction was to squint into his own Crown Vic and reassure himself that Cobin had followed his orders. Then he approached the Chrysler. Dillon powered down his window.

"Well?" The ADA asked, again in a tone Tully was quickly tiring of.

"Fredrickson thinks it's a heart attack."

"A heart attack? So no foul play?" Dillon sounded unsure if this was good or bad. Tully could almost commiserate though he suspected they were at different ends.

"Unless you can come up with a really good motive..." Tully abruptly stopped himself. Dillon could come up with a motive and probably several suspects with it, best to just wait and keep quiet.

Dillon considered for a moment then nodded. "So you still have a prime suspect." he said, apparently deciding this was a good thing.

"No," Tully said stubbornly. "I have two homicides with very thin leads and a few coincidences."

"So now you believe in coincidence? I thought cops weren't supposed to like that?"

"There's a process to any investigation that has to be followed." Tully said getting tired of this merry-go-round.

"So?"

"So, you can go home, you're not needed tonight." Tully said.

Dillon nodded slightly, then powered up his window.

Tully straightened slowly, feeling the strain all along his back. He hated getting old. He crossed the street and got back behind the wheel.

"Well at least Dillon should be happy." Cobin remarked, watching the Chrysler's taillights grow dim.

Tully didn't say anything, it felt like an exhaustingly long night, despite the fact it was only just 9:30. He didn't want to talk to Cobin, not out of the personal issues of the past years but simply because he was tired and didn't know what to say. Apparently Cobin sensed that and felt like humoring him this once; he stayed quiet as Tully piloted the Crown Vic back across town to the Cobin mansion.

In the driveway in front of the house Tully spoke.

"The mayor doesn't like you very much, neither does Howard or the DA, you've got a lot of cards stacked against you." Wesley fought the urge to ask Fineas how he felt. "We've got personal things and our personal relationship is more or less over, you understand that?"

Wesley considered his options. The truth of the matter was, no, he didn't understand, especially after that evening. But he knew that particular tack would lead nowhere so instead, he nodded.

"Okay," Tully said. "I don't think you killed Odette Boswell or Marana Epcot and I don't have any evidence to tell me otherwise. The thing is if there's another murder, one that links back to you, regardless of how shaky the evidence is I will have to bring you in and the DA is going to try and charge you. If you were a smarter, less stubborn man I'd tell you to go away, go to Vegas or somewhere with constant surveillance. But I know you. Tonight I'm going to sleep here and tomorrow you're going to go with me to the station then I'm going to take you back to my house and you are going to stay there all day. We are going to see if we can make it another day without a murder. If there is one you'll have the alibi I need to clear you."

Wesley swallowed hard. "Thank you." he finally said. It was the best he could do at that moment.

"I mention this only in the spirit of securing my alibi," Wesley said as Tully covered the hall couch with a blanket. "What's to keep me from ducking out during the night?"

Tully got the blanket situated and moved on to positioning the pillows. It was nice to be in a house big enough to have a couch in the hallway. Situated, he turned to Cobin.

"The alarm covers the windows right?"

"Yes." Wesley said.

"So I'll set the alarm after I lock you in your room."

"How do you figure that?" Wesley asked eyeing his bedroom door. The keyhole was on the outside, the turn key on the inside.

"Lock it with the key, leave it in the lock, the lock won't turn with the key in." Tully explained.

"Really?" Cobin asked and examined the lock. "Well if it's good enough for the jury..."

"Let's hope it doesn't come down to that." Tully said.

"You do realize this whole situation is almost making me wish for another murder just to clear my name? Seriously messed up." Wesley said.

Tully agreed.

"What if I just let you re-program the alarm codes?" Wesley asked. "Do that and set it to go off if any exterior doors or windows are opened?"

Tully considered. Locking Cobin in his room had a certain appeal but he supposed the alarm should be adequate.

"I mention this because I don't know where the key is."

Tully nodded.

"Alright."

"If we're using that method you really don't need to sleep out here, you could take one of the guest rooms."

"Don't push it." Tully felt far more confident of his testimony if he could say he was in sight of the door all night.

"Okay." Cobin said gamely and walked to the alarm keypad and began the procedure for resetting the codes. "Just make sure you use one I don't know."

Tully didn't think he was going to get much sleep on the couch, but it proved to be comfortable enough and he was extremely tired. He was duly surprised then when the screaming of the alarm system woke him in the pre-dawn hours.

He sat up immediately, with dread a solid mass in his stomach.

He reached for his gun, half expecting it to be gone, but it was there and half a second later Cobin was pulling open his bedroom door and flipping on the hall lights.

"Radburt!" he exclaimed.

Last night they'd both forgotten about Radburt who was likely downstairs in the back hall furiously pounding in the old code, growing more and more hateful of modern technology.

Tully stumbled off the couch and preceded Cobin down the stairs and through the house to find Radburt right where expected, shouting at the alarm keypad.

Tully brushed past him, tapped out the six digit code and jabbed reset. The system chirped and the siren stopped.

Tully found himself breathing hard, slumping against the wall while Radburt ran his gaze between Fineas and Wesley trying to determine just what was going on.

Five seconds later the telephone started ringing.

"That's the alarm company. You want to take the call?" Cobin asked.

Tully nodded. That way he could ask for a log of the system activity without a warrant, just to make sure the system had been running all night.

He started for the phone.

CHAPTER 11

Wesley found himself compulsively tapping his finger against the door panel of the Crown Vic as Tully piloted the car into town.

He hadn't been to the station since that night three years ago. Tully had made sure he didn't go back, despite his deserving to several times. Wesley found himself wondering for the first time what kind of flack his old friend had taken for that.

Of course, the last time he'd been in the county lockup he'd been beaten to within an inch of life. Fineas had found him at the last second and dragged him out of holding; had applied constant pressure to the most serious wound, slowing the flow of blood and saving his life.

The scar across his stomach throbbed at the memory. Jake Barry had been the duty officer that had somehow missed the small switchblade in Bob Jefferson's boot.

Now they were turning into the parking lot and Tully parked next to the impound lot in his reserved space.

Wesley frowned eyeing his Mercedes and wondered if now would be a good time to ask for it back. Probably not yet, though Fineas seemed to be warming up to him ever so slightly. Still, the words of last night hung in his mind.

This was not reconciliation.

Wesley didn't want to jeopardize anything that may have been starting.

Tully opened his door and waited for Cobin to join him outside the car. He'd noticed his ex-partner's nervousness expressed most obviously in his rare silence. This was stage two then, as stage one consisted of glib jibes and sarcasm and he almost wanted to say something comforting. He reminded himself of what Cobin was to him now and silently led the way into the station.

Marge more than made up for any silence on his part.

Tully had held the office door for Cobin, who reluctantly stepped through.

Marge, at her computer glanced up, did a double take, checked discreetly for handcuffs and Tully's expression then leaped up from her desk chair and covered the distance in two bounds, where she stopped and looked at Cobin. Tully hoped she was reconsidering her position. She smiled and embraced Cobin slowly.

"Wes, it's good to see you again. We've missed you." She said pulling away from Cobin and looking him in the face.

"I've missed you." Cobin said with a sad smile, "I've even missed this place." He slowly looked around the squad room behind the reception desk.

Barry wasn't there but Imahara and Stark were both staring incredulously at Cobin, then they looked to their boss for guidance but none was forthcoming.

At least there was no kill order being given.

Cobin waved to them.

Down to stage 1. Tully thought.

"Come on." he said and led the way behind reception, across the squad room to his office, past the two deputies who turned to watch them walk across the office but continuing to stare dumbfounded.

Tully pushed open his office door and Cobin followed him in. He closed it behind them.

Tully crossed to behind his desk and Cobin took a seat at one of the two chairs facing the desk unasked.

"So, what happens next?" Cobin asked as Tully turned on his computer.

"Would you wear an ankle bracelet?"

Cobin rolled his eyes. "Are you kidding? No."

"It would make things a lot easier. And they really aren't that inconvenient anymore, it's not like you'd have a perimeter or anything."

"No, it's not the device it's the implication."

Tully had to bite his tongue hard.

"You can track my phone if you need to know where I am."

"You'll sign the release?"

"Yes."

"Okay," Tully said reluctantly, at least it was something. "If I let you spend the day at my house…" Tully broke off, unsure of where he was taking this question.

"Will I be a good little boy and not break anything?" Cobin chimed in. Tully gave him a warning glare that, for once Cobin heeded.

Any further comments were interrupted by a knock on the door. Before Tully said anything the door opened and Stark stuck his head through.

"Everything alright in here?" he asked.

Cobin smiled exaggeratedly and batted his eyelashes. Stark ignored him.

"Yes, Blaze, everything is fine." Tully said.

"Oh, okay, good." Stark said but didn't close the door. "Uh, so, could I talk to you for a second?"

Tully sighed and motioned for him to come in.

"Um, actually, we," Stark gestured to the squad room and presumably Imahara. "We wanted to talk to you." He then not so subtly bobbed his head toward Cobin. "About C-O-B-I-N."

Wesley gave him an incredulous look. "Hey," he said cheerily. "C-O-B-I-N, that's my name too!"

Tully waved him down when he opened his mouth again.

Tully stood and followed Stark into the squad room leaving Wesley alone in his office.

Wesley ran his gaze around the room. Not much had changed in the intervening years. There were a few plants that had changed their shape or been entirely changed out but the general décor was the same.

Wesley's gaze rested on the fax machine, then on the computer, now up and logged in. He glanced to the door and wondered if anything else had changed...

Tully found himself in the squad room with Imahara and Stark eyeing him closely.

"So what's the deal with butcher boy?" Stark asked.

Tully bit his lip.

"Cobin is here confirming his alibi's." he said calmly. "Now, am I to assume since no one has called me that nothing news worthy happened last night?"

"There was something about a storm system." Stark said. Imahara looked suitably disgusted but kept quiet.

"I was thinking more along the lines of murder." Tully wondered how he ever relied on his staff.

"No, we haven't gotten any reports in, do you think he struck again?"

Imahara asked, clearly deeming it advantageous if he took over the conversation.

"Or, she." Tully added to make the point he had no one person in mind. "There just seemed to be a pattern of every night this week. Have either of you talked to the press?" he asked abruptly.

"Marge fielded some calls, I soothed over a few concerned townsfolk when I was on patrol. I said the killer seemed to mainly be targeting people from out of town."

Tully winced. "We really, don't know much of anything."

"Except both of the stiffs are tied back to Cobin." Stark put in.

Tully ignored him. This definitely wasn't the time.

"Just keep me informed and I'd like you to run two patrols."

"You think there's another body?" Stark asked almost gleefully.

"I really hope not Deputy, that would be depraved and ghoulish." Tully said flatly. Stark didn't get the connection. "Who's supposed to be on patrol anyway?" They were short staffed this week and so really Stark and Imahara shouldn't have been around at the same time this early.

"Um…" Stark looked at Imahara who stared right back.

Tully checked the clock. "Lance, call Reese and see if he wants to start his shift an hour early and get those two patrols going. Call Barry when you go on and tell him he can start whenever."

"Sure thing." Imahara said.

"So, what is it about Cobin?" Stark asked.

"He's not a suspect at this time. If you wanted to do something useful you could look into his past associates and see if any of them have a motive for murder."

"Right." Stark said and nodded with an odd expression to convey his seriousness. He turned toward his desk.

"Deputy?" He turned back. "After your patrol." Tully reminded him.

"Oh, yeah." Stark said and started for the door. Tully sighed and returned to his office.

Cobin was leaning back in his seat when Tully reentered his office. Tully found this fact disconcerting and ran his gaze around the office to see if there was something obviously out of place. Even when he'd been one of the good guys Cobin had a history of messing with things if left unoccupied for too long and here he appeared to be sitting in the same spot.

"Did S-T-A-R-K put away the torch and pitchfork?" Tully ignored him, which was slightly worrying, slightly annoying.

"Do you remember special agent Casale?" Tully asked. He was surprised to see a look of mild alarm on Cobin's face.

"Casale?" he asked woodenly. "I have a vague memory, yes."

"What is it?"

"What?" Cobin asked, recovering most of his composure. "Why did you ask about Casale?"

Tully thought the scene over but couldn't find any reason for Cobin's reaction so he filed it away, then shrugging if off for now.

"I was just thinking maybe there is some way you could... I don't know... Maybe..."

"You want her to baby sit me?" Cobin asked incredulously.

"For lack of a better phrase, yes."

"Exactly how does that constitute a federal case?"

"I call and ask for help, or maybe you could do some paperwork for her team?"

"I think the background check would make most temp agencies a little nervous about letting me work at Quantico. Is this just because you don't want me at the house?"

"She's not at Quantico anymore, but honestly? Yes, to a certain degree, but I also think you need to leave town."

"I thought that's what I'm not supposed to do?"

"If you're in Washington D.C. no one is going to accuse you of murder here."

"And what if I got to Virginia and the murders stop?"

Tully had already thought about that. Of course no more bodies would be great but it would also make Cobin even more of a suspect. It would also make sense if someone was framing him for the murders but the D.A. would never buy that.

Ultimately, they needed another murder while Cobin had an alibi from someone other than his hired man. If he was being framed then the real murderer had to think Cobin was still in a position to slip away and commit the crime.

The logistics made Tully sick.

And there was still a little part of him, entirely detached from any emotion and quite a bit of reason that said Cobin *was* the murderer, both then and now.

It was that part of him that made him look for any other way that didn't involve leaving Cobin alone with Loren and Caroline.

He considered taking the day off, he was owed a few personal days. There were probably men out there in his position that would consider babysitting Cobin part of their job, despite the fact they spent the day watching football. Actually, he knew men who had done just that to get the Super Bowl off; just spend it with your favorite convict.

But Tully was not one of them.

"Well, then it looks like we're at an impasse because I have an appointment to interview Marana Epcot's boss, but you need a solid alibi."

"And I can't stay at the house?"

"Caroline and Loren are both at work this morning." Tully was honestly relieved to be able to say.

He'd talked it over with Caroline the night before, he'd gotten her opinion and she was all for having Cobin at the house. But Caroline thought the best of everybody, especially Cobin.

He was also worried because it would be like his wife to see some spark of interest between Loren and Cobin and do something, something subtle, but something nonetheless, that could leave him with a fresh mess to sort out. The less time together the better he'd decided.

"What time is your appointment?"

"Sometime around 11:00." Cobin whistled, consulting his watch. "I guess we'll have to take my car."

Tully stared, trying to judge if Cobin was actually serious.

He was.

"Uh, how exactly do you think I could possibly justify taking you with me? You might not be *my* prime suspect but you pretty much are to everyone else in this town."

"Yep, thanks to the *Gazette*. I'm thinking about suing for libel, I can add your name to the suite if you want?"

That morning's article on the murders was particularly scathing and Tully wasn't exactly placed in a favorable light since he hadn't brought Cobin in immediately.

"I'm not taking you with me." Tully said firmly.

"Then what am I supposed to do?"

"I guess there's always Howard, based on last night I'm sure the two of you have plenty to talk about."

Cobin ignored the remark. "Fineas you're the only one who can give me a believable alibi, I'll go with you, we can take my car and get there faster, and then I could just wait. It's not like I could drive back, bump someone off and pick you up again before you're done."

Tully sat, his expression vacant, as he went over the arguments against it in his mind. He had plenty of them.

For one thing his objectiveness could be called into question if he spent too much time with Cobin.

But there weren't a lot of other options.

Radburt was out, he didn't trust any of his Deputies and the D.A.'s office had always just been a jibe.

"We can't take your car." Tully said eventually.

"Why? You said I can get it out of impound, I just can't drive it."

"Busted taillight." Tully reminded him.

Cobin stared at him in disbelief. "You're turning down the AMG Mercedes because it has a cracked taillight?"

"That's illegal." Tully opened his desk drawer.

Cobin shrugged and reached for his phone. "I'll get someone to come and fix that while we're out." He sounded annoyed.

Good. The feeling was mutual. Then Cobin shrugged and Tully didn't much like the smile that had replaced the scowl.

CHAPTER 12

The black and red Bell 427 lacked livery to declare it property of Cobin Enterprises, which was just as well.

In the end, anonymity was the only reason Fineas had agreed to take the helicopter. And he admitted to himself as they touched down at the airfield, the quick jaunt was much preferred to a couple of hours in the car.

A blue Ford Fusion was waiting for them just beyond the landing pad and in ten minutes more Tully was signaling the right turn into the parking lot of the West Haven *Tribune*.

The paper's headquarters building was a rectangular, four story concrete building built sometime in the early eighties Tully would have guessed from the fake stone adornments.

He gave his name to the guy in the security booth and parked the Fusion in a visitor's space.

He turned to his passenger.

"I'm going to take the key. Just so I know you can't leave the parking lot. I'm going in to talk to the editor and maybe some of her co-workers. I shouldn't be more than an hour."

Cobin nodded. "Lock the doors and if anyone grabs me scream and knee them in the groin?"

Tully scowled at the younger man. Cobin looked apologetic for once again bringing up their past.

"Just don't leave." Tully said and got out of the car.

Fineas was directed upstairs to meet with Epcot's editor in his office, the man, Preston Brats was giving him ten minutes and would meet him at the elevator doors.

Fineas already didn't like the arrangement or the man much and he was still in the elevator.

Brats lived up to Fineas' dislike.

The man was tall, wearing an expensively tailored suit and his dark hair was shellacked in place. He possessed that singular ability to walk with his nose held high and scowl at everyone he perceived to be his lesser.

"Please, Sheriff, follow me." he said and led the way across the office floor, past rows of staffed cubicles. The place was abuzz with ringing telephones and chattering voices. It was not an environment Fineas thought he would excel in.

They almost reached a row of offices against the far wall when someone called after them.

"There you are!"

Tully turned in surprise to see Cobin coming up behind him. The fact that he was there was enough to make Tully clench his jaw, but Cobin was also wearing a shaggy wig and glasses. For a surprisingly simple disguise it worked well at concealing his identity.

Cobin turned to the secretary that had evidently led him upstairs.

"Thanks. Sorry about that Boss, I got turned around at the elevators." He then leaned past Tully who was still just glaring at him.

"Hi there," he said to Preston Brats. "Lance Imahara, his deputy." He nodded to Tully. "Quite a place you've got here!" He glanced over his shoulder and looked as if the view from the fourth floor was the most amazing thing he'd ever seen. Then again, for Imahara it may well have been.

"Thank you." Brats said stiffly.

"What are you doing?" Tully demanded in a hushed tone, turning to face Cobin.

"Sitting in on the interview for the investigation." Cobin returned, dropping his voice to a whisper, like Tully.

"Are you completely insane? You can't!" Tully hissed. Then turned to Brats, "Sorry, just a little technicality." And turned his back to confer with Cobin.

"You need to go back downstairs and wait in the car."

"I thought I came along to have an alibi, what if I get accused of killing someone in the parking lot?"

"The deal was that you wait in the car!"

"I said I *could* wait in the car." Cobin pointed out. "And I thought you just meant don't leave the complex." Tully ignored him.

"I am sure they have security cameras in the parking lot. I cannot run my investigation with you here, if someone makes you this could all be inadmissible."

"So then you think this interview will help me?"

Tully just glared.

"Well, what are you going to do now, admit you brought the prime suspect with you to interview the victim's boss? I promise to not interfere, but I deserve to hear this, too."

Tully tried to read his onetime protégé, trying to see some dark angle but coming up short. He decided to let it play out, risky though it was, with a room full of journalists making a scene seemed worse.

"I'm trying to figure out what to call you without insulting your mother." Tully said finally.

"Ask Jake, he's got a whole list."

"Gentlemen, is everything alright?" Brats asked with a pointed glance at his watch.

With a final glare at Cobin, Tully turned and nodded. "Yes, sorry to keep you."

"Not at all." Brats said with total insincerity and gestured for them to follow him.

"This is going to bite you in the butt." Tully promised as they followed Brats, Cobin nodded sagely.

Tully was angry, but for some reason, not quite furious. It was because, as much as he tried to block the thought, it reminded him of how Cobin worked his cases; with tenacity and skill at bending the rules when everyone else was defenseless to stop him.

Brats was just as useful as Tully had expected, which was to say the discussion just went in circles for 8 minutes, buying time until the full 10 was up.

Tully was trying to figure out some way to get a real answer out of the man.

Brats didn't so much seem deliberately blocking, more just totally uninterested. That or clueless.

"So, did Miss Epcot have any ongoing stories that might have made her someone's target?"

"Well, of course on going articles are highly sensitive in nature. But I am sure that Miss Epcot followed all of the usual necessary protocols to ensure a productive and safe report was carried out." Tully couldn't decide what to scratch in his notepad.

"Could you give me an idea of what those protocols are?"

"Oh, just standard procedure, similar to many papers, but, as I am sure you can appreciate, our exact formula is somewhat privileged trade information."

Tully opened his mouth to ask another question when Cobin chimed in.

"Would it be possible for us to talk to Marana's copy editor?"

Tully tried not to openly glare at Cobin, but he wanted to strangle him.

Brats didn't answer for a moment, considering, then leaned forward and pressed a button on his desk, summoning his secretary.

"I trust then, that we are done here?" he asked.

Tully nodded stiffly. "For now."

Brats motioned to his secretary.

"Take them to see Mr. Mills." he commanded.

"Thank you for your time." Tully said without much feeling and led the way out of the office.

He grabbed Cobin by the arm once they were out of the office.

"What were you thinking!" he hissed in his ear as they followed the secretary.

"That I might make good on my alleged murderous tendencies if I had to listen to that guy ramble in circles any longer."

"You crossed the line and you know it!"

"What? I just expedited things! Besides, you always used to send two officers on every interview to make sure all the right questions were asked."

"But you're NOT an officer, are you, and the only question ended my interview!"

"It's not like you were getting anywhere. Now, you're making a scene."

Tully released his grip on Cobin's forearm and gave him his sternest glare. They'd reached the elevator and they rode down to the second floor in silence.

Rupert Mills, or Rue, as he introduced himself, was a much different character. His outfit clashed, light blue jeans, heavily worn, an orange and yellow stripped shirt and olive green suspenders. His brown hair had no style to the nappy tangle.

Tully was nervous as the secretary opened the door that he might be the one left introducing Cobin, which he couldn't get out of without lying to a reporter. Fortunately the secretary introduced them as Sheriff and Deputy, knocking it down to a lie of omission.

"Thanks Pearl." he said to the secretary then turned to Tully.

"You're the Sheriff, the boss of that cop that went psycho, right?" Tully forced himself to not glance left at Cobin as they took seats facing Mills' desk.

"Who, Wesley Cobin?" Cobin asked.

"Yeah, that's the whack job." Mills said.

Tully watched out of the corner of his eye, but the kid seemed calm enough.

"We call him the spawn of Satan at the station, on account of his father being just as screwed up as he is." Cobin's flippancy was making Tully nervous.

Mills nodded his approval. "Oh good, so no love lost. So I guess you're here about Marana? Shame, real shame, she was just a great reporter."

Tully just smiled. "I'm just trying to figure out what was going on prior to her death." he explained. "Do you have any idea what she was working on?"

"Oh, her story? Well I can tell you this, for about two week Marana was working on this piece, great piece by the way, something to do with some cops down in Charleston, real slime balls, ripping off old women or orphans or something like that. Anyway, it's a real golden story, but then she gets this call or something and she's back on this Cobin guy. Then next thing I know, she's calling in to get some time off, says she wants to personally follow up something and hands her other story off to one of the juniors and Marana never hands anything off, she's just that way."

"Do you know what the phone call was about?" Fineas asked.

"Not a clue, like she'd actually tell someone anything about a lead? Fierce with her stories, scared most of the kids working here and a lot of the old guys, too."

"Do you have phone records for what number the call came from?" Cobin asked.

Mills laughed. "Yeah, sure, like that would ever happen."

Fineas saw Cobin twitch.

"So, she didn't say anything about what angle the story was going to take?" Cobin pressed.

"What? Like the guy's innocent or something? No, way, not Marana! I mean, I'm not trying to speak ill of the dead here, but she was not one to admit if she was wrong on anything, her goal in life was to never print a single retraction. If she wrote it, he did it."

"But how do you even know she was on Cobin again?"

"She told me, or at least implied it. That was good enough for me! She calls in and says she's gotta' meet a source, that was two days ago, I gave her my blessing, wished her luck and told her to call me in a couple of days when she had something. Then I went upstairs and told the bossman to get ready for a new front page story."

Cobin started to ask another question but he glanced first at Tully. He caught a quickly concealed look of concern and shut his mouth.

Tully took the interview back.

"How many people would you say are out there that would have wanted Miss Epcot dead?"

Mills laughed again. "March 1999, her first minor story, pretty much everyone she featured since then."

"But, anyone specific?"

"Oh sure, I've got a whole file of them, but I thought you guys already knew it was that Cobin guy." Mills said and held up a copy of the *Gazette*.

Cobin rolled his eyes.

Fineas concluded the interview with Mills and picked up copies of Epcot's recent agenda, stories she was working on and recently published pieces, then they made their way back to the elevator and out to the parking lot.

"So, why Imahara?" Tully asked as they got back in the car.

"Seriously? I didn't have the hair for Blaze and I couldn't stand Jake's moodiness at the moment, plus he might follow up at some point and that wouldn't be good, not that I think Preston Brats would have noticed if I had green hair and orange nails."

"He's a reporter."

"No, he's not, paper pushing executive with an editor's title. Mills probably would have thought the look was real trendy. Which, by the way, you were planning on interviewing the copy editor, weren't you?"

Tully didn't answer and masked his involuntary head shake by putting on his seat belt. He started the car, annoyed that his best officer had to have turned out such a screwed up mess.

By 1:15 the Bell was back in its hanger and Tully was slipping behind the wheel of his car. He looked across the Cobin hanger to the black Lincoln in the corner, easily 40 thousand dollars' worth of car just sitting, awaiting to escort company executives to Cobin Manor.

"Company policy," Cobin said, catching Tully's gaze. "It goes with the chopper."

Tully shook his head. "The amount of corporate waste..." he muttered.

"I know, I know, I think we should just use a car service."

"You're the CEO can't you change that?" Tully asked, starting the car and shifting into drive.

"On paper? Yes. In practice? I could never run the company."

"Why, too much on your plate already with the remodeling?"

"No," Cobin sighed, he sounded forlorn. "The board of directors would never go for it. I might be out of prison and have money in the bank but from now on I'll just be a wealthy investor so far as Cobin Softworks is concerned. They've even proposed buying me out."

Tully considered this news in silence.

He knew Cobin had never intended to run the company, but he also knew what telling a man like Cobin he couldn't do something would do to him and he had some sympathy for him.

"So, what's the plan?" Cobin asked as they cleared the airfield security booth a headed back into town.

Tully checked the car clock and sighed.

"Caroline gets off work at 2. I suppose I could drop you off at the house then we can figure out the night when we get to it."

Cobin looked at him surprised. "Really?"

Tully shrugged. "I've already talked to Caroline about it. Just, stay put, don't touch anything and... behave, alright?"

Cobin nodded and Tully was haunted by the ghost of the boy he once knew.

CHAPTER 13

Wesley hadn't known what to expect when he arrived back at the Tully household.

He'd hoped the hollow place in his heart where this house and the people in it would have filled, but instead he felt the loss all the more acutely since it had been made very clear to him this wasn't an arrangement that would last. And yet, another optimistic part of him thought things could still change. Maybe once he convinced Fineas that he was innocent he could have some semblance of his old life back, even if it meant transitioning to the role of family friend instead of part of the family.

Fineas pulled into the driveway, behind Caroline's Mustang. He shut off the engine but neither of them made to get out of the car.

Wesley was surprised to see Loren's car in the driveway but after going inside he'd found out that she also had the afternoon off.

"Well, as much time off as Loren will ever give herself." Caroline explained over a cup of tea.

"Not much has changed then..." Wesley said with a smile.

"No, I'm told she gets it from her mother." Caroline answered with a smile.

"Oh, there's no doubt about that." Wesley smiled, but it wasn't in his eyes. As they continued to talk he realized just how much he'd missed this interaction and how much his heart ached at the thought of losing his surrogate mom again.

Wesley retreated to the living room. He felt an acute tightness in his chest that did a few deep breathing exercises to alleviate the strain.

Once he could breathe again he flipped on the TV and let its mindless pull take him.

Unfortunately he found himself growing bored with sitting around. Strange, perhaps, since at home he could spend entire days watching the television. Then again, that was for something like a *Star Wars* marathon or *Lord of the Rings: Extended Edition*. And his home theater's 1080p HD-Projector and 7.1 surround sound was a much more cinematic experience.

He also wasn't normally mulling over interviews and case details that his freedom could later depend on. That meant taking a nap was totally out of the question.

Maybe Caroline would need help with dinner, which gave him a better idea.

"Hey."

Wesley lifted his absent gaze from the floor and tried in vain to stop the goofy smile he felt tweaking his lips when he heard Loren's voice.

She was standing at the foot of the stairs looking at him, she trudged across the room then went limp and flopped onto the couch just like she used to when she was a little girl.

"Finally, I'm done!" she said.

"With?"

"Oh, right." Loren turned to him. "I'm working part time now, and with the other part I'm doing some marketing research for a consulting firm."

"Sounds fascinating."

"Well it definitely doesn't feel fascinating. You have lunch?"

Wesley nodded, though the in-car dining hadn't been much on the way back to the airfield.

Loren looked at her watch and groaned. "I might as well wait until dinner at this rate! Will you be sticking around?"

Wesley nodded. "I think so, probably, Radburt has the night off but even then your dad doesn't think he's my best alibi to begin with seeing how I pay him generously on a regular basis."

They fell into silence and Wesley kicked himself because now Loren was thinking about the suspicions against him.

Wesley vowed to himself that he would tell Loren whatever she wanted to know, but her next question caught him off guard and reminded him why he'd loved her.

"One thing I can't understand." Wesley swallowed. Waiting for it, "Why did you sell the Audi? I liked the Audi."

Wesley blinked and searched for an answer to the question he hadn't been expecting. She always could lighten a mood. "Trust me," he said. "The Benz is better."

"I don't know," Loren said skeptically. "I've seen it around town and it looks awfully chromed out and very 'look at me'."

"Do you not remember the size of the wheel arches on the Audi?"

"And you went with black metallic? That only looks good right after it's been washed."

"You know most people think the Mercedes makes me look much more respectable."

"Well, they just don't know you like I do. I suppose it's an automatic?"

"Ah," Wesley said.

"Not even a dual-clutch?"

"Well, no, but..."

"I rest my case."

"I thought you said marketing research, when did you become a lawyer?"

"Same time you became a lazy bum." Loren returned immediately.

"Ouch!" Wesley rubbed at his chest, illustrating his hurt. "I said I've been remodeling."

"That house of yours hardly counts as a full time job."

"And how would you know, maybe I've done a lot of adding on."

"What and then more remodeling? Weak, even for you."

"Fine." Wesley said and that topic was concluded. "So in a very non-mooching, lazy bum kind of way, could I borrow your car to go to the store?"

"My car, my precious machine in your hands? I don't know if you could handle it."

"I haven't forgotten how to shift in eight months." Loren gave him a look that made it clear she wasn't so confident.

"Why don't you just take your precious Benz?"

"Because it's not here." Wesley said simply. Leaving out the part it was locked in the impound yard and Fineas had his license.

"Okay, you can take my car." Loren conceded.

"Thanks, I'll get you a lollipop while I'm out."

"But I don't like lollipops."

"You'll get used to them." Wesley quoted the next line and stood up.

"You tell mom?"

"No, it's a surprise."

"And you remember how that usually works out?"

"I have to go right back and get what I should have gotten in the first place if I'd of just asked first."

"Huh, you haven't forgotten."

"I don't know if I should, it sounds like the system works."

"Wait, a minute, did you just invite yourself to dinner?"

"The invitation was implied, besides I'll be cooking."

"Heaven help us all."

"I'm leaving now." Wesley retorted heading for the kitchen.

Fineas drove back to the station feeling the best he had in several days.

He knew that he'd broken his own rules and that he was probably letting his guard down but he realized that he had actually missed working with Cobin.

Obviously, it wasn't something that was going to become a habit or something, and the interview with both editors hadn't exactly cleared anything up, but it had allowed room for the possibility of something else.

Epcot had left to work on a big story after she was tipped off by a source, possibly Odette Boswell based on the e-mail, or maybe not. Now that he had a time and date that she'd called in he could check her phone records. The techs should also have been able to copy the files off of her laptop and decrypt them. Perhaps they would give him a new direction to lead the investigation.

It all sounded plausible, except for one thing.

Both women had died in his town.

Eliminating the subject of a big story outside of their city limits dropped the numbers exponentially.

Epcot usually wrote about police, all they had was the county sheriff's department, which meant about eight people total. There was the D.A.s office and the mayor in other public offices and the crime lab. But that didn't mean she couldn't be writing about any ordinary citizen, or, Tully realized, Boswell herself.

Perhaps the con-artist had earned her own story and they just decided to meet somewhere small and secluded, maybe Epcot hopped for a chance at a follow up story on Cobin but that wasn't her primary reason for being there.

There were other alternatives was the point that Tully was trying to make with himself.

He pulled into the parking lot and made his way toward the office, trying to inhale deeply the fresh air and enjoy the short walk.

"Oh, good," Marge said as he stepped into the reception area.

"Good afternoon Marge." Tully said with a smile.

"Hmm, good mood?" Marge wondered, mirroring his smile. "I almost called, but a man with a repair service stopped by to work on Cobin's Mercedes, I went ahead and let him, I hope that was alright?"

"Yes, yes, that's fine. Actually if you want to get the paperwork ready I think Cobin will pick it up tonight." Marge arched an eyebrow but didn't say anything.

Tully continued toward his office, looking out over the quiet squad room, he pushed through his door and took a seat at his desk.

In his inbox were several file folders and another external hard drive. He read the labels, phone records, the hard drive keyword results and index, as well as some more lab work from the M.E.

He picked up the hard drive and the index, which he flipped through, heading straight for e-mail. There were over 100 individual sub-files in the e-mail client, Tully skimmed the list, then opened his top drawer to get a highlighter.

He frowned.

Greeting him was the photo he'd taken from Boswell's apartment, the one that showed her wrapped around Cobin.

He'd almost forgotten about it.

With that single glance he felt his doubts returning.

Wesley actually came within an hundred rpm's of killing the Mazda as he backed out of the driveway, though to his credit he'd never driven the car before to be familiar with the clutch engagement.

From there on out it went smoothly and he was delighted that no one tried raining on his parade the entire trip. It was as if he were any other citizen with no unusual back story. It was great. The only mishap came when, on the trip back, he turned on the CD player and was treated to Nickelback starting in on *How You Remind Me*.

He shut off the player and was assaulted by a flash of memory.

By the time he returned to the driveway he was composed again and could unload the cargo area with steady hands. He bustled the three grocery bags up the back steps and into the kitchen where he deposited them on the table.

"Hey, there you are, I was just about to call LoJack." Loren said her head buried in the refrigerator.

"The temptation was there but I resisted." Wesley said.

"It's the six speed I'm telling you." Loren answered and shut the fridge. "What ya get?"

"Sorry, it's only for people with distinguished taste."

"Bite me." Wesley rolled his eyes.

"Were we always like this?"

"Worrying, I know."

At that point Caroline walked in.

"Oh, good, you're just in time." she said.

"Yeah, I had to go two places and that was after I remembered about Kitman's being... closed."

They were all silent for a respectful moment.

"Loren, can you help me out?" Caroline asked setting to getting the kitchen prepared.

"I'd love too, but I just remembered..." she glanced at Wesley, feeling awkward. "I mentioned to Dillon I'd see him after that case today, not for dinner, just to drop off something."

Wesley's face gave nothing away, but it hurt.

"Actually that was the point of my picking stuff up Caroline, I'll be cooking. With some help, if you don't mind."

Caroline and Loren exchanged looks.

"I'm better now." Wesley assured them. "Besides, you got a new kitchen out of it last time."

"And I like this kitchen just the way it is thank you." Caroline said, but she handed Wesley an extra apron.

For Fineas the rest of the afternoon was a long drawn out internal conflict.

In his scouring of the data from Epcot's laptop he found a string of index references to Wesley Cobin. Many of them were involving her original stories or stories written by other people, as well as some photos and video clips of interviews and news footage. None of this was revelatory but it set the tempo to destroy the goodwill Tully had been feeling earlier that day.

Then he found the really bad stuff.

The most recent document that Epcot had been working on was titled *Murder and Freedom*. It wasn't hard to see that it was about Wesley.

Most of the story was unwritten but what was there was worrying enough.

"Three years ago, multi-millionaire and police deputy Wesley Cobin was

accused of murdering his partner Michael Carlyle. The evidence against him was overwhelming and the eyewitness testimony scathing. It was more than enough to convict any average citizen. But Cobin was both connected and rich enough to buy his way out, he assumed when the trial had ended that he had gotten away with it and has been casually enjoying freedom and his millions ever since. However, for some the past is not so easily pushed aside. And now they're talking, past friends and lovers. What they're saying could be enough to bring Wesley Cobin's happy days of corruption to their just deserved end."

The article contained a few notations, but it was clear that this was just a teaser. They hadn't found any notebooks in the car with Epcot's body. It seemed likely that the killer had taken them, especially if they contained the testimonies promised in the teaser.

The problem with that though, was that Cobin was the only one to benefit.

Epcot's phone history was just as worrying with repeated calls to a number tied to a burner phone that they were still trying to get a name for.

Additionally there were several calls placed to the Cobin Manor, all of them answered but lasted only seconds.

Tully needed to ask about them but Radburt would probably be the one to speak to.

But the most troubling for Tully was the comment about "friends and lovers". He found himself pulling out the picture again.

Cobin and Boswell.

It didn't seem possible! The one thing that he had been sure of, through the whole ordeal, was that Wesley loved Loren!

He caught himself.

Wesley.

Tully squinted at the photo.

He knew that he'd created a new persona for the boy he'd used to love. They were almost the same person, except for one thing.

He focused just on the smile.

It was familiar, self-confident and assured. It was Wesley. *Cobin* had never been quite as sure of himself, the same man, but wearing his scars more openly.

This picture was of the Wesley he thought he'd known.

Only he hadn't.

If Cobin could have been cheating on Loren then, there was no telling what he was capable of, including these latest murders.

He sat back and reviewed the time line.

The first murder was so close, the estimated time of death was 2AM, Cobin would have barely had time to leave his house and get to the beach and murder Boswell. Barely, but he could do it.

Then there was the second, Epcot had left a full day before she had turned up dead in the parking lot. Where had she been?

He dug out her mobile phone records and ran down the numbers, the calls to the Cobin Manor landline were highlighted in yellow. The burner calls were red. He searched the list for the call she made to Rue Mills and tapped it absently as he eyed the surrounding numbers.

He found the call from Odette Boswell which they already knew about. Again, he studies the names of the surrounding callers.

The first outgoing call she'd made after hanging up had not been to Mills but to an Atlanta number. The printout hadn't been correctly formatted so the only part of the name he could make out was Y. NIB...

He tapped the number thoughtfully and reached for Odette Boswell's file.

He opened it and pulled out her phone records, zeroing in on the Atlanta prefix.

Boswell had called the same number.

Y. NIBOC was the name attached to the number.

Niboc? Tully wondered.

Then the shoe dropped.

He sat at his desk for a few minutes, feeling unable to move as he confronted the possibilities. He knew what he had to do, there was too much evidence now, but, for the first time, he wondered if he really could.

It was then he noticed the flashing light on his phone.

He had a message.

He pressed the button to see the call log. The last call was from Fredrickson.

The file in his inbox!

Reaching to the corner of his desk he picked up the report and flipped it open.

It was a revised medical work up on Odette Boswell, he skimmed, not seeing anything relevant, he turned to page two and saw Fredrickson's red Post-it arrow.

He dropped the report and hit the desktop with his fist. Tully got to his feet and grabbed his gun and car keys.

Fredrickson had revised the Time of Death.

He now put it at 10 PM.

CHAPTER 14

Fineas resisted the urge to use the light and sirens on his way home. He didn't call for backup either. The only thing he had done was speed dial Barry on his way out the door and told him to get a subpoena for all calls and voicemails logged for "Y. Niboc" of Atlanta.

As he approached home Tully began to worry about what scene he might walk in on.

His mind conjured up images, progressively more horrific, from stand off to murder-suicide, until he nearly ran a stop sign and took out a car entering the intersection.

He slammed on the brakes and forced himself to be reasonable.

A mental image of Cobin filled his mind and he concentrated on the picture, trying to force him into some act of violence against Loren or Caroline but suddenly it seemed absurd.

He might not have known Cobin as well as he'd thought, even to the point of Mike's murder, but he fundamentally refused to believe he was a threat to Loren and Caroline.

It was impossible.

As he pulled into the driveway, a new worry played in his mind, and as he crossed the kitchen threshold he saw it was a reality.

Cobin was with Caroline in the kitchen putting the finishing touches on dinner.

Caroline was smiling and it was clear that Fineas had just walked in at the end of some sort of joke.

He'd warned her about this! He should have known it would happen. They were getting reacquainted and Caroline was losing track of the person Cobin had become.

It was easy to do; Fineas had been doing the very same thing. His worry now was if Caroline was losing sight of what it could do to Loren.

Then he remembered her car wasn't in the driveway. Maybe she'd been out most of the day?

He could always hope.

He ran scenarios through his head. He could take Cobin in then, or question him in the family room, but neither way seemed right. This wasn't something he could afford to mess up. Keep the situation calm, take Cobin home and wait for a judge to get him the subpoena.

"Wesley, this is good." Caroline said a few minutes later. They were in the dining room, their plates held cautious portions of Pasta Carbonara.

Wesley beamed with satisfaction.

Sure, the note of surprise in Caroline's voice was a little disappointing, but he pretty much deserved it after his previous attempts at cooking. Her appreciation of the dish was huge.

Loren, who had just returned as they were heading into the dining room was the next to sample the dish.

She still looked skeptical. Her expression changed as her fork reached her mouth.

"Wow, not bad." she muttered and served herself more from the dish.

Wesley smiled.

Fineas ate without comment.

Caroline sat on his right, Loren on his left so he faced Cobin at the end of the table. He tried not to look at him.

He'd come home to get rid of Cobin, only to find him taking dinner off the stove. Tully was forced to wait for a better time to spirit him away.

As he ate he had to admit it wasn't half bad, but he didn't think Cobin needed to hear him fawning over the meal.

Conversation seemed to keep stalling throughout dinner.

Fineas seemed overly edgy, more disturbed by Wesley's presence then could easily be accounted for.

Wesley assumed he must have been working the case, maybe even looking at Mike's murder today. Maybe the reasons for the animosity and alienation had been freshly renewed.

Regardless the atmosphere managed to turn an excellent meal sour in Wesley's stomach. He was tempted to speak, oh so tempted, to say something that might tip the scales back in his favor, desperate enough to lie. Instead he kept largely silent and soon Loren and Caroline were insisting on taking plates and handling the washing up.

That left Wesley and Fineas alone, which was worse.

"So," Wesley began, only to realize he didn't know where to head the conversation. "I guess I'll be heading home soon?" he asked.

Fineas gave a non-committal grunt.

"Did something happen I'm missing?" Wesley asked, unable to take it anymore.

"Did something happen?" Tully repeated back to him. "No, nothing *new*." he said with emphasis.

So, his mood was over Mike, not this latest rash of murders.

"Is there something you want to ask me, or..." Wesley shrugged.

"No, something you want to confess?" Tully asked.

"Look, Fineas, obviously there's something that wasn't there this morning. I would like to try and enjoy my desert, so..."

"Fine! Did you have an affair with Odette Boswell?" Fineas spat the question as if it tasted bad.

Wesley gave him an exasperated look. "An affair with Boswell? Are you kidding me? Loren and I were engaged! What exactly would make you ask me something like that? You know me, like it or not, and you know damn well I would never cheat on Loren!" Wesley hissed. He realized he was using present tense but didn't care; it was all the same in his mind.

His glare was hot and searing, enough to convince Fineas he was telling the truth. It shook Fineas' resolve slightly.

"Who want's ice cream cake?" Loren asked from the doorway.

Her smile fell when she saw Wesley's still raw expression.

The phone rang.

Fineas jumped up from his chair and went to answer it.

Loren sighed.

"I am so sorry." Wesley said.

"For what?" Loren asked.

"For everything."

"It wasn't all bad." Loren said with a shrug. "Now do you want some cake or not?"

"Yeah," Wesley said with a sad smile. "I'd like that."

Loren and Caroline returned with the cake.

Caroline at least was still happy.

"This is my first attempt using this recipe." She said as she set a generous slice in front of Wesley.

She waited as he picked his fork up and cut into the cake.

"This is great!" he said as the cold of the ice cream mingled with the chocolate and mint flavors and some underlying flavor that he couldn't quite identify. It was wonderful, smile inducing even.

Fineas returned from answering the phone very dour.

Wesley looked up and the smile died. He knew what that look meant.

Loren and Caroline looked from Wesley to the door and caught Fineas' look, they exchanged worried glances.

"Again?" Loren asked.

Fineas didn't answer, nor did he break eye contact with Wesley.

"Just tell me you didn't leave the house today." he said, almost holding his breath, hoping there was a chance he was on the wrong track.

"I didn't leave the house." Wesley said. His appetite was slipping as he wondered what connection he had to the latest victim. He looked down at the cake on his plate and froze. "Oh." He groaned. Fineas looked up at him immediately.

"What did you do?" he demanded, sounding almost fatherly.

"I went to the store." Fineas shut his eyes.

"I told you not to leave the house!"

"I asked him to go." Caroline said defensively.

"No," Wesley corrected. "I invited myself to go."

"Did you walk?" Fineas asked hopefully. If he'd walked that should be easier to come up with some witnesses.

"I borrowed the car." Fineas' glare was liable to bore through marble and it was leveled on Wesley's head. He was tempted to make an issue of his driving without a license, but he didn't feel like getting into it right now.

"I didn't think about it being a problem because everything had been happening at night, this was in the middle of the day."

"Fredrickson's not there yet but it looks like a change in M.O. I want you..." Outside there was a commotion; a racing engine, the chirp of tires and the sound of shattering glass.

Fineas leaped to his feet and hurried down the hallway. He cleared the hallway and crossed the living room in three bounds. He shoved through the screen door.

On the steps he saw a car turning the corner without any lights on, moving way too fast. The engine sounded big and American. Most of his attention was on the small fire in his front yard.

He deviated to grab the hose from the side of the house and ran towards the fire in the grass.

Wesley was already there stomping out the corners of the small conflagration which was working on the mailbox.

Fineas turned the hose on and drenched the flames.

Around them neighbors appeared.

It was Wesley who noticed the rock.

Apparently they'd been aiming for a window but the rock had glanced off the clapboard and landed harmlessly on the lawn. He carefully rolled it with his foot to read the message painted on it.

Murderer

His stomach knotted. He was well acquainted with rocks like these, though he'd usually found them on the passenger seat of his car, the rock having just been hurled through his window, sometimes while he was in the car.

"Molotov cocktail." Fineas said when Wesley approached him. "Go get a broom, we need to clean up this glass."

"There's a rock, too." Wesley said. Fineas nodded.

"It's alright now!" He called to his neighbors. He noticed their stares, mostly directed at Wesley as if he was some exotic and dangerous creature.

Fineas could sympathize to a certain extent.

After the mess was cleaned up he called in a patrol car to come sit on the house, then he took Wesley with him and together they rode to the latest crime scene.

CHAPTER 15

Fineas deliberately avoided telling Wesley who the victim was. He needed a cold read on the kid.

This was his best shot at making a ruling, if he thought Wesley had done it or not.

They stopped just outside town at a small park on the edge of woods. It was temporarily closed for repairs on the playground. Some teenagers had stumbled across the body and had fortunately been compelled to call it in.

After dealing with the vandalism at home and waiting for a patrol they were the last to arrive.

As they made their way across the park almost every eye was fixed on Cobin, a fact he and Tully both noticed.

Jake Barry looked especially fierce.

"I'm guessing I won't like this." Wesley muttered but Tully's face was implacable. He felt the old distance settling between them again. Earlier he'd been hoping he might be Wesley again before the night was over.

"Where is she?" Tully asked Barry.

"Why don't you ask him." Barry suggested, nodding to Cobin.

"Not now, Jake." Barry pointed to an obscure part of the playground, hidden by taped off play equipment.

"I remember coming out here years ago." Wesley muttered to Tully as they crossed the playground but he didn't get a response. It was all happening again.

The body was still on the ground, covered by a white plastic sheet.

Fredrickson stood with his back to the swing set as a few battery powered lamps illuminated the scene better.

"Ah, Sheriff, I haven't done more than..." Tully put up a hand. First things first.

A tech handed over a box of booties which Tully and Cobin fitted over their shoes, then, together with Fredrickson they walked over to the body.

Fredrickson stood behind and slid the sheet away from the victim's face.

Wesley stared impassively for a moment. He recognized her but his brain stalled the connection for as long as possible.

He took an unconscious half step backwards and had to physically fight not to open his mouth in a gasp. He covered his mouth with a fist as, for a split second, he thought he might be sick.

He glared at Fineas, who looked as impassive as ever.

"You could have warned me." he said icily.

"No, I couldn't, I needed your reaction. I assume you know the victim?" he asked.

"It's really her?" Wesley asked, directing his gaze at Fredrickson.

"According to the ID we found on her."

"ID?"

"He's not trying with this one." The M.E. said. Wesley was grateful Fredrickson hadn't implied it was him.

"Fineas, you have to know I..." Wesley broke off, there was no point.

"So it is her?" A voice called from the edge of the crime scene tape. Wesley recognized the voice, yet turned anyway. Dillon Howard stood, watching, just over the line.

"What is he doing here now!" he yelled to Tully.

"Come on." Tully said and led Wesley away from the body of Missy Carlyle, the widow of Michael Carlyle, Wesley's murdered partner.

Wesley ignored the conversations that floated around him. The only thing he could think about was Missy and there really was no point looking around because everyone here thought he'd killed her and they hated him.

Missy had been extremely well liked at the department for the exact same reasons she'd been such a horrible wife. She was gorgeous, knew it and wanted everyone else to. She flirted with just about any man breathing and was constantly reminding Mike that she was out of his league.

Wesley had quietly hated her for it. There hadn't been any love lost between them, at least, not in the end. She'd testified against Wesley claiming he was constantly arguing with Mike and that was just the nicer, less damaging testimony.

"You're going to hang for this."

136

Wesley looked up to see Jake Barry standing over him.

"Thanks for the vote of confidence, buddy." Wesley didn't really care at the moment what happened.

"You know, up until now I could have almost sympathized with you. Boswell and the other one got what was coming but now I will make it my mission to bring you down."

"Could you record this for me, I have a feeling it could be useful in my murder investigation."

Jake smirked. "I'm not touching you this time."

"Well, that's a pleasant relief; I always wonder where those hands have been." The smirk stayed.

"I suggest you enjoy what's left of your miserable life this side of barred windows and bad food."

"Guess so, your sister still around?" Jake's smirk flat-lined.

Wesley sighed and raised his hands in apology. "You know what, I'm sorry, that was over the line. Maggie's a great girl. Did she ever get that position at Webber?"

"No, what?" Jake asked, puzzled by the sudden shift in attitude.

"Before all of this happened, she was trying to get a job working at Webber and James, paralegal right?"

"I'm not talking about this." Jake said. He stomped off, leaving Wesley alone.

"I hope you've still got that same legal team on retainer these days." Wesley sighed and turned, this time, to see Dillon standing beside him.

"Added a few actually, thought you'd appreciate a new challenge." Wesley said dryly. He stood up. Apparently sitting was no longer a viable option to be left alone. He walked back towards the crime scene. Dillon followed him.

Wesley tried ignoring the shadow that followed him over to the swing sets.

He stood in the sand, watching CSU processing the scene on the other side of the playground.

The setting was so wrong. The brightly colored play equipment at odds with the brutality of murder.

Wesley dropped his eyes to the sand, which must have been recently groomed, because there weren't as many footprints as he would have expected.

He noticed one set of prints. From their size obviously an adult had made them.

He was interested in how they terminated.

He stood next to them and tried to reproduce the marks by rocking in one place. He stepped back and compared the two prints.

He was reaching conclusions when Dillon interrupted.

Tully was talking things over with the chief CSU technician and Fredrickson when they heard the cry of surprise and then the sound of flesh-to-flesh contact as a punch was landed.

Tully sprinted forward, felt his knee catch, then steady. Moving fast was getting harder and harder. He arrived just behind Barry as one of the crime scene techs shrieked. "No! Not here you idiots!"

Wesley was standing over Dillon who was bleeding from his nose.

"Don't you ever talk about her that way again!" Wesley said coldly.

"Cobin!" Tully shouted and dashed forwards to grab Wesley by the arm and drag him back away from the scene and Dillon, who now sat, stunned and bleeding.

Apparently coming out of his shock the ADA touched his nose, tried lunging forwards. Barry stopped him at a look from Tully.

"What was that?" Tully roared at Cobin.

"He..." Wesley started to speak, then cut out. "He called me... something."

"Something?"

"Uncomplimentary."

"So you just contaminated my crime scene over name calling?" Tully seethed.

"I guess." Wesley said in a hollow voice.

"You're going home now." Tully commanded grabbing him by the arm and leading him back to the car.

Wesley looked back at Dillon but no one caught the look that passed between them. One of uneasy understanding as well as a veiled threat.

"Good, this place isn't fun anymore. We going back to your place?" Wesley asked, striving, apparently for annoying nonchalance.

"No, I think it's time for you to go home since obviously you won't stay in one place anyway!"

"Yeah, probably best, I could snap at any time. So, back to my pad!" Tully's gaze was heavy on Wesley. Something had just happened, but he was too distracted to want to puzzle it out. Instead they just got back in the car.

"What do you think about Dillon?" Cobin asked. He'd been quiet since they'd left the scene and Tully had thought maybe his fit of whatever had passed. Maybe he really was unstable?

"What do you mean?" Tully asked warily.

"What do you think about him? His character? How is he with Loren?"

"He didn't break her heart." Tully said, not looking at his passenger.

"And he loves her?"

The question seemed dangerous but Tully knew he had to answer, lest silence be misinterpreted.

"Yes."

"You have no worries about him and Loren?"

"What's it to you?" Tully snapped.

"Loren deserves the best." Cobin said simply. "I'm not trying to win her back, Fineas. But I need to know she's going to be happy with him."

"You act like you actually have some kind of say over that. No one can guarantee happiness."

"Believe me, I know that, but it's important to me."

"Really?" Tully asked, annoyed now. "Because you have a very strange way of showing what's important to you!"

Cobin didn't say anything for a few minutes and Tully thought it might stretch the length of the car ride, but then he changed the conversation.

"Was Barry ever reprimanded after he broke my arm?"

"Why do you think he hates you so much?"

Cobin chuckled. "My looks, my money, though I really thought that it had something to do with my 'alleged cop killer' title."

Tully listened very carefully. Cobin had just said alleged, which implied it was wrong.

"Alleged?" Tully asked quietly.

"Well, no conviction, you can state anything as fact. And you know what, I don't think it's the right terminology. What is it when one cop kills another?"

"Betrayal." Tully said with icy finality and an edge of disgust in his voice.

He wondered how many years the emotional roller coaster of the past few days had taken off of his life? Cobin was sinking to an all-time low or at least, the lowest in the past couple of years. Old wounds were flaming up again and Fineas felt the betrayal and anger welling up in him again.

He looked at Cobin, trying to decide if he was man or monster, fighting emotion with reason and making himself sick.

But something was different.

The last crime scene had changed Cobin, and it wasn't for the better.

"I don't want you coming back to the house." Tully said suddenly.

He waited, silently hoping Cobin would say something to try and make him reverse his decision, to give some sign he cared.

Cobin was silent.

The silence Tully found even more infuriating.

"I don't want you talking to Caroline and I don't even want you to think about Loren." He sounded strange to his own ears, savage almost. "That's all completely over and it has been since that night." he added with finality.

"Day." Cobin corrected.

"What?"

"It has been since that day. It happened at night, I was dragged in at 10:57 PM, I left interrogation at 5:34 AM and you didn't write me off until then. You looked across the squad room and our eyes met and I knew from that point on you were gone and my life was over."

"No!" Tully slammed on the brake pedal, throwing them both against their seat belts. The car shuddered as the ABS system modulated the brake forces and brought the car to a dead stop.

"No, your life was over the minute you decided to shoot your partner three times in cold blood! It was that second when you took the life of a man who thought of you like his brother that your life ended. It was then that your forfeit every single right and claim you had to me or my family. It was in that second that I lost a son!" Tully shouted. He almost choked. It was the first time he'd said it out loud.

His knuckles turned white as he strangled the steering wheel, keeping his hands busy, not giving them a chance to find his gun or Cobin's neck. His chest heaved with the sudden rush of adrenaline, making his breath shudder.

Cobin said nothing, just looked through the windshield into the night. His lips were a flat line, clamped tightly shut, bottling up all of the things he wanted to say.

After the peak of near homicidal rage had passed Tully felt drained and completely spent.

"I think I'll walk the rest of the way." Cobin said.

Tully just nodded, still breathing heavily.

Cobin opened the door, stepped into the night, shut it behind him.

Tully took his foot off the brake pedal and turned the car around, going back the way he'd come, he checked his mirror and saw Cobin nearly engulfed by the night.

They hadn't exaggerated the danger earlier. The fervor had died down but given the opportunity there were still people in town that might take the vigilante route, as proved earlier that evening. But at that second he didn't care what happened to Wesley Cobin.

CHAPTER 16

Hot tears seared Wesley's cheek as he walked along the road. He wasn't prepared for it. He didn't have a flashlight or a reflective jacket. Then again he didn't really want to stand out.

He could put on an air of not being afraid, he could even handle a beating but it was different when he was alone, especially in the dark. He found himself turning around more and more frequently.

You really are becoming paranoid. He warned himself. But he knew there was something to be paranoid about. If he was right about what he'd seen.

He pulled out his phone and speed dialed home.

The phone went unanswered.

Radburt was at the cottage or still out for the night.

He'd told him he was staying at the Tully's again and Radburt wouldn't be expecting any trouble. He probably thought it was a welcome nod to normalcy because, of course, Wesley hadn't told him he suspected Fineas had been charged with keeping an eye on him. He didn't even know if Radburt knew he'd been a suspect in the murders.

Am a suspect, he corrected.

Wesley continued along the side of the narrow road.

This was a bad idea. He decided. Back in the car it had made sense, in the same way that death had always made sense to him, even before that night three years ago.

But he'd forgotten what it was like to reach that edge.

The final tipping point. The place where life became something of value again, became something worth fighting for.

Behind him a car was approaching.

Only fifteen minutes ago this had been exactly what he'd wanted. Now

Wesley found himself down in the ditch, getting out of sight, suddenly gripped with terror at the thought of the people no doubt coming for him.

This had seemed cleaner, possibly even more humane.

He'd been abrasive enough. He'd caused enough damage and sometimes wondered if he wasn't in control anymore.

But not now!

An old truck rattled past and disappeared up the hill. He let out his breath and continued on.

He tried to figure how long a walk it would be. Forty-five minutes maybe?

He tried to guess how long he'd been walking. Ten minutes? There wasn't much in the way of landmarks to gauge progress just a sliver of moon gave scant illumination.

Finally he reached the top of the hill then and saw the old truck off the edge of the road.

The truck! With a jolt he recognized it and froze. He tried to think of a weapon he had on him, something previously overlooked?

His Swiss army knife was the only thing that came to mind. It seemed more dangerous to have it out then be armed only with his fists.

Again he thought back to occasions he'd stared death in the face, to when he'd wanted it, but it was the same result, now he wasn't ready to give up.

It was funny what a quiet walk and some introspection could do.

He thought of Loren.

He'd wanted to protect her.

He would go on protecting her.

He would do whatever it took.

But before all that, he realized they needed to talk.

No, he wasn't ready to go quietly into the night, so this time it was going to be a real fight.

He was done taking their hits.

It no longer served his purpose.

He thought through strategies, trying to imagine how many there were. He was be able to take on one, maybe even two. He unconsciously traced the scar on his belly. Then there had been five.

Foliage rustled and Wesley thought he saw a figure standing there, then three. They stepped onto the road surface and into the weak moonlight. One of them toyed with a length of 2x4. Another hefted an aluminum bat over his shoulder.

"Hello Cobin." One of them spat.

"Good evening gentlemen." Wesley said back, his reply annoyingly weak as he faced the abbreviated Jefferson gang.

"We hear you've been real busy lately. Real tough guy, aren't you?"

"I think you might be confusing me for someone else." Wesley said trying his best to be amiable, knowing he was seconds away from a total thrashing. Knowing life's little ironies he probably wouldn't survive this one.

"Do you realize no one will miss you once you're gone? Next week at your funeral, if you get one, no one's going to show up."

Considering he was a dead man any way Wesley decided to argue the point. "I wouldn't be entirely sure of that. I've actually been building a list and I think I might be up to five." His back talk was apparently unexpected because no return taunts were hurled. On the other hand they didn't look any less determined. He thought about his other cards. Reason? Not going to fly. Professed innocence? Yeah, right. Run? Appealing except they had a truck.

They stepped forwards as a group with one agenda. In the distance Wesley could just make out the sound of an engine. Judging from the sudden fidgeting around it wasn't just his imagination and it obviously wasn't their backup. Bat and 2x4 vanished behind backs for the moment and Wesley back tracked to the opposite side of the road.

He had to stop that car!

Fineas took the turn into his driveway with too much speed and the Crown Vic slammed unhappily over the sidewalk, he experienced a twinge of fear when he realized how quickly he was gaining on the Mustang and stood on the brakes, halting the big cruiser and shoving it into park.

He sat in the car, engine running, while he tried to cool off.

He knew exactly what had happened.

Over the past few days he'd gotten too comfortable with Cobin. He'd lost sight of what he'd done and the price he was supposed to be paying for it. He'd forgotten who he was really dealing with.

He tried to relax but the anger was nestled vice-like between his shoulders.

He shut off the engine and got out of the car, trying to hold himself back from slamming the door but not quite making it.

His new car was taking a lot of abuse over this situation.

Fineas turned towards the house and saw Caroline watching him out the kitchen window.

He looked down, ashamed and made his way to the back door.

Neither of them spoke as he came in and stood leaning against the door.

"Dillon call?" he asked eventually.

"Jake, actually."

"Really?" Fineas asked, surprised. Was his deputy even beginning to have doubts?

Doubts about what? Tully reminded himself.

"Is it happening again?" Caroline asked.

Fineas shook his head. "The trial's over and he didn't do this. And no matter what I do, nothing is going to change that fact. He got away with it. He decided to kill his best friend and then he got away with it and never paid the price."

"Fineas…" Caroline started, but he cut her off.

"He got away with it and yet I'm the one that keeps coming across as the bad guy!"

Caroline shook her head. "Don't you think that poor boy *has* paid a price, don't you think he keeps paying it every day of his life?"

Fineas looked at his wife in surprise. "Well he sure doesn't seem to express it much." He said harshly. "Either way that's not the way the world works, you can't just feel bad about it. There are rules that are supposed to be obeyed!"

"Is this what this is about now, rules? Rules you think make the world tick."

Fineas tilted his head, trying to see his wife's perspective. They'd never talked much about what had happened. Granted, he hadn't really allowed it, but Caroline had never objected before.

"Fineas, there are still things about that night you don't know, things you've had to suppose."

"Things backed up by scientific, physical evidence. Then we can talk about his attitude."

"What would you do if someone killed me and Jake Barry came through that door and accused you of being my murderer?"

"That's not the same thing and you know it. That's not what happened!" Fineas said, disturbed at the very thought.

"But just suppose for a minute, how would you react?"

"I don't want to do this. I can't stand the thought of…"

"Fineas," Caroline said firmly, and then softly asked, "What would you do?" Silence settled between them as Tully thought.

"I don't know, I'd get angry, I'd prove I didn't do it."

"And what if you were locked up, what if you couldn't?" he didn't answer.

"What if no one believed you but you had the power to get yourself cleared. What if you had the money to beat the system, to get you out so you could keep going, keep looking for the truth?" Tully wouldn't look at his wife.

"That's not the way it was." he said softly, Caroline just frowned sadly shaking her head as she went back to washing dishes.

He looked down the hill, was blinded by the headlight bloom and waved feebly. He considered throwing himself in front of the car and getting everything over with quickly but the thought was too unappealing even to dwell on. In the end he didn't need to anyway because the car slowed as it neared the crest of the hill. The driver whipped the car onto the oncoming shoulder and for a minute Wesley thought he was going to be purposely run down. He stepped back into the road and then he recognized the Mazda.

Loren stopped the car and leaned over, pushing open the passenger door.

"Get in!" She called and Wesley obligingly fell into the car, he resisted the urge to wave at his would-be assailants.

Loren found first gear and dropped the clutch. The front tires slipped on the loose surface of the shoulder, then hauled them forwards with a flashing from the traction control light. She threw the car into second gear with equal violence.

"You okay?" Loren asked and they were the sweetest words Wesley had ever heard.

"Yeah," he said and found his voice shaky. He noticed there was also a tremor in the fingers wrapped around the door pull. "I think I'm right in saying you just saved my life. I love you." He blurted.

"I know." Loren said.

"Really?"

"Yeah, I do."

They rode in silence for a moment. Loren checked the rear view mirror, but no one was following them.

"Never actually stopped." Wesley said softly.

"Nope."

"Bummer."

"Totally." Loren agreed.

"Well at least we cleared that up."

"And that's a very good thing."

"It was for the best."

"So you say."

"What would you have preferred me to say?"

"The truth would have been a good place to start." Loren said and shifted into sixth and a comfortable cruise.

"The truth was too complicated." Wesley said.

"Is it still too complicated?"

"I don't know. I don't know about much of anything anymore."

"Do you know who you are yet?"

"Actually, I think I'm making some progress on that one."

"You're not a murderer." Loren said emphatically so as not to be mistaken as a question.

"Is that what you think?" Wesley asked.

"It's a fact. One I've known a long time."

"It never would have worked out between us Loren, there was no way, you would have been just as much of a target as I was and your dad, his career would have been over."

"His career? Right because that's really what I was worried about at the time, thank you for that consideration."

"I'm sorry."

"And I forgive you."

"This is an odd conversation." Wesley said after a moment of silence had settled between them.

"I think we both knew what we needed to say, we just needed the opportunity."

"Would it be too much to say we're square now?" Wesley wondered.

"I don't know, three years is a lot of time to cover in thirty seconds. But it's the right first step."

"So, where do we go from here?"

"I think you should go home." Loren said sensibly.

"I know that, but…"

"I know what you mean. But I don't have an answer."

They both thought on her words for a while, just the thrum of the engine between them.

"I did a lot of things wrong." Wesley said slowly.

"You got that one right."

"I was way too proud for one."

"Are you still?"

Wesley continued with his thought before answering. "I didn't think I could make a mistake, fail at anything. Now I know I can."

"Does that help?"

"Maybe."

"Do we need to talk about Dillon?" Loren asked, not softly but matter-of-factly.

"Only if you want to ruin the whole evening." Wesley said a little too caustically for polite conversation.

"Need I remind you I just saved your life?"

"That doesn't mean we couldn't have just enjoyed the drive home. What is there to talk about?"

"The fact that he was the prosecutor of your case and now he and I are engaged to be married for starters."

"I *would* like to know how that happened, but not right now."

"We'll talk later, about everything."

"Ships and shoes and sealing wax?"

"Of cabbages and kings."

"Sometimes we have really cheesy dialogue." he said.

Loren snorted. "We have history, it's different." she corrected.

"So, for now the only question,"

"Yes?"

"Do we have a future?" He saw Loren wince.

"You and I, happily ever after?" she took a deep breath. "We aren't the same people, Wes."

"So, we've both changed, I've grown up, you've... actually I can't figure out what you've done." Wesley said with a grin, lightening the mood.

Loren swatted at him. "We'll always have something. It's always going to be... different. But before we get to that, you've got to come clean with my dad. You've got to finish this, whatever it really is."

"And then?"

"I don't know." Loren said. "You don't want to talk about Dillon, so..." She shrugged.

There was a lasting silence between them, as Wesley weighed the dangers of lies and truths and the facts that he now knew. He could change so much depending on what he said.

"I'll tell you." Wesley said eventually. "I'll tell you everything." Loren was quiet, also sensing the gravity of the statement. Then she nodded. And Wesley told her everything.

Tully was waiting for Loren when she walked in the door two hours later. It was like a flashback to adolescence to find him at the kitchen table with a view of either front or back door in easy range of his scowl. Before he could say anything Loren beat him to the punch.

"Dad, I'm twenty-six and living at home by choice, just remember that."

"What were…" Loren held up a hand.

"It's late and I'm really tired."

"Then I'll make this brief. Where were you?"

"Saving Wesley from the locals."

"You were with Cobin?" Loren shook her head.

"I was with Wesley Dad, he's not the persona you've created, he's Wesley."

"The day…"

"He didn't do it. Not then, not now. I know the whole thing." Tully bit his lip. He'd already resolved he wasn't going to do this again. He took a calming breath. His daughter headed him off again.

"It's over."

Tully furrowed his brow. "What's over?"

"He's changed, he'll talk about it. It's a waste and it never should have happened but it did and everyone's had to live with that."

"What are you saying, first he didn't do it, now…"

"You need to talk to him yourself. You need to listen and you need to ask him what happened. You never actually asked him before."

"What was there to say?"

"A whole lot, as it turns out, starting with he didn't do it." Loren turned and made her way down the hallway heading for the stairs and her bed, leaving Tully in the kitchen wondering about what should have been.

Wesley stood on the porch for a few minutes after Loren dropped him off, staring after her car, going over the night in his head.

This wouldn't be the longest day of his life he knew, but it would probably end up being a close second.

They were fast approaching the endgame and if he didn't step things up soon he could easily see himself behind bars again. He hadn't been expecting to lose Fineas again, he had thought, after their day trip, things were beginning to mend then Fineas had come home and accused him of having an affair somewhere between three, or five years ago, with one of the women he would classify as a mortal enemy.

He hadn't been expecting that one and it had rather knocked him off his game.

The thing that had him worried was that Fineas hadn't given him any information to work with. Up until that point he'd managed a parallel investigation with, what he thought, was basically the same evidence. He'd obviously fallen behind.

Behind him Radburt opened the front door.

"Shouldn't you be coming inside?" Radburt asked, worry in his voice.

Wesley turned to his old friend. He'd called Radburt before launching into his explanation of events to Loren and given him a brief and to the point update.

"Yes, we've got work to do." Wesley agreed, though he knew Radburt's concern was to get him behind a securely locked door.

He doubted anyone could pull off an ambush of the house given the copious amount of up-lighting that decorated the property, but the dead bolts and security protocols would buy him more time.

He could even go all Kim Dotcom and lock himself in the panic room if they came for him.

"I think I've gotten everything together, it's in the office." Radburt said and Wesley followed him inside the house.

Radburt quickly shut the door and crossed to the alarm keypad. He put the house on lockdown, which would trip the siren if any door or window in the manor was opened or broken.

Wesley didn't think it really necessary but he didn't stop him.

Upstairs in the office Wesley couldn't help but smile, for a man who hated technology Radburt looked to have done a good job setting up the three OLED televisions and tying them to the DisplayPort hub. He'd also loaded Wesley's Murder Boards and had each displaying on a screen.

Wesley picked up the iPad which was serving as the control pad since none of the OLEDs were touch screens. He opened the board for Missy, which was awash with question marks.

He tapped a side tab to open her phone records, which slowly loaded, he then tapped *compare* and added Boswell and Epcot to the list.

Numbers in common appeared in triplicate across the big screens.

Wesley sighed at the ease the software made of managing all three investigations.

He might not have directly run the company, but having close ties to a software company certainly had its advantages.

By the morning he hoped to be caught up with Fineas.

By the time they arrested him, he had to be ahead.

CHAPTER 17

Phineas barely slept that night. His mind wouldn't stop turning over Loren's words of earlier.

He didn't do it.

Could it be true?

No doubt Cobin could work up a compelling enough story, especially for Loren, but what would be the point? And what a change that would have been from his earlier behavior that night, his flippancy over Mike's death. And now Missy.

There was a clear trail connecting Cobin to all of the latest murders and he was clearly hiding something, but even finding Missy didn't alter Phineas' original feeling that Cobin wasn't behind these murders.

He'd go see him tomorrow morning, before he went in to work. Loren said it was over. He hoped she was right.

"Sir, telephone," Radburt said, breaking Wesley's stream of concentration.

"What?" Wesley asked curtly. Actually there hadn't been much to break and since Radburt interrupted it was obviously important.

"I believe you will want to take this." He handed Wesley the cordless.

"Hello?"

"Hello, this Wesley?" The female caller asked.

"Yes."

"Good, this is Deanna Casale, Fineas' old partner."

"Special Agent Casale, it's good to hear from you." Wesley relaxed a little.

"I hear things are rather interesting your way?"

"Oh, accused of murder, no one believes my innocence, the usual."

"Oh, uh huh," Deanna said off handedly.

"Yes, it's like the money, the looks, were all for nothing when no one..."

"Okay, Wesley, shut up now."

Wesley shut up and almost smiled.

"If I got an accurate read on you the last time I met you I'm guessing you're at the stage where you're basically an ass to everyone you meet, including you're friends. Fineas is trying to work through a couple of things involving his feelings toward you and I would imagine that your attitude is not helping which means you're shooting yourself in the foot."

She could read him well. No wonder Fineas used her as a sounding board.

"Actually, I..."

"Don't interrupt please. You two have a lot of unresolved issues and you're not going to get through those in a day but you've got to let all of that go until you get the mess you're in now straightened out because you're both out of time."

"What do you mean?"

He knew he had a limited time frame, but why Fineas?

"I have a few connections, I've been keeping an eye on things and someone just called in the state police. The murders are now under their jurisdiction. I know that you were the best deputy that Fineas had and I know that the two of you have a good working relationship when it's not fouled up with the confusion of the past three years. Just so we're clear you understand that no one knows about this conversation?"

"Yes ma'am."

"And Cobin, if you killed any of those people, or if you should break Fineas' expectations of your character in a way so as to hurt him or his family, know that it will be my mission in life to hunt you down and bring you to justice in whatever way I see fit. Capish?"

"Loud and clear."

"Good, I enjoyed our little chat." Casale said and hung up.

Wesley slowly handed back the telephone to Radburt.

The State Police.

What were the odds he knew the officer they were sending?

The phone rang at 7 AM. Tully had overslept, or more accurately, had just fallen asleep about 4 AM, and was only just then fastening his belt.

Caroline had picked up on the unease between father and daughter in the two or three minutes they were both at the kitchen table together, but remained mute about it. She brought the cordless phone into the bedroom and handed it to her husband.

"It's Jake," she said. "Sounds urgent."

Tully took the phone, already feeling his stomach knotting in dread.

"Go ahead," he said simply.

Barry sounded agitated as he spoke up. "Sheriff did you know about this thing with the State police?"

"What thing?" Tully asked. He'd been expecting word of another murder and was somewhat relieved to hear something different.

"Trust me you'd know what thing if you'd heard. You better get down here." Tully hung up. He didn't like being left in the dark but it sounded as if Barry was trying to be evasive. Tully wondered what that could have meant.

He cinched his belt and headed for the door.

As soon as Tully turned the corner he saw the problem. Parked in front of the municipal building were two Ford Expeditions and a Dodge Charger decked out in state police livery.

Tully also noticed the District Attorney's blue Jeep and started to worry.

He squinted at the building, trying to make out any signs of movement. So intent of it he found himself wandering into the other lane and had to jerk the wheel back to avoid an oncoming burgundy Lexus.

His new car wasn't going to last long if he kept driving like that!

He pulled into the lot and parked quickly, then hurried inside. He had a feeling of foreboding, like he knew what was coming.

A few minutes later his worst fear was confirmed.

There were eight men from the State police looking busy in the squad room and it looked like the conference room had been sequestered as an office. In amongst the State lackeys stood a tall and burly man Tully recognized as Commander Luton Briggs, a man with whom he'd butted heads with before.

In the background he spotted Barry looking disapproving and Blaze looking dazed and confused. Then he spotted Jackson Bell, District Attorney, it was to him that Tully headed.

The DA didn't notice Tully at first, his attention being on Briggs as the man snapped out rapid fire instructions to his men.

"Sheriff!" Bell said, sounding startled and rightly so.

"My office," Tully said. "Now!" He added when the DA didn't immediately snap to. Bell pursed his lips then fell into step behind Tully.

Tully caught Briggs' eye when he looked back from his office. The State Commander seemed to shoot him a smug expression, but that may have been Tully's imagination. He reached down to unlock his office and discovered it open. He gripped the knob tightly and very carefully opened the door so as not to heave it in frustration.

Bell followed him into the small office and Tully took equal care in closing the door, then he turned to face Bell and in a very controlled, very annoyed tone, asked: "What did you do?"

Bell gave him a sympathetic look and started in.

"Fineas this is nothing personal and this is no reflection on your abilities as Sheriff, we just decided this case was getting too complex and, in light of your personal connections to certain persons involved, we felt calling in the State Police was the right thing to do."

Tully stared at the District Attorney. "First of all," he said icily. "What personal connection? Have you noticed how many people live in this community? This is the smallest county in the state! I've got personal connections to just about everyone here. Second, what gives you the right to decide when I need more help?"

"Fineas, I'm acting in the best interests of the community. We don't want any mistakes on this one." The bold faced implication being there had been numerous mistakes previously.

Tully wanted to go on ranting but he knew this decision couldn't be reversed at this point. The damage was done and the only thing left was to maintain as much control as possible. That and bring in a backup plan.

"Then what's going to be done about the case now?" he asked.

"The case notes have been reviewed as well as the forensic evidence we're starting to get back and I believe the officer in charge is about to make an arrest."

"Who?" Tully demanded.

"Again, it's no reflection on you personally Tully, we just needed swifter action, people are dying."

"Who are they arresting?" Tully asked grimacing. Had he overlooked some glaring flaw, anything aside from the obvious, maybe he'd missed another suspect somewhere in the background checks, anything that didn't end with them arresting…

"Wesley Cobin." The DA declared. "They have enough to hold him. The arrest will be made this morning."

Tully gave him a scathing look. "You are aware of the personal connection Commander Briggs has with your prime suspect don't you? I frankly find that more biased than my background given the fact I was with the prosecution on arresting Cobin the last time."

"You have nothing to worry about. Commander Briggs is very professional, I'm sure. He won't let past dealings influence him now." Tully snorted. His experience with Briggs led him to believe exactly opposite, but he saw no point in arguing that out with Bell.

"I need to talk with Cobin first." Tully said flatly making it clear these were his terms and not a request.

"That's not my call, but I wouldn't recommend it." Bell said.

"Excuse me?"

"You have a close relationship with the suspect and I don't think it would look good to anyone if you were talking to him just before his arrest, unless of course you could offer up a compelling reason to not arrest him?" Tully was silent, boiling beneath the surface.

"My duty is to protect the citizens of this county, all of them, including Wesley Cobin and to do that I need to interview him."

"Oh, don't worry, you'll get a chance, we've got the interrogation room prepped."

"He's not going to talk on camera."

"How could you possibly know that?" Bell asked skeptically.

"Because I've been through this before." Tully said testily.

"Exactly, you've been through this and he's still a free man. You can no doubt see our concerns."

"You cannot do this!"

The DA's smile turned into a look of pity as he placed a hand on Tully's shoulder and lowered his voice. "Fineas, you never understood the political aspects of this job. I have more political clout than you do. People higher up look to me for certain things I can do for them, not because of the things I do for the people. I recommend you learn that or you are liable to have a very short term in office." The DA removed his hand and pushed past Tully and through the door.

Tully closed his eyes and tried to breathe. Resolved, he went to try and patch things over with Commander Briggs.

Briggs was not interested in patching anything over.

"Corruption is like gangrene, Tully." Briggs was explaining. "Murder is worse, you were reluctant to cut off Cobin the last time this happened so you didn't dig deep enough and in the end you lacked the compelling evidence needed to convict. Fortunately for the people of Coolidge County I've dealt with this before from my own team. Twice in fact. You take the person out at the knees and watch which way they try to crawl."

Tully blinked. He remembered reading about one of the instances Briggs was referring to. Unless his memory had glaring holes in it he was pretty sure the accused in that case had been innocent but the hack job Briggs had done left the officer without a job anyway.

"Don't you think you're acting a little too soon?" Tully ventured. "Shouldn't we be waiting for something more concrete?"

Briggs was not impressed.

"The only way you can get a man like Cobin is to shake him, rattle him, mix things up. If he knows he have enough to nail him beyond a shadow of a doubt he'll split, or he'll call in his big dollar legal team and then it'll be just like your investigation three years ago."

"It wasn't my investigation." Then, like now, he'd been pulled off the case for the final interview, only then he'd been replaced with a dull and straightforward man requested by the preemptive Internal Affairs group.

Compared with Briggs IA seemed like a positively benign force.

Four years ago the department and Briggs had been involved in a drug trafficking case. Wesley had been taking point and he'd ended up embarrassing Briggs with superior police work.

Briggs didn't take embarrassment well and Tully had, of course, sided with his deputy.

Now Briggs had his chance at revenge on both of them and Tully had no doubts this would become a personal vendetta.

"Well, in any case, if Cobin is guilty and he gets away, it's your screw-up, not mine." Tully said and returned to his office to plan.

CHAPTER 18

Radburt happened to be passing one of the front windows when the security system chimed its proximity alert.

He looked down from the second story to the entrance of the driveway and saw the State Police Expedition lead the charge up the driveway, lights flashing sirens off.

He hurried to the foyer.

Wesley met him there, looking grim, but determined.

"Everything is done!" Radburt said hurriedly. "If they search the house?"

"Garage and my old room, I don't think it's going to be a problem. If they start tearing anything up?"

"Historic property, call Edwards, I know." Radburt said.

Wesley nodded his approval.

"The computers are clean, it would be better if they didn't get the iPad and the router needs reset, the hardline is clean but the cache could still..."

Radburt produced the router. "Already thought of that." He said and dropped the plastic box on the floor and stomped on it with what Wesley thought was a hint of glee.

"It could have just been wiped." he said dryly, looking at the smashed device.

"But why risk it?" Radburt asked eyes a gleam.

"Well, make sure they don't find it." Wesley said thinking smashing the device was probably more suspicious than just flashing the memory.

"Don't worry, and the backup is installed, you've been streaming movies all night."

Wesley blinked.

"You had a back-up router?" Radburt nodded, then picked up the pieces of the router and hurried back into the house. Wesley shook his head wondering what hidden depths there were to his friend.

He hurried to peek out the etched glass set high in the front double doors.

Through the haze it looked like there were three vehicles total, all with State Police colors.

He ran over everything in his head, looking for things he may have overlooked or forgotten. So far, running on just two hours of sleep was working but he knew he had another long day ahead.

With a sigh over what was to come he turned and hurried upstairs.

Seconds after he reached the top of the stairs the doorbell was rung repeatedly and someone pounded on the door.

So it began.

Tully knew he should have at least a few hours before Cobin was actually in any real danger.

If Briggs really charged him then they would process him before interrogation, all Tully had to do was keep him out of the general lockup.

If it was anything like the last time he could expect a long time in the interrogation room, especially since this wouldn't be a surprise. That said, Cobin didn't know to expect Briggs that would probably just make him more uncooperative.

That should give Tully time to look for any other possible scenarios.

His earlier suspicion of Cobin had waned after his denial of the affair, along with his reaction to Missy's murder and Loren's claim it was all for nothing.

Something was definitely going on and Cobin knew more than he was willing to share, but it might not be murder.

It wasn't until sometime after 12 noon that Wesley found himself, once again, in the familiar interrogation room.

He'd spent a lot of time there, though most of it had been spent on the other side of the table. He stared straight ahead ignoring the two way mirror set in the far wall. He knew Commander Briggs was probably spying on him through it trying to decide the best means of action.

Let him try. Wesley thought and leaned back in the chair.

He made a mental note to thank Marge for insisting on adding cushions to the metal chairs in the room. Back when he'd been against it but it really was a good idea.

Briggs in charge had been an unpleasant surprise, even if he'd been expecting the hot headed buffoon to be somehow involved he hadn't expected to see him standing in his foyer with *Commander* on his lapel. Exactly how Briggs had managed the upgrade Wesley had no idea and decided it just showed the corruption of society nowadays.

He wondered if it had been a matter of Briggs building a case against one of his superiors. The man didn't know the meaning of the word loyalty and had been befuddled at how deeply it seemed to run between Wesley and Fineas on his last visit. That particular drug trafficking case hadn't been straightforward and some subterfuge had been called for. Briggs had wanted to arrest him then, but Fineas had convinced him it was part of the plan, which it was, though "plan" sounded too orchestrated, it implied Fineas actually had an idea of what Wesley was up to. Wesley supposed his subsequent murder trial and televised falling out with Fineas just proved what Briggs believed about the world.

That actually stung more than his being pulled in for questioning.

Briggs hadn't arrested him yet, he was going to make full use of his time to hold Wesley without charging him then he might start small and build from there.

That's what he'd done before when he'd interviewed the wrong witness.

Wesley began going over his story, but, surprisingly, he didn't get far.

The interrogation room door opened and one of the State Police detectives entered and launched into a series of background check alibis, taking his questions from an open file.

The first question caught him off guard.

"Where were you this Monday between 9 and 11 PM?"

Wesley blinked. He thought the TOD on Boswell was around 2 AM Tuesday morning. That was the one murder he almost had an alibi for, depending on Missy's pathology report.

"Between 9 and 11?" Wesley asked, "I was at home."

"Can anyone confirm that?"

"Up until about 9:30."

"I see." The detective said.

"Do you own a .32 caliber revolver?"

Wesley gave the detective his best, "try harder" look. "No." he said flatly.

"How about a nine-millimeter?"

"What does it say in the file?"

"Do you own a nine-millimeter handgun?"

"No." Wesley said.

"Do you own a .45 caliber handgun?"

Wesley sighed. "Yes, as you know by my file since I've got a permit and registration on it."

"You claim to not own a .32 revolver and a nine-millimeter, but do attest to owning a .45 caliber Beretta, is this correct?"

"Yes." Wesley said. "Any chance of getting a sandwich or something?"

The detective didn't reply. "So, if we found a .32 or a 9 mill at your house you would deny that these guns were yours?"

"You didn't." He said flatly. "Because I don't own either."

The detective grunted something, then closed the file and stood up.

"So, am I being charged?" Wesley asked.

"Depends, are you likely decide to walk out of here?" The detective asked.

"Well, if I don't get lunch in the next half hour yeah, then when you charge me, my first act will be to call my legal team. Then I'll just have them grab a Grimaldi's pizza on the way down from New York."

The detective eyed him.

"Go on," Wesley made a shooing gesture. "Go tell Briggs he'd better make up his mind quick." The detective glared at him and flipped the lights off as he left the room.

The two way mirror became translucent as the light died revealing the adjacent room to be empty.

"Wow, very mature of you!" Wesley called as the door shut.

Obviously the detective was used to suspects being handcuffed and stuck in the chair.

He reached under the table for the auxiliary light controls that he knew were mounted on the interrogators side of the table when he had a better idea.

He stood up and walked toward the mirror, the only source of light in the windowless room.

Looking through the mirror he eyed the empty room and the computer at the far end, screensaver bouncing across the display.

He moved to the corner of the room and pressed on the adjoining wall, hoping that no one had thought to lock it.

They hadn't and the semi concealed door opened a crack.

Wesley reached his fingers through the gap and pulled.

The gap widened.

He hurried into the observation room and over to the computer at the far end. He knelt to pull the micro flash drive from his sock.

By feel he reached it around the back of the computer tower and plugged it in.

The computer chimed and the hardware detection icon appeared in the lower right of the screen.

He almost couldn't believe they weren't securing the log-in.

Grabbing the mouse he navigated to the start menu and pulled up the local network, he glanced at the name, knew it was the right one. Then he confirmed the drive letter assigned to the flash drive.

He launched command prompt and keyed in F://autoloader_execute

Execute? The prompt asked.

Y he keyed and then hurried back to the interrogation room, closing the door securely behind him.

A second later the overhead lights came back on and he collapsed into the chair.

The outer door opened.

It was a smug smile he offered to Commander Luton Briggs as he entered the room.

Briggs entered looking confident and self-satisfied. He grabbed the interrogator's chair and spun it around to straddle it backwards. He smiled at Wesley while a tech placed a recorder and a microphone on the table.

"Wesley Cobin, you've agreed to speak without a lawyer present?" Briggs asked.

"For the time being," Wesley said. "But I reserve the right to choose when I want legal counsel."

Briggs continued to smile.

The tech checked that the recording levels were good and left the room.

"You know why you're here?"

Wesley hesitated only for a second. "Because it just wasn't the same here without my sparkling personality?"

Briggs' smile remained fixed but Wesley caught the warning in the Commander's eye.

He made a point of ignoring it.

"Let's talk about the night of the seventh. What were you doing?"

"I did a lot of things the night of the seventh, you'll have to clarify."

"Then give me a detailed rundown."

"What times constitutes night, I mean is this a Night and Weekends phone plan night or after dinner or at sunset?"

"Let's say after six PM."

"Really? Cause I usually think six thirty, seven."

"Answer the question." Briggs said tightly.

"Alright. I had dinner about six twenty, Radburt, my valet, cooked it. It consisted of mashed sweet potatoes, green beans and four slices of turkey breast. I had butter on the potatoes and some brown sugar, there was a wonderful glaze for the turkey and the beans were served with ground bacon, if I remember correctly. To drink I had sparkling pear juice, it was actually quite good a little bit too much…"

"I think we've established that you had dinner!" Briggs snapped then the forced smile returned. Wesley wondered why the man even bothered with the pretense; he was just getting warmed up.

"Oh, okay, I thought you wanted a detailed summation. So, I had dinner till about six forty, I read a book, I went for a drive, came home and went to bed, end of night on the seventh." Wesley sat back folding his arms behind his head.

"When you say you went for a drive?"

"Now you want details?" Wesley asked in feigned exasperation. "Alright. Once in my car I applied my seatbelt, I checked the mirrors to make sure they were properly adjusted. Then I placed my foot on the brake and pressed the engine start button. My car has a keyless starting procedure where I just need to have the transponder on me to start the car. Then, since I had already removed the car from the garage I shifted into drive, I know some would call that a travesty but with a 6.2 liter V-8 engine it's not really…"

Briggs cut him off by slamming a palm on the table top.

The techs would love that. Wesley thought.

"This is your last warning Mr. Cobin. You are being intentionally obtuse and I will not have you making a mockery of this investigation. That night were you involved in an altercation with a Mr. Jebadiah Jefferson?"

"Define altercation?"

"Did you hit his car?"

"Oh, right, yeah that happened too." Wesley could see the effort on Brigg's part to restrain himself. He was impressed the man was even trying.

"Leading up to that incident were you exceeding the speed limit?"

Here Wesley did hesitate. He knew the question was going to come up but he hadn't reached a decision on how to answer.

"I may have been over the limit."

"Do you know how far over the limit?" Wesley shook his head.

"Could you have been doing over 100 mph?"

"No." Wesley said.

"But you just said you didn't know how far over."

"What?"

Briggs glared hard, the smile was gone now. "Do you know what speed you were traveling at?"

"Between seventy and eighty."

"Thank you." Briggs said dryly. "Now, following the collision were you assaulted by Mr. Jefferson?"

"Yes." Wesley said.

"What?" Briggs asked and consulted the papers in front of him. "But according to this official report you said you weren't assaulted."

"Of course I said that, there was one officer and two Jefferson's. The whole family is pretty much insane and as the state patrol car was pulling up Jeb said if I squawked he'd kill me or someone close to me. I kept my mouth shut."

Briggs eyed Wesley for a long minute, likely trying to decide if he should back up the tape and try again.

"So, now you're saying..."

"That Jeb Jefferson threatened to kill me if I told the truth." Wesley smiled encouragingly at Briggs.

Briggs continued to stare, flames flickering behind his eyes.

"Alright, I think we're done for now." He stopped the recorder and tapped the rewind button once then made his way to the door.

"Hey, do I get lunch for being a cooperative little boy?" Wesley asked.

Briggs slammed the door.

Tully had watched the interview from the observation room and was waiting at the interrogation room door when Briggs opened it.

"My turn." he said and reached for the door handle only to be stopped by Briggs.

"No."

"I was told I'd get a chance to talk to him."

"And now I'm saying that you don't."

Tully clenched his jaw. "This is still my district, my station."

"And he's my suspect." Briggs cut in. "Maybe if you'd made the arrest I'd let you talk to him, but from what I've seen you tried everything in your power to keep him out of that room, which in my mind, raises a lot of questions, questions that you probably don't want me to ask out loud."

"I want you to remember that you threatened me." Tully said evenly.

Briggs smiled. "Should I be taking *this* as a threat?"

"As fair warning."

Briggs snorted. "Do you really think he's innocent, or is this because you feel responsible for him and therefore could never admit to his guilt?"

"I had my chance to let him off and I didn't take it." Tully said. "I played my hand and lost and now I'm beginning to think it came up that way for a reason."

"But now we aren't talking about something that happened three years ago; I've got three bodies with his name all over them. We're hauling in all his cars and we're going to go through them with a fine toothcomb, we're getting the tracking data from the vehicles, from his phone and I'm going to get the evidence I need to make sure that he'll never see the free world again."

Tully thought about offering Briggs some advice having an idea of what he meant by "fine toothcomb" but his advising against something would just make Briggs all the more determined.

"The only thing I would like from you is one answer. According to your men and your reports he lacks a solid alibi for all three murders. He knew all of the victims and had something against all of them. According to phone records two of the victims were in contact with him and each other. They had something on him, something that could put him away and they were going to use it. He killed them to keep it quiet. Now, as soon as we can match his Jeep to the tire tracks from the beach and find his .45 for testing he is done. Oh, and," Briggs paused with a smile. "We found blood at the last crime scene."

Tully was stunned and he knew it showed plainly on his face much to Briggs' amusement.

"You found Cobin's blood at the scene?" Tully asked, quickly regaining his composure as Briggs lost a measure of his.

"It wasn't Cobin's, but because he instigated a fight with the Assistant District Attorney to contaminate the scene and make much of what was found potentially inadmissible."

Tully fought hard to keep from rolling his eyes.

"Oh, and Sheriff, don't think I missed Cobin's little slip up."

"Really?" Tully asked. Surprised Briggs was letting it stand on the record.

"Yes, he was going well over one hundred miles an hour, but those speeds would have meant immediate jail time, which, since you didn't lock him up makes you accountable for the second girl's murder. If you'd followed the rules she'd still be alive."

Tully found it best not to say anything since the mixture of relief and loathing made a bad combination.

Briggs motioned to a uniformed officer who looked barely out of his teens.

"Son, I want you to guard this door. No one goes in without my say so, you understand?"

The kid nodded.

"There." he smiled as he brushed past.

Tully shook his head. If he wanted in interrogation he could just go in through the observation room, though Briggs likely hadn't even noticed the door. He'd also missed the hole in his accusation, Tully was only responsible if Cobin was the killer and that was something that he planned to find out before the night was over.

CHAPTER 19

Tully went and got a cup of coffee which he drank in the squad room since his office had been sequestered and he didn't want to let Briggs out of his sight.

It was then that he decided to see what other "evidence" Briggs thought that he'd uncovered.

Tully left the desk he was sitting at and stepped into the conference room, which was empty at the moment. He casually leaned against the conference room door and ran his eyes over the whiteboards the state police had strung up around the perimeter.

He paid most attention to the one that featured Cobin as a suspect.

There were several featured articles of evidence.

They had testimony from people at the store Wesley had picked up groceries yesterday, confirming that he had a window of opportunity, though they had yet to question Caroline.

There were the phone records, calls and text messages from Boswell and Epcot to the same burner phone and they'd caught Y. NIBOC, the subpoena on which turned up a billing address that happened to be Cobin Softworks of Atlanta. They were still waiting for any recorded calls from the carrier's voicemail database.

Tully tried to remember anyone he knew that worked for CallCOM that might be able to get him the voicemail first. The only person he could think of was the youngest Jefferson brother who worked part time at the company's local outlet. That wouldn't be any help.

Of course, he realized, the fastest way to check was by going directly to the source.

Tully peeked out the window to the squad room and looked for Briggs.

The Commander was strutting back and forth between desks looking self-important.

Tully left the conference room and made his way to the far end of the squad room and let himself into the station's evidence locker, which also held personal items of those they brought in for questioning.

He picked up the envelope that Wesley's stuff was in and, with only a momentary hesitation, broke the seal.

He carefully emptied it onto the counter.

There were three items, the Mercedes key fob, wallet and phone.

Tully picked up the phone and tapped the wake key on the side.

A lock screen greeted him. Suddenly his face filled the screen. He blinked. So did his face.

He realized then it was live feed from the camera on the front of the phone.

It used facial recognition to unlock.

He thought he remembered reading somewhere that holding a picture of the owner in front of the camera would sometimes trick the device into unlocking but he doubted Wesley's phone would be susceptible to such an easy hack.

He grimaced. It had been a long shot at best.

The phone unlocked.

Tully furrowed his brow at the device.

It didn't take long to figure out what had happened, but really, a grimace was what Cobin went with to lock the phone?

He ran his eyes over the screen, then returned the keys and wallet to the envelope and resealed it, slowly making his way back to the squad room.

It was 1:30 in the afternoon and both Lance and Blaze were lounging at their desks. Barry had left at 12:00 but he said he'd be back by 5:00.

Tully made his way over to Blaze.

"Deputy I need you to go to Lou's and pick up a chicken club sandwich and fries and a strawberry lemonade."

Blaze stared dumbly at Tully.

"You want me to go get food?" he asked.

"Yes, and it's an order not a want."

"Um, I don't think that's in my job description." Blaze said.

Tully's glare was hard. "What job is that?"

"Uh, this one." Blaze said sarcastically.

"Oh, okay, sorry it's a little hard to tell. I thought maybe you meant the job where you leak sensitive case details to the press."

Blaze suddenly sat up straighter.

"Um, I'm not sure I know what you mean." The unnatural reddening up his neck said otherwise.

"Chicken club. French fries. Strawberry lemonade." Tully reiterated.

Blaze nodded. "Oh! Right!" he said, standing up and looking around for his car keys.

Tully picked them off the desk's cluttered surface. "To be continued." he said.

Blaze snatched the keys and hurried for the door.

Wesley sighed contentedly as he sipped the last of the lemonade and crumpled up the Lou's Drive-Through bag.

He got out of the chair and made his way over to the door, which he knocked on.

It opened a crack and he handed the trash to the kid on the other side.

"Thanks." The junior officer didn't reply, but he dutifully took the trash and shut the door again.

Wesley paced the room a couple of times before returning to the chair, when he did he closed his eyes and began counting his allies and trying to predict the outcome of events. The whole investigation needed to be carefully orchestrated in order for everything to work and there were a few pieces he still didn't know. Those pieces could be his undoing.

Right now though, all he could do was wait.

Tully was at one of the extra desks in the squad room, trying to lean back in the chair and look nonchalant as he waited for his phone call to be connected.

He wanted Briggs to notice, but not to get in his way.

On the line the ringing stopped.

"This is Detective Jones."

"Hello Detective, this is Sheriff Tully."

"Yes, good afternoon Sheriff. What can I do for you?"

Tully swallowed, wondering if this lead was worth pursuing or if it was just misdirection.

"I wanted to thank you for all of your help for one," Tully said.

"I heard you made an arrest?" Word traveled fast.

"The State Police have made an arrest." Tully corrected.

"I see."

"I'm not entirely convinced they have the right individual."

"Really?"

"They're outsiders, they think it gives them a fresh perspective but it just means they don't have the background right."

"Yeah, sounds like the state police." Jones commiserated.

"At least they aren't feds I suppose," Tully said, mustering as much distain as he could and hoping Dianna would forgive him.

"Tell me about it!"

"I think they're missing something."

"Probably, they come in and act like they're running the show, just like that!" Tully tried not to smile, it would throw off his inflection and he didn't want any of the State officers to see it.

"Is there anything I can do?" Jones asked.

"Well, I know you're probably busy with your own cases and I wouldn't want to add to your work load..."

"Hey, if you can embarrass the State boys it's worth it." Yep, Tully's evidence as to Jones prejudice had been right on the money.

"I can't get the landlord, Lorenzo Washington, out of my head." Tully said of the man he'd never met.

"Washington?" Jones asked. "Right, Boswell's building manager. Talked to him real briefly, didn't have anything to say but I drug it out just because it annoyed him."

"Did you happen to run any kind of background check?" Tully wondered.

"Naw, I don't think so. Didn't seem relevant at the time. You think there's something to find?"

"I don't know." Tully said. "Could just be his attitude making me think he's hiding something."

Over the phone Tully heard Jones talking to someone in the background.

"Hey, Miguel, do we have anything on a Lorenzo Washington? Well then why didn't you say something earlier? I know what I said..." Jones came back louder. "Sheriff? Can I call you back in a few minutes, I wanna check something out."

"Sure." Tully said and gave Jones the number and the desk extension.

As he hung up though Tully knew Jones had something, he just hoped it was something he wanted to hear.

Jake Barry was back in the office by 4:00, leaving Tully to wonder how much sleep his Deputy had actually gotten over the past 24 hours. He was glad to have Jake there though, since he could hover around the fringes of the State Police operations, collecting information to pass on to Tully.

At the moment Jake was the only deputy he could trust, both Lance and Blaze were starry eyed over the possibilities transferring to the State police could bring, promises that Tully had no doubt Briggs was falsely holding out to them.

The problem was that he also knew in matters concerning Wesley Cobin's freedom having Jake as his only ally was a bad thing.

So far though, Jake was remaining dutiful, even if he seemed a little disappointed there was nothing new to reveal about the investigation to add weight to the case against Cobin. And that was definitely the only lead that Briggs seemed interested in pursuing.

"Their suspect pool is exactly one name deep." he revealed to Tully, who nodded. It was hardly a surprise. "Still," Barry said. "They are just following the evidence."

"What evidence there is."

"Who else is there?" Barry asked, trying to keep his voice down as they were trying to appear non-conspiratorial against the far wall of the squad room. "Expecting a call?" he asked.

Tully realized he kept eyeing the phone, waiting for it to ring.

"Just a follow up with Jones. Probably nothing." He wanted to down play it just in case Barry decided to be a double informant.

"I've been thinking about the original case." Tully confided, casually watching his detective's reaction.

"Boswell?" Barry asked, but it was obvious he knew what Tully meant.

"No, Mike. Did we miss something?"

"Yeah, we didn't catch him sooner." Barry answered acerbically.

"Eyewitness testimony, prints on the murder weapon." Tully continued. "Testimony, well, we know how reliable that actually is. Prints? It was Cobin's gun, never denied it. Never wiped it down either."

"Because he thought he could control us!" Barry snapped. "He thought he could just walk away, that he could play us for fools!"

"Maybe." Tully allowed. "You alright?"

"Why?" Barry asked, a little too sharply, even given the previous subject matter.

"You just seem a little edgy."

"Fine. I just want this to be over."

"You and me both." Tully murmured, though the outcomes they desired were likely at odds with each other.

"I'm going to get some coffee." Tully said. "Need anything?"

"No, I'm burning off 8 shots of espresso right now." Barry answered.

Well, now Tully knew how he was still awake.

After getting his coffee Tully returned to the squad room.

Briggs had to be getting ready to make his move. It had been almost five hours since he'd sent someone to talk to Cobin.

It was one of the State Police officers who noticed the truck and cursed in surprise.

Tully turned towards the front facing windows about the same time the racket of the racing, poorly maintained V-8, penetrated the well-insulated room.

Surprisingly within about a second it had everyone's attention.

The Jefferson's old Chevy pickup had leapt the sidewalk and was accelerating across the parking lot towards the building.

Then people started to panic, diving away from the windows, but Tully watched calmly as the truck surged towards them.

He cut his gaze momentarily toward Barry, also standing his ground.

Their eyes locked for a split second then Barry looked at the ground.

Tully frowned. Jake's impartiality it seemed, was at an end.

Before it could plow through the front of the station, the truck slowed slightly and then veered towards a parked cruiser.

The impact sounded inside as a solid pop.

The cruiser leapt sideways and jumped the curb in front of the building while the truck came to a standstill, puffs of steam spilling from the grille.

"What the hell!" Briggs shouted, staring open mouthed, the only State officer to have also held his ground. "What kind of crazy…"

Tully frowned and took a sip of the too strong coffee.

Briggs shouted orders to his men, which also got Imahara and Stark to jump to attention. Lance led the charge outside.

"You should have told them to duck." Tully remarked casually.

"What?" Briggs demanded. Tully took another sip and watched as three state uniforms and Lance approached the truck. Jeb Jefferson slid from the driver's seat and said something. Lance made a reply and stepped towards Jeb.

"Lance." Tully said with a trace of disgust.

Jeb threw a casual punch that took Lance solidly in the chin and sent him sprawling backwards into Briggs' men. Tully sighed. Two more of the Jefferson clan climbed from the truck as a fresh wave of uniforms surrounded them.

"Now you really can't put Cobin in the general lockup." Tully said.

"Why the hell not?" Briggs demanded.

"Because you're going to be locking him up with the Jefferson boys and they'll kill him."

"I don't know that." Briggs said. "Law's the law for a reason." Tully shook his head.

"You're not hearing me."

"And I'm kind of liking that, Sheriff. One thing you seem pretty consistent on is ignoring the rules, don't think I don't know Cobin's covering for you. So far as I'm concerned you might as well be in this together. Now if you'll excuse me I have an investigation to run."

Tully gripped his mug tightly but let the moment go. He wouldn't make any headway with Briggs, nor would he be officially allowed to talk to Wesley before they got a confession or felt they'd gathered enough evidence he couldn't get away. Now, once they were done talking he figured he had an hour, two at most, before Cobin was being loaded into an ambulance, headed either for the ICU or the morgue.

CHAPTER 20

Briggs didn't return to the interrogation room until after the Jefferson's were dealt with. He'd left Cobin alone for almost six hours.

It was the kind of technique that might have made a difference with a regular civilian but Tully knew the only thing being achieved was giving time for Cobin to think up more biting retorts.

Before heading back into the interrogation room though, Briggs talked to Imahara, who had finally removed the ice pack and was now just tenderly poking his swollen chin.

The interchange made Tully apprehensive and, since Jake had evidently slunk away in shame, the Sheriff had no spy.

He figured it out though when Briggs let himself into the records room.

Briggs was going to bring up the past, probably in an attempt to get Cobin riled and make some kind of slip.

Tully wondered how far back Briggs would go.

Bringing up Mike's murder seemed like thin ice, but maybe Cobin's alleged change of heart would yield something new. But if Briggs was planning on bringing Herod Cobin into the picture he wasn't going to get anywhere and Tully for one, would like him even less.

He headed towards the observation room, at least Briggs hadn't ordered him not to watch, and waited to see which hand Briggs decided to play.

"Let's talk about why you did it, shall we?" Briggs said, this time he was seated correctly in the chair, glaring across the tabletop at Cobin.

Wesley took note of the file Briggs dragged out and set on the table. He read the orange name strip Cobin, H.

"Don't you dare." he said, enunciating each word carefully. Predictably Briggs ignored him.

"It's almost understandable when one takes into account whose son you are."

Behind the mirror Tully grimaced and felt sick. This was wrong of Briggs, regardless of what Cobin was accused of.

"Your father, Herod Cobin, let's see, successful business man, went into real estate." Briggs snorted. "He owned three homes all right here? Hardly my pick of places to settle down, but then I can't credit him with much taste. He only seems to have had a few problems in his life. Success, reasonably good looks, a smooth talker by all accounts, yet somehow this combination proved fatal to the seven women he murdered, including your mother. Quite brutal too. I'd imagine you probably wondered if you were somehow to blame? Did you notice how, let me see, Jessica Rawles, your babysitter, right? Did you notice that her death corresponded to an argument you told the investigating officer you had with him? You probably wondered if you'd been a better son, were more cooperative, maybe he wouldn't have needed to kill anyone?" Wesley sat very still. There was no snappy retort this time.

In the observation room Tully weighed his options for ways he could stop the interview. Briggs probably didn't know what he was doing but Cobin was just going to get angry and Tully was going to have flashbacks centering around the orphaned Wesley Cobin that he'd taken in and raised, who he and Caroline had tried their best to fix. In the end though this was up to Cobin to end the interview, he just had to ask for his lawyers.

"Of, course even when the police were running their investigation it was mostly your eyewitness testimony that provided the ammunition. Maybe if you hadn't abandoned him, as it were, he wouldn't have gotten so mad that night and maybe he wouldn't have tried killing you and your mother?"

Tully felt gutted as he saw Cobin sitting there because he was seeing eleven year old Wesley and the walls that he'd so carefully built around his emotions connected to Wesley began to crack. They'd been through all this guilt and self-doubt before and recovered only with countless tears and cookies.

If Briggs didn't back off they might end up back there and Tully knew if Wesley cracked, it would be over for him.

If he saw the boy he loved showing through then he was over.

From the look on Wesley's face he knew it was seconds away from happening, when Briggs played the wrong card.

"Of course, we have to consider your mother too. If she hadn't had that affair with the accountant, well, I see where that messed you up later in life."

Tully winced and watched the oncoming emotions shift at once on Wesley's face. There were a few things you didn't mention around Cobin. If his mother, you better be saying something nice and if you brought up the alleged affair you were taking your life in your own hands.

Wesley had always had a temper but he didn't react with violence, the two times that Tully had seen him on the brink of exploding had once involved a string of slurs against his mother, the other had been similar directed towards Loren, when they first started dating. The second time hadn't bothered Tully overmuch since he'd been jumping in to defend Loren.

Later though, after Wesley was on trial for murder, the memory had haunted him.

Now though, he noticed subtle differences. Cobin was still very mad, but he wasn't on the edge of control. Briggs should have noticed and backed off but instead he kept on poking for a verbal response.

Tully wished the response he got was "I want my lawyer", even if those words here were considered the classic admission of guilt.

With a sudden jolt he realized what he had just thought and then rewound that to the night three years ago…

Tully sat at a desk in the squad room that gave him a view of the interrogation room door.

He couldn't reconcile with any of his feelings. The evening's earlier numbness had faded away, replaced with a gnawing doubt.

Wesley couldn't have killed Mike! It wasn't possible. He knew Wesley, even though it had been his investigation, even though he'd found the evidence, he'd seen Wesley's reaction he couldn't reconcile it. He wondered if this was what if felt like to lose your mind.

Swirling, screaming thoughts over a black pit.

He felt on the brink.

He checked his watch. 5:31 AM. He wondered if Caroline and Loren got any sleep.

Oh Loren! What was going to happen now?

It had been almost seven hours since they'd told him to leave the interrogation room and he was haunted by the look he'd seen on Cobin's face when he'd complied.

Pleading, abandonment, fear. Why? Why would he be afraid if he was innocent?

But that was the thing, wasn't it?

He couldn't be innocent.

There was the gun.

Wesley's own gun was the murder weapon.

Missy placed him at the scene, drunk and angry. She said it was a pattern, then she'd clammed up. He wondered what else she had to say.

Eyewitnesses at the bar confirmed that Wesley and Mike had argued.

At the scene, Mike's gun was kicked to the side, just like Wesley might have done.

Maybe it had been self-defense? What if Mike had turned on him?

But there were two shots.

Wesley could hold his alcohol reasonably well, Mike less so. If Mike had gone after him Wesley wouldn't have needed a gun to stop him, let alone two well-placed .45 rounds.

5:34

The door opened.

Fineas jumped to his feet.

They led Wesley out in handcuffs.

"Get a phone, he lawyered up." Someone said.

Across the room their eyes met and Fineas felt himself fall into the pit. The numbness returned and somehow his heart didn't hurt anymore. He looked away.

In the interrogation room, unaware of the ground he was treading Briggs continued on.

"That's a lot of responsibility to bear for a boy, a stigma too. And so maybe, after your life was ruined, once you found that you couldn't help yourself. You found out that Odette Boswell, the one person you couldn't punish for her crimes, like you couldn't punish your father, you found out she was close-by. You knew she'd shown an interest in you, you contacted her using a payphone here in town," Briggs pushed a sheet of paper containing phone records with a highlighted number from a payphone on the corner of Main and Peach. "You arranged to meet, she came expecting a moonlit walk on the beach, but instead you killed her.

Now you've got a taste for it so you move on to Epcot, you get her into town but I'm guessing something goes wrong so you end up shooting her in her car. Maybe she just happened to be at the grocery store at the wrong time and you spotted her.

Then you decide to go after the woman that made you look bad, the one whose eyewitness testimony should have landed you on death-row and you killed her, too. And so they all got what they deserved, punishment for their crimes against you."

Cobin sat quietly, arms folded, after Briggs had finished.

"That was the wrong point to bring up." Cobin said. "And then you blew any emotional control you had by talking too long."

Instead of getting annoyed, Briggs smiled at him. Then closed the file in front and took back the phone records, signaling an end to the interview.

"One more question, if you don't mind Mr. Cobin, how is your relationship with the Jefferson family?"

Wesley watched Briggs carefully for some sign.

"I just wondered since your father killed Angelica Jefferson?"

"Strained, as you can imagine." Wesley said through tight lips.

"That's too bad. It looks as if you're going to be spending some time together behind bars. That is, unless you want to tell me something?"

Wesley sat impassively, concentrating his full will power on not flinching or giving some sign of apprehension for Briggs' benefit.

"Alright then," Briggs said. "Let's get you to lockup."

Tully was deep in thought as Briggs left the interrogation room, leaving Cobin alone. For someone capable of making his face so impassive, he looked scared.

"That was wrong." Tully looked left, toward the door. He hadn't heard Barry enter the room, but he was there, leaning against the wall.

"You or Briggs?" Tully asked.

Jake didn't answer immediately. He wasn't ready to apologize because he was still convinced that Wesley Cobin was a murderer, but he also knew even that didn't justify his behavior.

"How are you doing?"

Tully was surprised by the question.

"Briggs brought up a lot of painful memories for me." he said honestly. "And I have a lot of unresolved feelings relating to them. You know the Jefferson's are going to kill him, right?"

Jake glanced at his feet. "I doubt Briggs would allow that."

"Then you put more faith in him than I do. He'd let it happen and then find some way of blaming us for it."

Tully turned to leave the room, pushing past his deputy.

"Fineas," Jake said. "I'm sorry. Alright? I thought I knew what I wanted."

"And now?" Tully asked.

"Mike and I went through the academy together."

"I know that."

"The thought that…"

"What if you gave Cobin the benefit of the doubt, just once, just to save his life?"

Jake looked into Tully's eyes and Tully saw a wall that he wasn't getting through, but he had to try.

"Mike loved him like a brother. You know that, I know that. It wasn't like Missy said. They also respected each other."

"That's what made it all the worse!"

"But what would Mike want? Wesley killed by the Jefferson's?"

"Sometimes justice…"

"Revenge." Tully corrected. "Cold, bloody, revenge. Do you think they care about what happened to Mike? They just want to hurt people and he's someone they can hurt that no one will care about. That's not what Mike would want. Do it by the book." he finished softly.

"We already tried that." Barry said and turned to walk away.

"So why did you call Loren?" Tully asked, remembering his conversation with Caroline.

"What?"

"You knew Wesley wasn't going to make it home. Caroline said you called the house and told them what happened."

"That was just about Missy." Jake said.

"Was it really?" Tully asked, trying to read his Deputy.

Jake didn't answer, just ducked his head and slipped away.

CHAPTER 21

It was a state officer that led Wesley to the holding cell at the very back of the building.

It was purposely disconnected from everything and featured meter thick concrete exterior walls. It had clearly been designed by an architect with an attraction to dungeons of old. It was also soundproof, which Wesley could attest was a very bad thing, because once a prisoner was put into the cage, he was largely on his own.

As the metal door to the room opened Wesley saw three other prisoners behind the bars, Jeb, Jay and Bo. It was the three he was expecting. The eldest brother, James, was the only moderate success in the family and he'd made a second job out of controlling the rest of his family. He was never tied to his brother's nefarious deeds, but to Wesley's way of thinking he was unquestionably the puppet master.

To the brother's credit they waited thirty seconds after the state officer left before they closed in around him.

Wesley tried to imagine the series of events that would follow. Any of the outcomes weren't pretty.

"Seems to me we've got some unfinished business." Jeb said as the gangs elected spokesman, after all he almost graduated from high school.

Wesley tried to think of a clever retort, something he'd missed... nothing came to mind.

"Before all of that though, could I get one final request?" Wesley asked.

Jeb eyed him as if expecting some kind of trap, but didn't immediately start the beating, so Wesley took it as a sign to continue.

"Why are you doing this?" he asked.

He didn't expect an answer and Jeb's leer didn't boost his spirit any, but that was one thing that Briggs had got him thinking about.

"We don't need a reason Cobin. You're a dog that needs to be put down." Jeb spit.

"Right," Wesley said, feeling a wave of fear creeping up his spine. "But, what exactly gives me that classification? Is this about Michael or Angelica…" he didn't get the name out before Jeb slugged him. He moved instinctively, making the blow more glancing, but still wildly painful. He knew he'd never get that lucky again.

Then the door opened.

Wesley turned to look, along with the gang, hoping against hope that it was Fineas.

It wasn't.

It was Jake Barry, just the man to turn a blind eye.

Jeb smiled. "Hey Barry, come to watch?" he asked. Jake wasn't smiling.

"Back off boys, Cobin's coming with me." Wesley didn't know if he should feel relief or greater dread.

Jake slipped the key in the lock and opened the cell door.

"Just give us five minutes." Jeb said.

"No can do, brass need him unspoiled." Jake said and grabbed Wesley by the arm, hauling him out.

"Just you bring him back, or else…" Jake turned back to Jeb and glared.

"Did you just threaten me?" he asked, which took Jeb off guard.

"Uh?"

"The next time you ask me for something, I'd suggest you not start the afternoon by ramming my cruiser, I mean, are you really so stupid you didn't see the big "State Police" decals on the other cars?" Jake slammed shut the cell door and led Wesley out of the room, firm grip on his arm.

"So, where are we going?" Wesley asked as Jake pushed him into the hallway.

"Copy room." Jake said flatly.

"Copy room?" Wesley asked. It didn't sound good. For one thing there were no cameras in that particular closet and it had an attached bathroom which featured easy to wipe down tile.

"It's the second most secured room in the building."

"Yeah." Wesley said nervously.

"Tully wants you locked in there."

"Tully?"

"So do you just parrot everything anyone says nowadays?"

"No, I just kind of expected some form of grievous bodily injury given our history."

Jake's jaw clenched, obviously biting off his reply. "You know they were going to kill you?"

"Ah, thank you." Wesley said. "Is this Briggs' version of waterboarding?"

"No, Briggs' idea was you go in and die, though he might not have realized they'd go all the way." Wesley swallowed, feeling suddenly more fear than he had when he was in the middle of the Jefferson's. He had been a few minutes away from being beaten to death.

"Wait." Barry said and halted before the copy room door. He took a few steps more, toward the end of the hallway and looked around, then came back and opened the door. He pushed Wesley through ahead of him.

"Briggs doesn't know?" Wesley asked.

"Now you're getting there. Stay here and don't make me regret this." Jake said flatly, then turned and left locking the door behind him.

Ten minutes later Tully left the squad room and made his way back to the copy room, where Barry was casually standing guard.

"Alright, Cobin's coming with me. I'll bring him back later." He said.

Jake looked worried. "That wasn't the plan."

"The plan's changed."

Jake sighed. "Fineas, I can't lie for you, I'm sorry, but I won't."

"And I wouldn't want you to. If Briggs asks you, tell him what happened. We'll hopefully be back in a couple of hours, he can wait that long to have me fired."

Jake frowned. "I hope it doesn't come to that." He said solemnly.

You and me both. Tully thought and unlocked the door.

Wesley was sitting in the cramped room's only chair next to the photocopier. He stood up when he saw Tully.

"Sheriff," he said, showing some surprise.

"Come on." Tully said and gestured towards the door.

"What's going on?" Wesley asked.

"Loren says we need to talk. In light of all of this I figured it might have been the motivation you needed." Tully said with a determined yet grim expression on his face.

"I don't want to talk here." Wesley said.

"I wasn't planning on it, you're coming with me."

"Did Briggs okay this?"

"What's it to you?" Tully asked annoyed Cobin wasn't just following him.

"I know what's going on. We already took a big enough chance today. I can't let you risk losing everything for me."

"It's my decision, I'm just doing my job, I have reason to believe there's some perversion of justice and in order to find that out I need to talk to you alone and in private so are you coming?"

Slowly, Wesley stepped forwards and followed Tully out of the room.

They took the side door, bypassing the reception area and the squad room. From the side exit they could easily reach the parking lot without being seen.

"I guess you got my message?" Cobin asked.

"I haven't found anything yet." Fineas said.

"But didn't..."

"That's not really what we need to talk about, is it?" Fineas asked.

They'd reached his car, which he unlocked and dropped behind the wheel.

"No, I guess not." Cobin agreed, slipping on his seat belt.

Fineas maneuvered out of the parking lot and turned right at the street, leading

East towards the coast.

If Cobin had some idea where Fineas was heading he never let on.

He didn't do much more than just stare vacantly out the passenger window.

They eventually joined the beach road and Fineas drove South, away from town and up into the clump of seaside hills that divided the beach.

Across the water the sun's light was just an orange glow and in the evening shadows Fineas almost missed the abandoned driveway.

He'd never spent much time at the house, though the last time he had been there was forever burned into his conscious.

He whipped the car left, off the road and up the hill.

The large and irregular slabs of concrete, leading up to the charred foundations of the Cobin beach house were marred by tufts of beach grass pushing through the cracks as nature sought to reclaim the driveway.

Fineas drove past the *No Trespassing* signs and the Danger notices to the top of the hill, where blackened pavement spread out, covering most of the hill side. The ocean view had been blocked by a few encroaching trees, but it was not hard to imagine why someone would have built a house up here.

He shifted into park and set the brake, then shut off the engine.

Silence rushed in as soon as the engine died, taking with it the headlight glare.

They sat for a few minutes, Fineas waiting for Cobin to say something.

"I've been told that I need to go back to the beginning, that I missed something, so I figured this is the beginning." he said.

"The beginning of what?" Cobin asked.

"Whatever you'd like. I figure we've exhausted the subject of your father and I know most everything since that up to about four years ago."

Cobin nodded slowly, but didn't speak.

"Loren seems to think that there's something I missed."

"I burned this place to the ground." Cobin said. It wasn't the confession that Fineas had been expecting and he wasn't sure how to react.

"What?" He decided was best.

"I loved the apartment. That's where I grew up. It was the only thing that we had, that's where my memories are. Then we bought back the Manor, but it wasn't gaudy enough. He built this place. I hated it. Mom hated it. It was cold and all hard angles." Cobin said, looking around at the foundation stones still left. "It was just water, steel and concrete. I never thought it would burn."

"So it was arson, but not anyone from town?"

"He loved this place so much. I thought it would be like punishing him."

Fineas bit his lip and wondered if this was orchestrated to play on his emotions, or if Cobin was genuine. He hated looking for motives.

"What about the apartment?" he asked, as coolly as he could manage.

"That wasn't me. That was the nail in my coffin really, after that I knew I couldn't go back. Forever outcast. The same as my father."

"How about that night?" Fineas asked.

Cobin was quiet again.

"September 22, 2008?" Fineas prompted. "Everyone I love seems to keep telling me I did something wrong but I'm working with the best I have."

"You saved my life three times." Cobin said. "I saved yours once, you condemned me once, by my count that's a life owed."

Fineas stared at him in frustration.

What was Cobin talking about?

"*Are* you crazy?" Fineas asked.

"And there it is again." Cobin whispered.

"What?"

"You never once asked me if I was guilty."

Fineas opened his mouth to object, but, as he thought back on that night, he realized that Cobin was right. The opportunity had never presented itself and it wasn't the kind of question he wanted to ask.

"I never wanted to see you lie." Fineas said.

"And you assumed I would have?"

Fineas closed his eyes and made a conscious effort to stay composed.

"Wesley," he said and almost lost control of himself. It had been so long since he'd said the name out loud and suddenly, for the space of about a second, the whole thing seemed ridiculous. What if it really was all built on a mountain of misunderstandings? But he had to play it cool.

"Did you tell Loren everything?" he asked.

"No."

So he may still be guilty.

"So you would have confessed?"

"How come you're so sure I'm guilty? You said this was the beginning," Cobin said, gesturing around them. "So what's the theory, I'm warped because my father killed people and see that as an acceptable way of dealing with problems?"

"That's not what I meant."

"Are you sure?"

"All the evidence…"

"There had been evidence that didn't match before, stuff that's harder to explain than just some fingerprints and eyewitness testimony. Witnesses in a bar, might I add."

"You never gave me reason to think otherwise!"

"Because I lawyered up? That was my only way out! I had a plan, but as soon as I left that room I knew I'd lost you. I was dead to you! I tried, alright, I tried."

"Don't put this all on me." Fineas warned.

"I'm not. It wasn't your case in the end. You stuck to the facts, you never went any further."

"Alright Wesley, what happened that night? Why is Mike dead?"

Wesley swallowed visibly.

"Because of something I did."

The car had been parked on Elm Street for a while now. The plain sedan drew no attention to itself and behind the tinted windows the driver felt safe from prying eyes that night.

He watched the house down the street and thought about what he was planning on doing.

It was for everyone's good really.

He just wished he'd chosen the exact manner earlier but he'd been unable to decide. He looked over at the passenger seat and the black ski mask laying there. Poking out from one edge of the black knit was the cold glint of the gun barrel.

CHAPTER 22

Fineas almost missed the slant of the confession. Wesley had said it was his fault, not that he'd pulled the trigger. It was something, but still not the answer that he was after.

"If I had done things differently that night then Mike wouldn't be dead." Wesley said.

"Not the question. Did you kill Mike?"

Wesley smiled sadly and realized the moment wasn't quite like he'd imagined it.

"No." he said softly.

Fineas let out a breath he hadn't consciously been holding.

"Alright," he said. He couldn't adjust his view on Cobin right away, but he could think of him as Wesley, at least until he got everything sorted out.

"I should have told you." Wesley said, finding himself getting choked up.

It reminded Tully of conversations with the scared, guilt riddled 11-year-old, but now the murder in question had pointed back to Wesley.

They sat in the silence of the evening for a while, both wondering what might have happened if one of them had talked or listened more.

The conclusion they both reached was the same. Right now it didn't matter.

Except, if Wesley was lying about not killing Mike, then nothing he said could be trusted.

"So, how about those holes?" Fineas asked. "You were arguing with Mike that night?"

"Yes." Wesley said.

"And you were drunk?"

Wesley hesitated. He'd asked himself that same question countless times.

"Probably."

"Then you *drove* to his house and went inside where you continued to fight?"

Wesley shook his head. "No. Well, sort of."

"And then Missy left?"

"I don't know. Look, I just… I'll tell you what happened, but first I want you to get another car over to your house."

A tentacle of fear gripped Tully.

"Why?"

"Because of certain unanswered events that night." Tully wanted to question him, but he picked up the radio handset and called in the request. While he did that Wesley sat still with his eyes closed replaying that night in his mind, at least, the parts he could remember.

"Alright, it's done." Tully said. "Now talk."

"Mike thought Missy was having an affair." Wesley said.

Tully sighed. He didn't like the way this was leading because it seemed Cobin was going to point the blame at a dead woman.

"I know, I know," Wesley said. "But that's what Mike thought. He told me at the bar. Well, mentioned it off handedly, he didn't mean to, then he wouldn't talk about it."

"So you got him drunk?" Tully asked.

"I don't know." Wesley said. "If that was the goal I didn't do very well because we were both buzzed when we left. But, yeah, during the evening I managed to get him to open up more. He thought…" Wesley paused, trying to figure out how to present facts without sounding like he was fabricating. "Mike thought she was having an affair with Jackson Bell."

"Bell, as in the District Attorney?" Tully asked in surprise.

"I know, it sounds off until you actually think about it, about Missy."

Fineas had to allow that Wesley had a point there. Missy was a bombshell and a flirt. She was power hungry. Bell was just so unattractive it made it hard to comprehend.

"Mike wouldn't say anything because he was afraid of losing her. I told him not to be so stupid. Very bluntly."

"So you didn't think it was true?"

Wesley rolled his eyes. "Come one, this was Missy! I assumed there were at least two other guys Mike didn't know about. I also told him that and that she wasn't the prize he thought she was. Also, very bluntly. Too bluntly. But in the end he admitted he thought they were together that night since he was supposed to be gone and that was the reason he wanted to crash with me."

Wesley stopped and shut his eyes again.

"So then what?" Tully couldn't stop himself.

Wesley hit the armrest lightly. "We went over to their house."

"And it was Bell?"

"I don't know." Wesley said at first then corrected himself. "No, it wasn't, he had an alibi. Someone was inside, the lights were on and there was Missy with a guy in the kitchen, at least that's what it looked like based on the shadows.

Mike was nearly paralyzed by it.

In that moment, yes, I hated Missy enough to think I wanted kill her. I was ready to storm the place and confront them but Mike told me no, he'd go in alone. I argued, probably what the neighbors heard since we were back in the car and I had the moon roof open and wasn't exactly using an inside voice.

He asked me not to humiliate him further, which hurt, but I saw his point."

Wesley shook his head.

"So I let him go in. There was some shouting. I waited a couple of minutes then went up to the porch. I hung back, but then I heard sounds of a fight.

I was afraid Mike might have lost it, so I went in.

The living room was a mess.

Mike was on the ground and Missy was looking back from the kitchen, this look on her face.

This look I will never forget." Wesley broke off, somewhat choked by the memory.

"What look?" Fineas asked gently.

"Satisfaction, I guess, excitement. Then she looked at me, she wasn't surprised or concerned, she just had this smug smile.

Before I left the car, I'd taken my gun, I don't know why, it was stupid.

Then I realized she wasn't looking at me, she was looking past me.

I grabbed for my gun. I'd forgotten about the guy.

He said something, something that should be seared into my conscious that should have haunted my every waking dream. But I can't remember it. It could have been Italian, maybe it was English and I just didn't process it or it was something completely different. The point is he knew what he was doing and he dropped me fast.

There was a light, this splitting pain in my head and then I woke up in my car in my driveway."

Tully looked over at him, unable to stop the skepticism. "So you don't know what happened?"

"That's what I know happened for sure. Over time there have been more flashes.

When I woke up I didn't remember anything from the night after we left the bar. I assumed my headache was part of the hangover. I went inside and cleaned up. Jake called and told me they'd found Mike. I assumed you wanted me on the investigation. When I got there Missy was relating how Mike and I had been arguing, that this wasn't the first fight. That he and I were…"

Wesley looked at Tully.

"I remember what she said."

"You told me to go home. Before I did I… may have threatened Missy. I knew something was up because of her lies. When I got home there was a note waiting on my porch. It said you and Loren were targets if I said anything. Somewhat ironically the hush note was what brought back most of my recall. But I never planned on staying quiet for long. I needed to get to you to tell you face-to-face.

By that time you'd narrowed down the ballistics to my gun, you came to get it, I couldn't find it and I really didn't care because I was trying to tell you there was more going on, you left. That night the Gazette announced I was the prime murder suspect. My apartment was burned down. My gun turned up, tests were run, and it matched.

I needed to talk things over with you, you were avoiding me, then you got pulled off the case, I was dragged in for questioning, I still couldn't remember everything and I'd promised Mike to look after Missy once so I wasn't about to say she did it without evidence. As a result my interview was full of holes. You believed I did it, which… killed me. After they booked me… Well, you know what happened that night. When my lawyers met with me in the hospital they said they could get me out of the charges if we went to court, by which point I didn't care anymore. And I think you know the rest." Wesley finished without any emotion, just a cold statement of facts.

Tully absorbed what was said for a while. The silence was filled with words that should have been said. More events that should have happened if one had been more trusting or one had been less stubborn.

"So it wasn't Bell?" Tully asked.

"Alibied, out, I looked into a few more, thought I may have even had something on Howard at one point, but I was forcing that."

"There's a problem with your story." Tully said, "The best you can do is saying that you were there but can't remember who shot Mike, with your gun..."

"Damn it Fineas, I didn't shoot Mike!" Wesley shouted. Then looked away, embarrassed, he'd known Fineas was just pointing out what case could have been made against him.

"I believe you," Fineas said quietly.

"I'm sorry, Fineas, I..." Wesley broke off.

Fineas cleared his throat. "So, what did you tell Loren?"

"Pertinent details, but not everything, like the threat."

"Did you find anything on the note?"

"I ran it, dusted for prints. It was printed on plain copy paper, nothing special about it, HP ink, no help there, believe me I've tried."

"And you don't know who it was, the guy?"

"I've had ideas, hunches, like I said, no one stuck."

"And the only other person who knew..."

"Is dead." Wesley finished.

"Except for the guy." Fineas pointed out. He didn't want them too distracted with what they'd lost to forget the murder might still be solved.

"It doesn't matter now anyway, at least not right now, double jeopardy, I'm safe from Briggs on that single count of murder, now it's the triple."

"Do you have any ideas how we tell the world you're innocent of these latest murders?"

Wesley smiled grimly.

"You have my list, anything on the landlord?"

"Still waiting on that one, I didn't want to risk the search myself so I have someone else on it."

"Have they tracked my phone yet?"

"Even if we do Briggs isn't going to like that, you could have just left it at home." Tully hesitated, wondering if he should show his hand. This whole conversation had been about the lack of transparency they had between each other and the damage it might have done, but did he bring up the cell phone? "How many phones do you have?"

"One." Wesley said.

Tully frowned. He was lying.

"Actually, I guess there's technically three." Wesley corrected. "There's my main phone, then a backup and a company BlackBerry that probably hasn't been used in a year or so. Of course there's also the Manor landline."

"All registered to you?"

"Obviously."

Tully nodded, disappointed.

"Well, for Boswell's murder you're the closest I have to an alibi."

"Not anymore."

"What?" Wesley asked, startled by Fineas' comment.

"Fredrickson revised the time of death to earlier that evening. She was dead before you went for your little joy ride." Wesley grimaced. "Fineas I didn't kill those women. You know what I'm capable of. That's one of the reasons you let yourself believe I was a murderer." Tully didn't like the sound of this. "So, knowing that part of me and knowing what someone out there did to my partner, my best friend, ask yourself this: If I was going to kill anyone who would it have been? And then, would I have just shot him?"

Tully's lip twitched inadvertently. Wesley had an excellent point, but, by his own admission he didn't know *who* had killed his partner.

"It also means the real killer, doesn't know about Mike's murderer."

"Not necessarily." Tully said slowly. "So far these murders have been in chronological order, first Boswell, the one you couldn't stop; then Epcot, the woman that led the mob against you; next, Missy, the woman whose testimony turned popular opinion. Shot three times showing escalation. Finally, the real murderer and the man having an affair with your partner's wife. Maybe the killer knows the whole story?"

Wesley shook his head. "The only person who could know is the person that killed Mike!"

"What if the first shot didn't kill Missy, maybe he got it out of her?" Fineas suggested.

"Maybe I got it out of her." Wesley said coldly. "It's what Briggs would think if he pieced it together."

"So, you think Mike's killer is the one behind these murders?"

"Maybe, but why wait? If he's afraid of me coming after him at some point, why let three years go by, during which I could have a flashback or something and ID him?"

"A good point," Tully said. He was watching Wesley closely, but out of the corner of his eye.

Wesley noticed.

It was the cop look.

Analysis by the part of the brain detached from emotion, the one that was still sizing Wesley up for murder. The part he may never be able to silence.

Fineas spoke next. "It would be an awfully big risk on the killer's part. It seems to me he'd have been better off just to shoot you if he was worried about you talking at some point."

Wesley agreed. "I've thought of that too. If it had been me," he said quietly. "And I was trying to fame, well, myself, there would have been two bodies at the last scene."

"Murder-suicide." Fineas said flatly.

Wesley nodded.

"If Missy's lover is supposed to be the killer why did he kill Missy?"

"You did actually meet Missy right?"

Fineas sighed. "I'll do what I can. Talk to Briggs, start the investigation fresh."

"You know that's not going to happen, right?" Wesley asked. "I'm being set up."

"Isn't that what we've already surmised based on your relationship with the victims?" Tully asked, somewhat put out.

"Yes, beyond that though, re-check the surveillance from Boswell's building, I think we might be able to identify the wheels on the car that picked Boswell up." Tully stared at Wesley.

"That's exactly the kind of thing I don't want to hear coming out of your mouth. How do you know that?" Then Tully remembered the picture. He couldn't believe he'd forgotten it after the sleepless night. "And would you mind explaining this?" he asked and removed the picture he'd stuck back in his jacket pocket. He handed it over.

"What?" Wesley said in surprise. "You…"

"What?"

"You don't recognize this?" Wesley asked. Then reached for his phone only to remember it was back in lockup. "It's Photoshopped, that's supposed to be Loren and me! Fineas, this is from our engagement party!" Wesley handed the photo back.

Tully examined the creased picture, concentrating on Wesley. Then he remembered the original and frowned, suddenly spotting the inconsistent light, the almost jagged edge around Wesley's head, the familiar pose.

He tucked the picture back in his pocket.

He had missed the sudden shift on Wesley's face as he contemplated what it meant.

"You just concentrate on cooperation and not getting put away for murder. I'll handle the investigating if you don't mind." Tully said and started the car. "I don't know what Brigg's will do but I'm in your court now."

"That's enough for me." Wesley said masking his features before Fineas had a chance to notice the recognition there.

Tully's phone rang.

He picked it up and glanced at the caller read out.

"Barry." he muttered, feeling his employment slipping away.

He flipped the phone open.

"What is it?" he asked.

"You need to get back to the station." Barry said.

"Briggs know he's gone?"

"No. Maybe. That's not the problem."

"Alright, I'm on my way, be about five minutes."

"Try to make it two." Barry said and hung up.

CHAPTER 23

Fineas marched Wesley through the front doors of the station.

All eyes swiveled towards them, including a very angry looking Briggs.

"He didn't do it." Fineas announced, not that he expected anyone to pay him any heed, but he hadn't taken a stand last time and he wasn't about to make the same mistake.

"Yes, we're considering that." Briggs said.

Fineas frowned, not comforted. He'd assumed Barry had meant they found something else on Wesley, now he exchanged surprised glances with his charge.

"Sheriff, if you could join me in the interrogation room?" Briggs asked. "We have a new suspect." he added.

Slowly, Fineas made his way across the room with Briggs, leaving Wesley in the squad room.

Wesley looked around the room of state police to find some of the locals. He spotted Barry and by his dour expression he knew something was very wrong.

That explained the lights and siren getting back, and the phone call.

He turned to find Briggs watching him.

"Fineas didn't do it!" he said, horrified such a conclusion had been made.

"Oh, we know that, too." Briggs said with a smile that made Wesley want to slap him.

"I just need to ask him a few questions about our new suspect."

"Who?" Wesley asked, dread slowly engulfing him.

He could only think of two likely names.

He closed his eyes.

"Loren Tully." Briggs said and Wesley felt something hot pierce his heart.

Tully felt like he'd been dropped in the Arctic Ocean. Just drawing breath was painful, let alone trying to speak, and then, he had to act as normal as possible lest his apprehension be cast in the wrong light.

It was too much to bear.

"Loren Tully was engaged to marry Wesley Cobin at the time of Michael Carlyle's murder, that's correct isn't it?"

"What case are you working on?" Tully asked.

"I'm getting to the pertinent details. Despite this connection I understand that she never attended the trial?"

Tully swallowed. "That's because I wouldn't allow it."

"She was… twenty-three at the time?" Briggs said, pretending to read over some paperwork. "And before the trial was over her residence had changed. There was nothing stopping her from going. It's also my understanding that she never believed Cobin was guilty."

"Again, what are you accusing her of?"

"Can you tell me, does she have an alibi for any of the recent murders?"

"She was at home for at least two of them." Tully said miserably.

"That would be your home, correct?" Tully didn't bother responding, Briggs wasn't really asking. "I've been by your house and from talking to a few of your deputies, all very cooperative and knowledgeable by the way, there's a second exit on the second story of your house. I would be surprised if someone couldn't slip out that way without the rest of the household knowing, there's no security system." Tully wouldn't concede this point but he knew it really didn't matter what he did aside for confessing himself, which he would do, but not just yet.

"Where's your proof of any of this? I'm sure close to half the town couldn't give you alibis for all three murderers."

"No, probably not. Fortunately for me not half of the town was engaged to Wesley Cobin."

"What do you mean?" Tully asked.

"We found this." Briggs said and pulled out a small evidence bag. Tully was careful not to react when he saw the contents.

"It was Loren's ring." Barry said and sounded appropriately miserable.

"Did she still have it?" He asked.

"I guess." Wesley said, still dazed from the accusation.

"She didn't give it back to you?" Barry demanded.

"No."

"That's kind of cold."

Wesley shrugged. "What happened, exactly?"

"They found it in the sand next to... next to Missy. Lucky for her you had the engraving done in French and just used initials so it took longer to ID."

"Who made the ID?" Wesley asked.

Barry shook his head.

"Who was it?"

"I'm not going to tell you Cobin. All I need is you to confess and keep Loren out of prison."

"I didn't do it." Wesley said firmly. "As for the other, don't worry, it won't happen."

"You're right, because Tully would take the fall first."

"That's not going to happen either. I lied about the ring, by the way."

"What?"

"I lied when I said she didn't give it back."

Barry looked at him. "You're saying she did give it back?"

Wesley shrugged.

Barry pursed his lips, not liking the situation but respecting Wesley for it.

"I doubt it will come to that though, if I sell the company I'd have nearly unlimited resources, at least for a while, and I'd do anything to keep Loren and Fineas out of prison." Wesley added.

"I think you're forgetting about her new fiancée. Howard's not exactly going to stand idly by."

"He's only the Assistant DA and Bell would watch both of them hang and I doubt Howard would put up much of a fight for Fineas."

"You can't impugn everyone's motives." Barry said.

"I'm sorry, but you have met our district attorney? Bell wouldn't risk helping his own mother if it would damage his political career." Barry wanted to disagree, he was conversing with Wesley Cobin after all, but he found he couldn't on the subject of Bell's ethics.

"You said us, who's on our side?" Wesley asked, shifting back to solving the case.

"You and me and Fineas I guess." Wesley closed his eyes.

"Great, what about Lance and Blaze?"

Jake rolled his head in the direction of the other two deputies. They were amongst a cluster of state troopers, apparently exchanging jokes. Blaze was presently doing a terrifying impression of a laugh, doubled over and hitching.

"No great loss anyway." Wesley said, also remembering earlier cases worked with the two juniors.

"One, question," Wesley said. "Why are you so sure Loren didn't do it?"

"Because she loves Howard." Jake replied. "Any motive she could have for killing these women points back to you and frankly she's not the kind of obsessed personality it would take. Besides she'd know these murders only make you look guilty, so unless she was trying to frame you for murder…" Jake tailed off. "Then again maybe she was trying to help out her fiancée?"

"You can leave Howard out of it."

"It really is something huh? I mean the man who prosecuted you and your ex-fiancée are getting married? Even if she wasn't involved in the trial, she's got to have some idea of what he did to you, this town just isn't big enough, hell, this state isn't big enough. I hated your guts and I still wasn't entirely comfortable with what Howard did to you."

"Yeah, you just tried to kill me." Wesley muttered. Barry ignored him.

"So I figure, it must be love."

"Too bad you aren't that efficient working your cases." Wesley retorted.

Barry moved them on. "Before we work together on this, there are some ground rules. You don't talk about your innocence, or your life, or anything not immediately pertaining to this case. Fineas seemed pretty convinced you didn't murder these three women even after whatever that was at the last scene. Therefore I'm not going to think about it. So don't you bring it up."

"Likewise." Wesley said and they shook hands.

"Oh, and I'll have to drive your car." Jake added.

"Really?" Wesley asked. "Cause I was just going to say you need to get my license back."

"That might work," Jake said with a rare smile. "If I didn't already have the keys."

CHAPTER 24

The state lackeys didn't really like the idea of letting Wesley walk out of the office a free man, but, as he pointed out he had been nothing but cooperative not having been charged formally with any crime and Barry would be with him the whole time, hardly a free man then.

Together the unlikely pair made their way across the parking lot toward the fenced-in county impound yard.

Jake keyed in the lock's code at the fence and together they hauled open the un-powered gate.

Wesley was mildly annoyed to notice he could have gained access to the yard any time since they hadn't bothered changing the lock combination since he'd been forced out.

They walked past a couple pickup trucks and a Ford Explorer to reach the Mercedes, which glistened in the moonlight and the sodium vapor parking lot light's orange hue warmed the chrome accents.

Wesley let out an unconscious sigh and dutifully crossed to the passenger door.

Barry took the driver's side and pulled on the door handle. He pulled again, but the door was locked.

"I thought this was some kind of keyless entry system?" he said, reaching into his pocket.

"It is, push the button." Wesley said.

"On the key?"

"No, the button on the door."

Barry squinted at the door.

"You really want to drive?" Wesley asked.

Barry didn't reply as he prodded at the door handle. In a second the interior lights came on and the door locks popped. Apparently he'd found the button.

Wesley opened the passenger door and dropped into the seat.

Jake joined him in the car and began feeling under the seat for the adjustments.

"On the door." Wesley said.

"What?"

"On the door, by the handle." Wesley heard the whirr of the side view mirror motor. "That's the mirrors, on the door, just ahead of the locks. The locks clicked as he spoke, then the seat started to move. He wondered if Barry was messing with him.

Barry adjusted the rear view mirror and played with the seat controls again; then he moved onto the side view mirrors as the cabin lights faded.

"Okay, then where's…" Wesley reached over and pressed the engine start button on the dashboard before Barry could fumble for it.

The engine rumbled to life with a growl not typical of a car wearing a silver arrow.

"Thanks, I can take it from here." Barry said and shifted into reverse, while turning in his seat. He looked back when the motorized hum began.

The infotainment screen rose from beneath its panel in the dashboard and displayed footage from the rear view camera.

"Nifty." Barry remarked and released the brake.

The Benz drifted slowly backwards and he maneuvered into the aisle, then dropped the transmission down into drive and gently rolled onto the throttle. They left the impound yard and parked, engine idling, on the side of the road while both got out and closed the gate.

Wesley considered making a dash for the car, he just had to get in and he'd be gone, but to what end? He didn't have an answer yet.

Barry got back behind the wheel and pulled the shifter back into drive. In so doing he not only pulled the lever down but also toward him. Wesley noticed this and opened his mouth to remark on it, decided it would be unappreciated and let Barry roll back on the power.

Since the Mercedes was still running in Sport mode and had just been manually shifted into first gear, and because Barry prodded it like he did his old Crown Vic, the Mercedes leapt forwards with a Berserker-like bellow from its quad exhausts and the tires yelped in pain. Barry stood on the brakes and all forward momentum was immediately lost, flinging driver and passenger forwards.

Wesley glared as they were both cinched tight by the seat belts. "One more time, and I'm driving." he warned.

Jake curbed the Mercedes on the end of Elm Street.

Wesley stared hotly at Barry and clenched his fingers against the door pull as the AMG wheels cried in agony as they were rubbed against the unforgiving concrete. It wasn't the behavior that annoyed Wesley it was the mechanical and cosmetic abuse to the car, an innocent, that angered him. If Barry needed that release Wesley wished the deputy would just punch him a few times and leave the Benz out of it.

"This is a bad idea." Barry said again but shifted the car into park nonetheless.

"I want Loren to know what's about to happen and neither of us can call or text or anything that can be traced because it'll make her look guilty. The only way to do this is face to face."

"But there are four state troopers sitting on the house," Jake said. "They've got it covered; if we get caught now then it's over for us." Wesley had to admit that Jake had a point.

"What if Briggs tries to play it cool, calls her down, says Fineas needs something, tries talking to her casually, gets her to say something and then uses it against her, I can't take that chance."

"Have a little more faith in the Sheriff, would you? He's not going to let that happen."

"I don't think he'll have much choice." Wesley said and reached for his phone.

"What are you doing?"

"Calling my lawyers, I'm reactivating Loren as a client." Wesley remembered he hadn't bothered to collect his things from the station.

"Can I borrow your phone?" he asked.

"She's not going ask for a lawyer because she's innocent and she thinks the…" Jake nearly bit his tongue off he stopped speaking so fast.

Wesley stared at him, a slight, but hugely irritating kink at the corner of his mouth. He knew what Jake had been about to say, that she thought the system worked. It was true, even the accusation against Wesley she thought was due to him not telling the whole truth.

Wesley sighed. "That's why we need to talk to her."

"Okay, but I still think it's a waste of time and an unnecessary risk."

"And you are entitled to that opinion," Wesley said.

"You realize if you get caught this investigation is over, right?"

Wesley paused. He'd thought about it but it had seemed worth the risk, but what would it accomplish? Loren would be on guard, sure, but maybe that would actually make her look guilty.

"Wouldn't it be better to get a handle on things then give her something to work with? It's not like Briggs can act too fast, you know the paperwork."

"Where do we go?" Wesley asked. Looking at the Tully house in the next block, wishing he could teleport into the front room.

"If proving Loren is innocent is our first task we should try and find her an alibi."

"Have you seen Dillon?" Wesley asked.

"No." He could tell Jake was thoughtful, he surmised it was surprise over Dillon's absence.

"He's over on the south side right?"

"Yeah, but he's probably at the office right now." Barry started the engine.

"What about the vandals?" Wesley asked.

"Who?"

"At Fineas' house, the Molotov cocktail."

"Oh, eyewitnesses put the deviants in a convertible Camaro."

"Jefferson's?"

"Do you really need to ask?"

"Shame about your cruiser." Wesley said. Barry remained silent. "I can't believe they tried that, I would have thought they could have puzzled together the outcome."

"It almost worked." Barry reminded him. "Maybe we should go see if James had anything to do with it?"

"No, not his style, too messy, they must have been freelancing." Wesley said and waited. "Talking to James would be a waste of time." he added.

"Well, I mean, of people with an axe to grind…"

"Oh come on, way too obvious." Wesley said.

"Who is the sworn and sanctioned deputy in this car?" Barry asked irritably and shifted into drive.

"The one at the wheel." Wesley muttered, turning to look out the window. He didn't want Barry to see his smile.

Jake turned the Mercedes up the dirt driveway that led to the Jefferson's property.

From appearances along the road, the place might have been abandoned, the mail box was unpainted, the land bordering the ditch was just overgrown scrub, the only sign of habitation was the driveway itself, well-worn and with an underlying layer of paving stones defining it.

Suspicions of abandonment were not quelled when one came in sight of the house a few hundred feet uphill. At one time nothing more than a tin roof shack, the place had been extended to five or six times its original size, but the distressed look of chipped and peeling paint and tin roofing material defined the entire complex, along with its numerous outbuildings.

The Xenon headlamps illuminated the one anachronistic item on the property, a gray Porsche Boxter.

Jake parked the Mercedes at the far edge of the circular driveway and shut off the engine.

"Parking brake." Wesley muttered.

Jake glanced at him and removed his foot from the brake letting the car roll back against the transmission with a jolt that made Wesley tighten his grip on the door handle.

Barry opened the door and got out of the car first, eying the house, from which there were multiple light sources. They both knew they were more than likely under surveillance from the moment they rolled onto the property, possibly even prior to that.

Wesley's gaze was fixed on the Boxter, he wasn't sure why, but something about the car unsettled him on a subconscious level.

Barry looked over his shoulder, wondering what was taking Cobin so long.

Wesley opened the passenger door and left the shelter of the car to join Jake as he made his way towards the porch.

"I don't want trouble from you." The deputy warned.

"If there's trouble, it won't be from me." Wesley retorted and together they climbed the steps, which didn't creak as loudly as one would have imagined.

The knock was answered a few seconds later by none other than James Jefferson himself.

"My, my, Deputy Barry, what an unexpected surprise." He said with a sticky smile. "What's the occasion?" He asked, ignoring Wesley for the moment.

"You know where your brothers are at?" Barry asked.

"No, the last I knew they were going to the store." James said coolly.

"County lockup actually." Barry said.

"Nothing serious I hope." James said.

"Actually, they rammed my cruiser, so it could be."

James looked out at the Mercedes. "Well, deputy you don't seem to have done too badly. Is this a prelude to asking to come inside?" James asked and opened the door wider.

Barry eyed the eldest Jefferson brother carefully. There seemed to be no hidden agenda in the face.

Barry stepped over the threshold, followed by Wesley.

The interior of the Jefferson residence was at odds with the exterior.

The walls were painted a soft cream, offset by low wattage lamps with dark brown and green shades.

The ceiling was open to the rafters but the tin roof was not exposed, a generous layer of insulation and plaster between the interior ceiling.

The furnishings, at least in the front room that James led them to, were of good enough quality, with an appealing Pottery Barn design.

The room should have been cozy, but reminded Wesley instead of a fly eating plant; careful design to put unsuspecting victims at ease before they were swallowed down whole. Maybe that was just the effect of having only one window, set high in the far wall.

"So, there was some kind of, traffic accident?" James asked as they settled into chairs around the room.

"Hardly, an accident." Barry said, letting his scorn show. "They drove into the parking lot and straight into my cruiser."

James frowned. "I wonder if there was something wrong with the brakes?" He suggested.

"They then assaulted deputy Imahara."

"A misunderstanding?" James suggested.

Barry pursed his lips but restrained himself. "That's not actually what I came here to talk about." He said.

"Oh, really, what else could you possibly want to know Deputy? I am an open book."

"Did you kill Odette Boswell?" Wesley asked. The question earned him a blazing look from Barry, but his attention remained fixed on James.

Jefferson smiled, "Mr. Cobin, I didn't realize you were back in any official capacity at the Sheriff's department. If I'd known I would have congratulated you."

"He isn't, he's a material witness helping us with inquiries."

"More of a consultant." Wesley put in.

"I see, psychic now are we, Cobin? That must account for why you have such a close connection to all these horrific murders?"

"I noticed you haven't answered the question." Wesley said stiffly.

"I didn't think you were serious, quite aside from the fact that I didn't know I was being questioned, am I a suspect in these murder investigations, Deputy?" James asked Barry.

"No, of course not, Cobin has no such authority, that's not why I'm here at all."

"I see, well, just to put your mind at ease, no I did not murder Ms. Boswell, the implication is simply revolting." James purred without the slightest hint of revulsion.

"I'm here because of a 1967 Camaro." Barry said. "Several eyewitnesses place it at the scene of an incident that took place yesterday evening. Someone vandalized Sheriff Tully's residence. There is a 1967 Camaro registered to you, so we were just wondering if you would shed any light on the matter?"

James looked thoughtful.

"Of course, I do have a '67 Camaro, but I don't think it's left the garage in some time. Do you have anything else, a license plate number perhaps, or a description of the driver?"

"Black with stripes, V-8, convertible, dead ringer for your car."

"Very interesting, of course, I believe there was something like 34,000 '67 SS models built, it seems like there should still be a few leftover."

"But the car is here?" Barry asked.

"I'm sure it is, there's no reason it wouldn't be."

"Would you mind checking on that?" Wesley asked, as impertinently as he could manage.

"Actually, I'm afraid you caught me at a bad time. Not that I haven't enjoyed this little chat, but if you wouldn't mind, it's getting late."

Barry considered protesting, but it wouldn't serve a purpose. He wasn't even sure why they'd come up here in the end.

It had seemed a good idea, but that had been mostly because Wesley had been against the idea. Now he wondered if he'd underestimated his "partner".

Wesley certainly didn't seem to mind, judging from his careful study of James Jefferson's face.

James led them back to the entry hall and out the door.

"So sorry I couldn't have been more help to you, deputy Barry."

Barry didn't say anything as he stepped off the porch.

"Oh, and former deputy Cobin, diga Olá para o seu pai." James said, speaking low, into Wesley's ear.

"Boa Noite!" James said and shut the door.

Wesley's fist was clenched so tight he felt his nails draw blood.

"I need a phone." Wesley said as soon as they were back in the car.

"What?" Barry asked.

"I need a phone, can I borrow yours?"

Barry reached into a pocket and handed him a Motorola flip phone. Wesley looked at it.

"Okay, I need a smartphone." he amended. "Or a computer, but it would be better with the phone."

"Where's your phone?"

"Back at the station, remember I didn't have time to grab it. I need my phone and I need to go to my house."

"What about Loren? What about proving her innocent?"

"She is innocent and I can prove that but I need the phone and I have to go home."

"Why? What do you need?"

"I need you to trust me." Wesley said.

Jake actually laughed as he started the engine and turned the car around.

"Trust you? Sorry, that's never going to happen Cobin, get used to it."

"Do you think I killed these last three women?" Wesley demanded.

"Do I think you killed them? I don't know. Tully seems pretty convinced you didn't, but he's not exactly impartial."

"Don't fool yourself Jake, this is a town of 2,000 people, no one is impartial. I didn't kill those women and someone is trying to frame me, someone who has to have been watching my every move, someone who hates me enough to feel no compunction in killing three other people just to watch me hang!"

They were pulling back onto the county road then.

"Who do you think it is then?"

"Oh come on? How long have the Jefferson's wanted me dead?"

"Probably since your father murdered their sister." Barry said coldly.

"And how many times have they tried to kill me?"

"Okay, point taken, now you listen, they tried to kill you, directly, not through some plot."

"So why not try something new, let someone else be the executioner?"

"What is this about? What did I miss back there?" Barry asked.

Wesley weight his options, he had been since crossing the yard to the car.

He didn't trust Barry's reaction so he couldn't tell him the truth, not yet at least.

"It's just a feeling." Wesley said lamely.

"Oh, gut instinct, well why didn't you say so, let's call Briggs and tell him he should just arrest the whole Jefferson gang because Wesley Cobin, former deputy all-star, has a bad feeling about them, never mind the personal agenda between the families."

"Not what I had in mind, but it works." Wesley said.

Barry snorted.

Wesley looked out the window, staring into the dark as they headed toward the lights of town.

"I also want to talk to Howard."

"Ho, ho, now there's an exchange I don't want to miss!" Barry said.

"Where do you think he is?"

"If he knows about Loren he's probably at the station, he hangs around there enough as it is."

Wesley's brow furrowed.

"Look, like I said I need to go to my house if not the station, I have a backup phone and I can get the Jeep, you can keep the Benz if you need wheels." Wesley said.

"Don't you want to head to the last crime scene, maybe find something that we all missed with your mad crime fighting skills?" Barry asked voice heavy with distain.

"No, I already know what you missed." Wesley said casually.

Barry's glare was searching, he assumed Cobin was just being flippant with him, but he couldn't be entirely certain he hadn't been serious.

"If you think I'm letting you go all free bird you can guess again." Jake said and took the next left, aiming the Mercedes toward Cobin Manor.

As soon as the car stopped moving Wesley yanked open the door and ran for the house.

For a split second Jake had to fight the urge to jump out of the car and run after him, thinking he was trying to escape. He had to remind himself they were on the same side, at least for now.

He turned off the engine and slowly made his way to the front porch.

"Radburt!" Wesley called as he hurried through the foyer and down the side hall heading for the kitchen.

"Radburt are you here?" he called again.

Radburt could have been out at his cottage but Wesley tended to doubt that.

"Wesley, master Cobin!" Radburt called from somewhere near the back of the house.

Sure enough Wesley found him in the kitchen, most of the silver in the house piled on the big table and the polishing accoutrements piled on the table.

"Oh, Wesley, I'm so relieved!" he said.

"Don't be, this is looking like a variation of plan B. Briggs is going after Loren."

"What?" Radburt asked disbelief plain across his face.

"I need you, we, need you. We need time."

Radburt nodded, he knew exactly what Wesley meant.

"I'll just grab my things." He said, then looked down at his suit. "Do you think I have time to change?" he asked with a frown. "I don't feel entirely formal enough."

"You look perfect." Wesley assured him. "Barry is outside, probably with the car, I'll be there in a minute." he said and headed for the garage access door.

In the garage Wesley snatched the keys to the 230SL, which gleamed from the far end of the garage. Next he took a supple leather jacket off a peg by the door and slipped it on. Finally he turned to a shelving unit and removed the bottom shelf, revealing a small niche. He removed a boxed smartphone and a shoebox, which held a few thousand dollars loose cash.

Not knowing exactly what he was planning for he stuffed his jacket pockets with wads of twenties, then returned the shoebox to the niche and pulled out another case. He hesitated, then flipped the lock and looked down at the 9mm carefully nestled within.

There were two magazines for the SIG and a small box of bullets. He took the magazines, attached one, left the extra ammo and returned the box to the niche, then recovered the whole thing.

He slipped the SIG into a specially designed pocket on the inside of his jacket along with the extra magazine; then he went to find Barry.

Radburt was doing an excellent job of keeping Barry distracted while Wesley made his preparations.

"What took you so long?" Barry demanded as he opened the driver's door.

"Legal papers and a phone." Wesley said, holding up a manila folder and the phone.

Radburt squeezed himself into the back seat of the Mercedes.

"Back to the station." Wesley said.

Barry chafed at what sounded like a command, but started the engine and swung the Mercedes around nonetheless.

"What position are we taking on questioning, sir?" Radburt asked.

"No questions whatsoever, I don't want Loren saying anything, she's going to want to, but you have to stop her, trust me, it's best for right now."

"Wait, what?" Barry asked.

"Radburt is going to be Loren's legal counsel until Denny, Sivil and company get here." Wesley explained.

"But he can't do that." Barry said.

"And why not, deputy Barry?" Radburt asked.

"Because you're a butler."

"Roles traditionally associated with, as you say, a "butler", maybe part of my duties, but I assure you I am also a licensed and bar approved solicitor." Radburt declared icily.

"Really?" Barry said, eyeing Cobin anew.

CHAPTER 25

Tully watched everything from his office.

He had been sidelined.

It was an obvious development, but he was shocked at how callously his two deputies were acting.

Granted, he didn't expect them to risk their careers for him; just their lives. It wasn't very comforting.

Furthermore the whole thing was totally ludicrous, as anyone with half a brain could see!

Aside from the paper thin motive, there was the total lack of evidence, barring the ring, which wasn't conclusive at all. Even Briggs had said the scene was contaminated when the fight broke out. There was blood in the sand, should they also assume that Dillon was involved?

What was to say Loren hadn't simply lost the ring in the park?

He didn't even know if she'd kept it, would have thought she hadn't, but in his heart he knew she had. That was just Loren she'd never be over Wesley even if she did love Dillon.

Speaking of Dillon, where the hell was he?

Then again he was probably arguing with his boss.

As in tune as the A.D.A. kept with the goings on at the department, he had to know Briggs was now looking at Loren as a suspect.

Tully looked down at his desk phone and casually pressed the speakerphone button.

He was greeted with silence and was freshly galled.

He'd been forbidden to call home and his phone had been very politely sequestered; now it seemed his desk phone had been cut off as well.

He looked at his computer and wondered if they'd left his internet on.

If his men had been in charge of the shutdown than it no doubt still be active.

He could send Loren a text message through e-mail.

He could warn her.

Warn her of what?

Well, tell her not to say anything.

Tell her not to trust Briggs or anyone in the department.

This would be cleared up; it had to be cleared up!

Loren wasn't a killer, especially not a cold and calculating sociopath capable of planning and carrying out a triple homicide, presuming of course, it was still just the three bodies.

He'd thought similar things about Wesley, he reminded himself.

He could now relate to what the night three years ago must have been like for Wes.

Tully felt sick when he considered his role in that affair.

If he had been innocent...

If, it was still *if* in his mind, years of conditioning speaking?

It had to be.

Wesley's case for his innocence was compelling, the emotions had all been there. But of course, emotions had ways of messing with people.

Boil it right down and Wesley had no idea who had killed his partner.

He admitted to being drunk, to having his gun, to blacking out.

What if he'd shot Mike, then blacked out?

What if it had been self-defense, what if Missy had turned Mike against his partner?

What if, what if, what if! So many what ifs!

Tully pounded his desk once in frustration and forced himself to sit down, to look at the case again. What was he missing?

His pocket vibrated and he suddenly remembered he still had Wesley's phone.

He pulled it out and turned it on.

He grimaced for the lock screen and tapped the notification.

New email. It said.

His jaw went slack when he saw the email account it was attached to.

Tully, F. His email! Wesley had tapped his email account.

He jabbed the screen and the message opened.

He skimmed through it.

The message had been forwarded to him. It was from CallCOM, the one message from the voicemail of Y. Niboc.

He tapped the link and the message opened in a media player.

"Wesley, this is Odette Boswell, how you been sweet thing?" Boswell purred through the phone's speakers. The voice of the dead woman sent a chill up Tully's back. "I've been better myself, it might surprise you but I actually made a few mistakes and I think the 5-0 is finally closing in on me. Oh, don't worry I'll have a new name before they get me. The thing is, before I disappear, I've had this excellent little proposition from an old friend of yours. I'm afraid my participation might land you behind bars for the rest of your life. Lucky for you, my candle still burns. I'm coming your way. Meet me at that charming little restaurant just off the highway at 9:30 this evening. Or else... well, you get the idea. Oh, and dress up, this is meant to be a date. See you then lover." The message ended. Tully didn't know what to think.

The vehicles had been towed away, but, in the excitement the parking lot had yet to be cleaned. As they made their way to the station doors, they crunched through the gummy safety glass littering the sidewalk.

The crunching made Jake grimace, a reminder of his smashed cruiser.

He was tempted to voice the idea of the Jefferson's as killers simply out of spite, let alone the fact, if, and it was a big if; if Cobin wasn't the murderer, they did possess the needed traits. After all, ramming his car had just been so they could get another chance at Cobin.

Marge had been sent home, so there was no one manning the front desk.

Wesley nodded for Radburt to hang back in the reception area and followed Barry into the squad room.

The place was a mess.

A chaos of confusion in a normally orderly space.

Files, and print outs were stacked on desks, which had been rearranged in weird groupings. The extra equipment the State police had brought with them seemed to have doubled. The State investigators seemed to be meeting in the office.

Wesley's heart clenched.

If he had to guess it meant they were getting ready to go get Loren.

He needed to act fast.

First he tried to spot either DA or ADA though neither one's car had been in the parking lot.

Probably building a case, or, for Dillon's sake, he hoped tearing one down.

He checked Tully's office and saw Fineas through the blinds, seated at his desk, watching the computer screen. The Sheriff looked bad, as could be expected.

Wesley wanted to reassure his old friend, but there was no time.

He spotted Lance against the interior wall watching the going's on inside the conference room.

He made his way over to him.

"Imahara," Wesley said. "I want my stuff back!"

"What?" Lance asked irritably.

"I want my stuff, everything you took, my phone, my wallet, pocket litter, you know the drill."

"Fill out a form." Lance replied, still staring into the conference room, basically ignoring Wesley.

"This is not what I pay you for!" Wesley snapped.

It got Imahara's attention if nothing else.

"Excuse me?" The deputy asked, bewildered.

"Of anyone in this pokey little village I pay the most in taxes, therefore I deserve the best service!" Wesley snapped. It was a common and totally skewed excuse he'd heard more than once during his tenure as a Sheriff's deputy. Sometimes it worked on the more gullible deputies.

Lance sneered at him and looked away.

"Did you hear Tully knows about Blaze's little side income tipping off the Gazette?" He asked.

Now he had the man's attention.

"It kind of makes me wonder if he knows about your little cash jobs on the side? I mean, I think the saying is still, justice is blind but you seem to have made a career out of peeking around that blindfold. For example..."

"Alright, alright, sheesh, I'll see if we have anything." Imahara said, finally heading toward the storage locker down the hall.

"And my license!" Wesley added, though he thought Tully had that, and he couldn't talk to Tully just yet. He felt bad for him, he knew exactly what he was going through, but he wasn't going to comfort him. For one thing, it would take too long, for another, a small part of him, a piece of himself he hated, wanted Tully to suffer, at least a little, to understand the desperation that had made him do what he'd done that night.

Briggs and a couple of his people climbed into their cars while Lance was off getting Wesley's stuff. He returned handed Wesley two envelopes which held everything he'd wanted except for his phone. He started to call the deputy on it when he remembered lunch. He glanced at the office and wondered if Tully still had the phone on him. He'd forgotten about it when they'd left earlier.

He stuffed his license back in his wallet and turned on the backup phone he'd grabbed.

The DROID showed a 45% charge, which should be enough. He also planned on taking his car back, he'd palmed the key fob of Jake the minute they'd entered the station.

Briggs had just left. They'd take the direct route, Wesley would go around and 451 horsepower said he'd get there first.

Wesley left the station without a word to anyone, hoping that Barry wouldn't notice.

As he pushed thought the front door he unlocked his phone and pulled up Translate. He set the phone to detect the language, he used the salutation.

"*Boa Noite,*" Wesley said, and waited.

Good Night. Translated from Portuguese.

He switched to Portuguese and spoke the phrase as best he could remember it.

"Dizer ola para oh supah," he said

Thai squid Ferrari driver coopsul.

He sighed, so it wouldn't be that easy.

As soon as he realized Cobin was gone Jake Barry ran to the front door.

Outside he heard the howl of a thundering engine. The sound was both distinct and familiar.

He reached the sidewalk in time to see the taillights of the Mercedes as it rocketed away from the station on a sonic boom of basso exhaust rumble.

A smile tugged at the corner of his lips.

As soon as he cleared the station and turned left on 4th street, Wesley reached under the dashboard and flipped a nondescript switch.

Instantly the road ahead of him was decorated with cycling red, blue, red, blue as police lights flashed from underneath the grille. The switch next to it activated a siren and the final button set everything to speed sensitivity.

Even with the highly illegal aftermarket lights and sirens driving like he was through town was extremely stupid, not to mention dangerous, but at the precise second he didn't care.

As bold a face that he'd put up, he was scared.

There was no reason money and power shouldn't be able to get Loren off, should the utter lack of evidence not do it, but he knew things didn't always work the way they were supposed to. Usually the system worked, sometimes people were too powerful for the system and sometimes a cop with a vendetta was more powerful then both of those.

He had to try and cut them off at the pass, just in case something went wrong, and in this case, the expression was more or less literal.

Wesley braked as lightly as possible to bring the Mercedes down from 60 to zero on the side street right across from the Tully's.

He shut off the lights and engine then ran for the small alley-like pedestrian way between the houses.

He reached the back fence and pulled himself over, knowing from childhood experience that the back gate would be locked.

He landed on the other side of the fence and ran for the back stairs, which he ascended as lightly as possible, then wrapped on the door to Loren's room.

"Loren, it's me!" he hissed and continued to knock.

He reached for the handle and, whispering an apology, tried the knob.

It turned.

The lights were on in the office, the screen saver danced on the computer, but there was no sign of Loren.

Wesley moved on to the bedroom door and knocked, then pushed his way through.

Lights were out in the bedroom, but from the light spilling from the office he could clearly see that the bed was made.

Loren wasn't there.

He crossed to her jewelry box and checked the contents. Assuming it would be with the rest of the rings, the engagement diamond was missing.

He reached into his pocket and removed the SL's key ring. From it he slipped an almost identical ring, though this was a wedding ring.

He put it with the rest and closed the lid, then hurried back to the office.

In his mind's eye he saw the state police Expedition baring down on them, they couldn't be more than three stop signs away!

He ran for the stairs, sorry if he startled either Caroline or Loren, but he was past worry.

"Loren! Caroline!" he called out as he reached the stairs and descended into the living room.

"Wesley?" Came Caroline's startled reply.

She was on the couch, or had been, now she was standing, staring at him.

"Where's Loren?" Wesley asked.

"What? Loren? She's upstairs."

Wesley shook his head. "No, she's not." he said.

Where was she?

The bathroom door had been open, he'd passed the spare bedroom too, she hadn't been there.

"You're sure she didn't go out or anything?" Wesley asked.

"Has Dillon called?" he asked hopefully.

"No, no phone calls all evening, what's going on?" Caroline asked.

"I can't explain and I am so sorry for that, I'm so sorry for all of this, everything is going to be alright, trust me." Wesley said, as much to reassure himself as Caroline.

"Wesley, you aren't making any sense, where's Fineas?"

"Some State investigators have taken over the case, you can't trust them, you can't trust anyone. Do you understand?" Wesley asked and made his way over to the side window.

He saw the flash of red and blue.

They had arrived!

"I have to go and I need you to pretend that I was never here, can you do that?" Wesley asked.

It killed him to leave Caroline like this, completely unprepared for what Briggs was about to unleash, but she needed to react as naturally as possible.

"Wesley,"

"Just remember that you know Loren and you know Fineas, you know me too, probably better than I know myself, don't forget any of that."

"But what do you mean Loren's not there?" Caroline asked.

"You don't know that." Wesley said quickly and then ran back up the stairs.

He heard the doorbell ring as he reentered Loren's rooms.

Loren hadn't run, he knew her, she never would. The only explanation was that she'd been taken!

He looked around the room, then grabbed his phone and switched the camera on, shooting as much video of the room as he could, not seeing any clues, but maybe he would.

He wanted to check the computer but he couldn't or it would look like Loren just left.

He opened the back door and looked out.

No one seemed to be covering the back.

He stared at the door knob and felt sick.

If they found his prints they'd think he'd taken Loren.

Did it matter?

What if the kidnapper's prints were on the knob?

He'd probably already smudged them.

Biting back tears he wiped the knob with his shirt, then descended the stairs and quickly and silently as possible.

He checked the gate as he left.

It wasn't locked.

He vaulted the fence and ran back down the alleyway.

He dropped into the Mercedes and closed the door.

Then let out a single shuddering sob.

Wesley forced back tears and, when next he blinked his eyes he only saw red.

There was only one name that came to mind and only one course of action to take.

He threw the car into gear and tramped the accelerator.

The car revved in place and Wesley kept pounding the accelerator, finally realizing the Mercedes was sitting in neutral.

He swore and shifted into drive, but his foot froze over the accelerator.

How good were they at their framing?

How well could they predict his behavior, how deep did this go?

He shifted into park and thought things through.

He thought about the drive over.

He thought about James Jefferson.

He thought about Loren.

He thought about his trial, the testimony, the behavior.

And then he thought he had an answer.

He unlocked his phone.

CHAPTER 26

Wesley drove across town, away from the station and the Jefferson's.

He'd obviously never been to Howard's condo, but he knew where the complex was.

The condos were white and contemporarily styled. They reminded Wesley uncomfortably of the old beach house.

He drove past them once, eying which ones had lights on and what cars were parked out front. He didn't see Howard's car, hopefully there would be some kind of directory to find which condo was his. The complex had been advertised as "high security", meaning the main door had a lock system, but Wesley wasn't too worried about that.

He parked a block away and walked back to the complex.

If the Jefferson's were involved there were, at most, two brothers unaccounted for. James wouldn't be getting his hands dirty, not this time.

However, Wesley doubted that he would run into any Jefferson's, they were involved, but they wouldn't have been trusted with this.

Wesley was wondering how it was going to be explained away to Loren? It would take a pretty strong excuse.

Wesley skirted the building and made his way to the back, past reserved parking spaces to the private garden around the back.

"Come on, just grab it and go!"

The voice was coming from a dark alley behind the condos.

Wesley heard it and froze.

It was unsettlingly like the voice of Jerry Jefferson, one of the unaccounted for brothers.

Wesley swallowed.

"Quit chickening out, just go for it!"

Wesley changed his course and headed for the alley, in a rush he entered the alley, too fast, as it turned out he didn't have time to grab the SIG.

He saw with relief it wasn't Jerry. But that was the last thing he saw before the world went black.

Tully paced his office.

There really wasn't room enough in his office to pace, so eventually he ended up back in the squad room.

Once there though the only thing he wanted to do was bore holes in the heads of his deputies, all three of whom were still hanging around.

He checked the clock.

It was after 10 now, Briggs should have been back.

At least the commander had decided to be upfront about the whole thing. He'd gone with his full force to bring Loren in, so she wouldn't be duped into saying something out of context.

Tully caught sight of movement in the waiting area beyond the front desk and went to investigate. It was still his station after all.

He found Radburt, uncomfortably huddled in one of the chairs.

"Radburt?" he said, surprised to see the man.

"Ah, Sheriff Tully," Radburt said and rose to his feet.

"I am so sorry to hear about all of this." he said.

"So you know about Brigg's idiotic theory?" Tully asked.

"Oh, intimately sir, I am your daughter's legal counsel." Radburt explained.

"Then what are you doing here?" Tully asked. He found himself wishing Radburt was at the house.

"I'm afraid it was a bit of a gamble but I knew a bit too much of the plan already, you see, Wesley had to do something, on the sly, you could say. We thought it best if I wasn't in any way implicated as being in collusion."

Tully sighed. He should have known Wesley wouldn't sit idly by, especially acting as a free citizen without any duties or obligations. He was somewhat at ease hearing it.

Wesley would keep Loren safe.

Tully heard vehicles in the parking lot and stepped back into the squad room to peer out the front windows.

The State Police vehicles were back.

He nodded to Radburt and then fell back, watching from the middle of the squad room.

Briggs climbed from the passenger seat of the Expedition and clearly slammed the door.

It was obvious he was not in a good mood.

He stormed across the parking lot to the side entrance then stomped into the station, marching straight for Tully.

"Where is she?" He demanded, his voice booming, enraged. "What did you tell her?"

Tully's surprise was genuine. "What are you talking about?" he asked.

"Loren Tully is not at your residence, she was there when two officers were stationed to watch the house, they didn't see anyone come or go and yet, your daughter is not there!"

Tully's forced himself not to look at Radburt, standing by the front desk.

Surely that hadn't been Wesley's plan? It was only making Briggs madder and putting off the inevitable.

"Bradley!" Briggs barked.

"Yes, sir." Said a wiry uniformed officer who stepped immediately to attention.

"I want Sheriff Tully's phone records and his internet history, I want you to find out how he contacted his daughter and I want you to reverse that method to find her. I also want Caroline Tully's phone records and I want you to trace her phone, we found your daughters phone but not your wife's." Briggs explained.

"Then I want someone to call District Attorney Bell, wake him up and get him down here!"

"Briggs, I do not know what is going on." Tully said, enunciating clearly. Fear building.

Wesley had to know better and Loren wasn't one to run from anything.

He thought about the worry in Wesley's voice when they'd been at the beachfront property, when he'd told Tully to get another car on his house.

What if someone had taken Loren?

"Briggs, listen to me, very carefully," Tully said quietly, in a tone that commanded respect and that even made Briggs stop shouting orders for a minute. "My daughter, even if she knew what was about to happen would never run. I can assure you that I had no contact with my family this evening and that there was no way for them to know what was in the works. If Loren is gone then she is missing and it would be a very smart life move on your part to start looking for her, not as a suspect but as…" Tully's voice cracked, "as a victim." he managed.

Briggs studied him for a while.

"Regardless of her status I am going to find your daughter." he said simply. "Do you have any suggestions where I should start looking?"

"Dillon," Tully said in relief looking past Briggs.

Dillon Howard stood next to Radburt, his eyes moving through the squad room.

He found Tully and started toward him.

Briggs turned to see what held Tully's interest.

When Dillon's eyes fixed on Briggs Tully thought he saw the glint of flames in the steely gaze.

"You idiot!" Dillon thundered across the room and Tully didn't think he'd ever been quite so glad to see his prospective son-in-law.

CHAPTER 27

By 3:30 AM they had established Loren Tully as missing.

Browser history and phone logs had cleared both Fineas and Caroline Tully, though Loren was still considered a person of interest.

Dillon Howard was more angry than concerned by the early hours of the morning. He'd already had one yelling match with his boss and things were not looking good professionally.

Fineas had tried going home, he'd talked things over with Caroline, wanting to comfort her but she'd sent him back to the station where he could be of more use.

All he'd done was sat at his desk or pace the room as the town was searched.

Briggs wasn't allowing him to join in, he understood why, but chafed all the same.

Furthermore the emphasis was being placed on finding her fleeing the county or state, not as a kidnap victim.

Tully racked his brain for possibilities.

The Jefferson's topped his mental list simply for being the craziest family in town and if they knew she'd been the one to rescue Wesley from their clutches the other night they might want a score settled, but Loren was not Wesley.

If they hurt her, the town would hang them, whereas they imagined free beer for life if they killed Wesley. It probably wasn't far from the truth.

Nonetheless he had ordered his men to take a look around the compound for any signs of foul play. They'd come back with nothing to report aside from finding the Camaro that had likely been at his house earlier and the fact that the James appeared to be gone. He had no option but to trust their judgment.

Radburt had allowed a cursory search of the Cobin property, though Wesley was apparently unavailable.

In fact Wesley was missing, too but Fineas had managed to keep that away from Briggs.

Wesley wouldn't do that to him, even though he was sure the boy had considered hiding Loren, not that she would have agreed either.

Of course, as Sheriff he had enemies but no one that seemed likely to kidnap his daughter, let alone while there were four men and two squad cars there watching.

The timing had to have something to do with it. It had to be someone connected with these murders and frankly that terrified him.

He didn't think he could handle the loss of Loren, he really didn't.

He checked the clock.

5:23 AM

He left his office to wear a fresh path through the squad room.

Bell and Howard were in the conference room again, the door was closed, but the window was rattling.

Briggs and a few of his men were going over maps of the area.

Suddenly, the conference door flew open and Dillon stormed out, his face was still, devoid of emotion.

"I cannot believe your complete and utter disregard for the rules, your lack of objectivity!" Bell shouted after him. "I hope you realize this means your career is over!" he bellowed.

Dillon's look was haunting. There was almost the ghost of a smile on his lips as he turned to face his boss.

The staring went on for a few seconds.

When Dillon next spoke it was soft and almost emotionless.

"I should have known." his voice just above a whisper, "All along and it was right in front of me."

Bell furrowed his eyebrows. He'd been expecting pleading, Howard begging him to reconsider. He was shaken by this turn, confused.

"Commander Briggs!" Dillon called.

Briggs looked up from the maps. Tully watched.

"Commander, if I were you I think I would have a team comb this man's car."

"What!" Bell demanded, flying into immediate outrage. "Absolutely not!"

"The vehicle that was used to dump Odette Boswell was a 2005-2009

Grand Cherokee was it not?" Dillon asked his voice still devoid of all emotion. "And the weapon in question, a .32 revolver?"

"That's circumstantial, do you hear me Howard! You will never work again!" Bell shouted.

"Finally there's the connection with the victim, I believe Mr. Bell's mother was one of the targets for one of Ms. Boswell's confidence schemes and I happen to know some people who would likely testify that Mr. Bell flirted with the victim while she was in town, in case you wanted a motive, too."

Tully stared, shocked.

Briggs almost looked amused as he mulled the situation over.

Dillon looked at Tully. The A.D.A.'s face was sallow; it was as if his will to exist was gone. Tully could relate, but Dillon's deflation seemed not entirely to do with Loren.

"Like you said, you could make a case against him."

Dillon left his boss arguing with Briggs over search warrants and looked out the front window.

Tully watched him, trying to puzzle together what he was seeing take place.

Did Dillon honestly expect the team to find some evidence in Bell's Jeep? Or was he just giving it back to his boss. Tully suspected the latter.

Outside the morning had gone from black to gray. In another hour the sun would be up.

And Wesley was still gone.

Somewhere a phone rang.

"Hey, Sheriff, it's for you." He heard someone say. "A Detective Jones." Tully couldn't explain the icy tendril of fear that almost paralyzed him.

Jones could just be getting back to him. But Jones also worked homicide.

Where was Loren?

Wesley came to still in the alley.

His whole body ached, likely the effects of whatever had happened when he'd blacked out. He didn't want to think about it.

The sky was gray, early light.

How long had he been out? Had it been exhaustion or was he drugged?

All questions for later he decided as he struggled to his feet and checked his pockets.

His wallet was gone but he could feel the SIG inside his jacket pocket.

He breathed a sigh of relief, simple robbery.

They'd also left the phone, probably knew it could be tracked.

He hurried back out to the street and was relieved to see the Mercedes still parked there. He tugged on the door handle. It opened and he fell into the car.

He could tell the glove box and center console had been rifled through but all he cared about was the silver key fob lying on the passenger side foot well.

He grabbed the fob and straightened in his seat, wrestled with the seatbelt, started the engine and jumped on the throttle.

Gray smoke came off in wisps from the rear Pirelli's as the car whipped around in a 180 degree turn and screamed off through town.

Wesley thought he knew the players.

He thought he knew what was going on and where to look next.

He knew who had killed his partner.

If not for Loren being missing Wesley would have turned left at Main Street and done something very stupid.

Instead he blasted toward the police station.

Tully was staring at the board in the conference room that established Wesley's professed guilt.

Four murders. Links to every one of them.

First Odette Boswell. They had the message, left on the voicemail of Y. Niboc's phone. The threat to reveal everything, the insinuated relationship, the meeting place, though they had yet to find anyone to place either Boswell or Cobin at the restaurant around 9:30, but then the place closed at 10:00 so there wouldn't been many witnesses. He had a call in to get the signal for Niboc's number traced. Maybe it would help.

Then there was Marana Epcot, the catalyst quite possibly, but it was of course the third, Missy Carlyle, who was filling in the blanks.

The burner phone that they'd been attempting to trace had originally been registered to her. She was the key.

She had called Epcot with some piece of information, had geared her up to go after Cobin again and then she'd gotten Boswell involved.

It was one of those phone calls that bothered Tully.

Loren's name on the list made him uncomfortable.

And now they had the second message and the fourth murder.

Lorenzo Washington was victim number four.

He had indeed been more than Odette Boswell's landlord. He was her partner in crime.

With the amount of paperwork he had in his possession they appeared to be running a con on the roommate, Lisa Cuthard. Apparently Boswell was holding off making the play until she was done with Wesley. That also explained the picture of Wesley and Odette, hadn't Jake said something about the guy being into Photoshop? At some point she must have filled Washington in because of the threatening new message they'd just pulled from Mr. Niboc's voicemail.

A couple of hours ago he was shot and killed with what was looking to be the same .45 that had killed Missy.

Because both Loren and Wesley had vanished, suspicion was high and Briggs wanted both of them brought in.

For Missy's murder Dillon had only been able to give Loren a partial alibi. It was physically possible she had driven to the park and shot Missy before coming home, but the whole idea was too absurd to be given any credence.

Tully suspected that Briggs had put Loren in the spotlight to see how Cobin would react.

Now she was gone.

If it was somehow related to Briggs directing attention to her Tully didn't know what he'd do to the man.

Tully reviewed the evidence, looking for only things he might find significant. He didn't like what he was beginning to see.

As the killings progressed, they became more in sync with Wesley's personality.

Boswell was weirdly removed from the others. First, she had been abducted, bound, driven to the beach and then executed. The gun was likely a .32 revolver.

Wesley didn't like revolvers.

Fredrickson's revised TOD allowed for the possibility that Cobin had shot Boswell then switched cars and gotten involved with the Jefferson's. It would have given him an alibi.

The problem was that the carpet fibers and tire impressions were from the wrong model year for Cobin's new Jeep.

Then Epcot; it was fast, a single shot to the chest with a nine-millimeter. The gun was more in character.

Next, Missy; shot three times with a .45. Clearly there had been an escalation as well as rage. The site was out of the way but this murder had been in the day time.

They'd recovered her cell phone and ran the SIM card to trace her calls, that wasn't something Wesley would have missed or overlooked.

Now Briggs would have to add Bell to his suspect pool but he was only good for the first murder.

Of course, they could be dealing with two or even three different killers?

Tully pushed himself, trying to force some new connection to appear, something he'd missed; something to save Loren.

Where was Wesley now?

He would have felt better if he knew where the kid was and that he could account for himself that whole night.

Trust might have been rekindled, but Fineas was still a cop and Cobin had no hard evidence to exonerate him.

He needed to get some air.

Tully stood on the sidewalk and looked at the impound lot.

He noticed dimly that the Mercedes was gone.

So that had been what Jake had been up to.

Tully was surprised and almost a little heartened by the fact that Barry and Cobin had evidently stood each other's company.

"Fineas," Tully turned to see Barry coming toward him, emotions playing across his face.

It was then that Tully realized Barry could have killed Cobin and dumped the car, thus accounting for both of them being missing.

"The state lab just called about a tire tread at the latest crime scene." he said without much excitement in his voice.

Tully let himself hope it might be some clue as to where Loren was.

"That was fast." he said.

"The tread pattern is from Pirelli P-Zeros." Jake said flatly.

Tully frowned. Those were high end tires.

"Optional OEM tires, care to guess on what car?"

Tully felt a weight in the pit of his stomach.

"A Mercedes-Benz C63. I'm willing to bet that Cobin is the only one for at least two counties with one of those."

"It's convenient," Tully said slowly.

"It's evidence!"

"It's obvious," Tully objected. "He knows we can pull information like that off a tread, he wouldn't be that careless!"

"I've driven that car, it's not that difficult to do accidentally. He could also make it there and back easily."

"Do you know where he is?" Tully asked, wondering again if Barry might have done something with him.

"Yes," Jake said and pointed down the road.

The black Mercedes was moving fast, but not very far past the speed limit, it whipped into the parking lot and made straight for them.

Wesley saw Fineas and Jake outside the station and pulled up to the sidewalk. He pushed open his door and got out, looking at the two men.

"Where have you been?" Barry demanded. Fineas just stared at him with a haunted expression. In it Wesley read the pain, the fear, the need. He knew what it all meant.

"Get in." was all he said.

"What are you hoping to accomplish?" Barry asked as Fineas headed for the passenger side door.

"I can't stay here and watch from the sidelines anymore." Fineas said. If Wesley was the kidnapper, going with him was the fastest means of getting to Loren.

"But what about what the lab found?" Barry asked as Cobin shut his door.

"It's no smoking gun." Tully said and dropped into the car. "Find other options!"

Frustrated, Barry watched the Mercedes pull away for the second time that morning.

He debated following, but chose instead to go back inside.

He wondered darkly if he would ever see his boss again.

CHAPTER 28

Fineas was silent as Cobin piloted the Mercedes west, toward the outskirts of town.

He didn't know what to say, and, since Cobin seemed to know where he was going he didn't see a need to interject anything. Either he'd figured out where Loren was or he'd taken her, in which case the outcomes was the same.

He thought about the murder board in the conference room, about the tire treads possibly coming from the car he now rode in.

At that precise moment he didn't care.

"We're going to get her back." Cobin said, breaking the silence as they left the last house behind and accelerated up toward Route 3.

"Is she safe?" Fineas found himself asking.

"No." Cobin said. He slowed the car as the road dead ended at Route 3.

He turned left, south, away from his house.

"Where are we going?" Fineas asked.

"I don't know yet."

Fineas blinked.

"What do you mean you don't know yet?"

"I'm still waiting on that call."

"What?" Fineas asked in confusion. He'd assumed Cobin had a destination in mind as he was assuming that he'd taken Loren there. He realized suddenly he had drawn that conclusion with his sleep deprived and stress addled brain it had reverted to familiar patterns. He was Cobin again and possibly the murderer both then and now, even though he hadn't even been the one to suspect Cobin, Wesley, in the first place.

"There's been another murder." Fineas said.

"Let me guess, Lorenzo Washington."

"I would much rather you hadn't known that." Fineas said.

"I didn't kill him."

"He left you a voicemail."

Wesley eyed Fineas strangely.

"No, he didn't."

"I heard the recording, or are you not Mr. Y Niboc?"

"Niboc?" Wesley asked.

"Registered to your company, don't deny it."

"I wasn't going to deny it, that's my line but I never got that message."

Fineas' phone rang.

"Tully," he answered.

"Hey, Tully it's Mario," the lab technician said.

"Do you have that trace?"

"Yeah, yeah, and a good morning to you too, or what about thank you for coming in at an ungodly hour and bending the rules for me Mario, you're the best." Mario said.

"Sorry, but this is serious."

"Yeah, yeah, so that number you want is still transmitting but it's on the move now."

"Can you trace it and give me directions?"

"Yeah." Fineas heard a keyboard clatter in the background.

"Huh," Mario muttered.

"What?"

"You're right on top of it." The tech said.

"Thanks, that's all I needed."

"You know it's a data line?" Mario asked.

"A what?" Fineas asked.

"It's a data line." Mario repeated. "It isn't used for voice calls. That's why I had such a hard time on the lookup, I mean this took me like fifteen minutes because it only transmits intermittently."

"Back up, what do you mean it's not for voice calls?"

"He means you just traced my phone through the 4G data connection." Wesley said. "Is that the number the voicemails were left on?" he asked.

Fineas look was the only answer he needed.

"I love that phone." Wesley muttered.

Barry made his way back into the station.

He noticed that everyone there seemed to be moving lethargically, likely the result of little to no sleep the past night. For him he was well past 24 hours without shut eye.

Judgment and decision making abilities would deteriorate, as would tempers, if they kept this up. Maybe that's why he hadn't dragged Cobin in or tried to stop Tully or followed them.

He made his way back into the squad room and turned right toward the secondary desk where Lance Imahara was looking through an oversized envelope, one of the kind they kept personal effects in. He was on his way to the break room for yet another cup of coffee, but he stopped as Imahara upended the envelope on the counter. A key fell out and clattered on the Formica surface.

Cobin, W

He read upside down.

Cobin had forgotten something.

Barry looked closely at the key.

The Jeep emblem was easy to see, and he assumed that it must have somehow slipped off Cobin's ring of keys. Then he realized the problem; Cobin's Jeep didn't use a traditional key.

He studied it anew and glanced down the hall to the interrogation room.

He picked up the key without a word and headed for the parking lot.

Outside he crossed over to the District Attorney's Grand Cherokee.

This is crazy! he thought.

But still he stood there, heart hammering.

He slipped it into the lock.

He was surprised by his reluctance to try it. He didn't think there was any love lost for Cobin; he knew what he'd done and even though he'd helped him out tonight it was for a greater good, or so he'd thought.

With a calming breath he turned the key.

The door unlocked.

Wesley brought the Mercedes to a halt pointing south on Route 3.

"Why are we stopping?" Tully asked, looking around the area for some sign.

"I still don't know which way to go." Wesley explained. "We could be heading in the wrong direction, it's safer this way."

Fineas frowned, he didn't like this idea. He had been more at ease when they were driving too fast.

"How long are we supposed to wait?" he asked.

His phone rang.

Back at the station fresh pandemonium had broken out as Briggs began shouting new orders and telling Radburt about his client's guilt.

Barry tried to consider the situation dispassionately but he kept thinking about Tully getting in the car with Cobin. He considered his options.

He had to find them!

Briggs finally issued a coherent order for someone to check the power seat controls for fingerprints since Wesley was noticeably taller than the district attorney.

Barry didn't wait for the results. He snatched the keys to one of the cruisers and hurried to the parking lot.

Tully pressed the green talk button on his phone.

"Tully, here." he said.

"Fineas, I have the property records you wanted."

"Casale?" he asked. "I didn't ask for a property record." he continued in confusion.

"Oh, yeah, that's me." Wesley interjected.

Deanna sighed. "Are you with him? Put me on speaker."

Fineas sighed and pressed the speaker button, wondering why Wesley insisted on being such a tightlipped maverick.

"For the record, Mr. Cobin, bringing up the Cheesesteak incident was not very professional."

"Yeah, sorry about that, I wanted to make sure you knew who it was."

"You know what?" Fineas said. "I'm not even going to ask."

"Did you find the records I was looking for?" Wesley asked.

"Eventually, sure. You were right there's a family farm off County Route 3. Not much to tell you except the taxes are paid every year. I wouldn't say it was hidden but he's not exactly shouting about it from the rooftops, nothing on social networks or anything like that."

"What's the exact location?" Wesley asked.

"About three miles north of town, there's a turn off to the left, looks like an old road but there are several other residences so it should be traversable. It's the second driveway on the right, leads uphill to a clearing and there's a farmhouse or something, odd location since there's not much in the way of farmable land."

"Thank you." Wesley said to Casale then added to Tully. "Hang on."

He dropped the car back into manual mode, killed the driver aids, and eased quickly onto the accelerator.

The Mercedes bugled as the nose lifted slightly, building speed.

"That's behind us!" Fineas said quickly.

"I know." Wesley said calmly then flicked the steering wheel right, clipping the gravel verge, then spun the wheel hard left and matted the throttle. The big V-8 bellowed and the back of the car kicked around as Fineas struggled to hold onto something through the 180 degree turn. Wesley backed off the throttle only for a second to let the tires settle, then pulled the upshift paddle and returned hard to the gas. The Benz charged ahead with another savage bellow as Wesley aimed for Route 3 North.

"I take it he's driving." Casale shouted over the bellow of the Mercedes.

"Yeah, thanks, I'll call you back." Fineas said and hung up.

As the speedometer passed 60 a siren began to wail and the road, still in shadow, lit up in alternating patterns of blue and red before them.

Fineas looked over at Wesley.

"Legal?" he asked redundantly.

"You have to admit useful and more responsible than the alternative." Wesley said.

They took a fast corner and as Wesley backed off the throttle the Mercedes popped and snarled on the overrun.

Tully decided even if Cobin wasn't unhinged, his car certainly was.

When they blasted through the stop sign at the junction of route 3 north and south Wesley pressed the trip computer reset.

The digital readout then began ticking off the miles.

"Put it up on the screen!" Commander Briggs snapped.

They'd found an almost perfect print on the underside of the power controls for the seat. It had been digitized and now they were loading it next to one of Wesley's on the big screen in the conference room.

Radburt stood next to Briggs while everyone else attempted to crowd into the small room.

Radburt ran his eyes around the crowd while the technician messed with getting a laptop to mirror its display on the television.

He noticed two missing faces, Jake Barry and Dillon Howard, he wondered if they were going to be a problem.

The TV jumped to life and the fingerprint pulled from the Jeep appeared on the left half of the screen, on the right Wesley's print appeared.

"Mirror it!" Briggs snapped as the prints were opposed to one another. "Index finger." he ordered and the print changed. He smiled broadly.

"It's Cobin's!" he said and turned to Radburt. "See your client is guilty, I'm issuing an arrest warrant immediately!" The Commander said smugly.

"I wouldn't do that." Radburt said, breaking into a smile of his own.

Brigg's grin faltered. "What do you mean?" he demanded. "The prints are almost a perfect match!"

"Precisely. It's backwards." Radburt said pointing to the screen. "Un-mirror it" he ordered. The tech looked from Radburt to Briggs. Radburt narrowed his eyes and the tech tapped the keyboard.

Someone in the room gasped. "He's right!"

"What!" Briggs demanded.

"That is Wesley's fingerprint, but he couldn't have left it because it's backwards."

Briggs studied the mirror image for a moment.

"No, it's because…" he imagined fingerprinting Cobin, then overlaid that with the man working the power seat controls and his face went slack.

"I would say it exonerates him, as clearly someone is trying to frame him." Radburt pressed.

Briggs just stared at the screen, unwilling to concede but seeing his case beginning to unravel.

"Commander, I would suggest you begin looking at people with access to the District Attorney's vehicle." Radburt took great pleasure in saying.

CHAPTER 29

Wesley drove flat out, glancing down to check their progress while the AMG V-8 competed with the siren for aural dominance.

Because the road was more or less a straight run, because the police lights were flashing and because the most important thing in the world for both men was finding Loren, the Mercedes was allowed to run unchecked well past 130 miles per hour.

Fineas hoped the blare of the illegally obtained siren kept animals from charging into the road and killing them both.

He had questions, many of them, but now did not seem to be the time for them.

At 2.9 miles, Wesley hit the brakes, not hard enough to engage the ABS, but enough to test that the seatbelts were still locking on cue.

The speedometer fell below 100 and both occupants began searching the left side of the road for signs of a driveway.

They found it at 3.1 miles.

Wesley added pressure to the brake pedal and judged the distance, then lightly flicked the wheel again and blipped the throttle. The tail rotated appropriately and they lurched onto the gravel side road.

Immediately Wesley began to accelerate cautiously as gravel rattled and pinged around the wheel wells and off the floor pan. He didn't even notice the sound.

"Alright, you want to tell me what we're doing?" Fineas asked.

"Getting Loren, the whole thing was planned and executed. It went without a hitch until people stopped getting along."

"Is there a short version?" Fineas asked wincing as they were jarred as the wheel hit a rut.

"James Jefferson killed Mike. He was the one having the affair with Missy." Wesley said.

He slowed the car to an agonizing crawl as they lurched up a three inch split.

He realized they were still in sport mode, and switched the suspension over to comfort, then drove faster.

"How do you know that?"

"He speaks Portuguese."

"So?"

"Remember how I said the guy who hit me over the head said something?"

Wesley reached his right hand into his jacket and retrieved his phone, which he handed to Fineas.

Fineas turned on the phone and slid the unlock ring across the screen.

"'Say hello to your father'? This is what he said to you?"

"Yes."

"So it's been James this whole time?"

"He's working with Howard."

Fineas swallowed, he didn't like Dillon as the villain simply because it was convenient for Wesley.

"Obviously, Howard wanted me convicted for the murder, as did Jefferson, at some point they got together. I'm assuming the Jefferson's did the killing. Maybe Howard didn't know what was going on entirely until he was involved." Wesley grunted as he whacked his head against his window.

"They staged the murders, Howard prosecuted."

"You know this how?"

"Piece by piece, Dillon is involved. He's the one that took Loren."

"Impossible!" Fineas said.

"The only reason Loren wouldn't have fought is if she knew the person. There was no struggle, I checked, and the back gate was unlocked. I don't know what he planned on doing, but then the Jefferson's crossed him. I think they got him to kill Washington to make sure he wouldn't get away, then they grabbed Loren and now they're willing to kill her."

Fineas felt his blood freeze at the thought.

He watched Cobin wrestle the car up the driveway and wondered if he could tell a lie from the truth anymore.

Suddenly the second driveway appeared, branching off on the right.

Wesley turned the wheel and added more power.

The hill could be slick, if so the car might get stuck. They couldn't afford the time.

He gunned the engine and they sailed up the hill.

The house was clearly run down and long deserted.

Wesley accelerated right up to the front door then braked hard.

He worried for a minute that they would slide into the house then the tires found some resistance and the car slid to a halt. He set the parking brake and got out of the car, followed by Fineas.

Wesley ran his eyes around the ramshackle house and the yard in front of it.

The grass was sparse and straggly, shrubs had long ago run wild and what might have at one time been a garden was a jagged pile of fence posts.

Heading to the front door Wesley reached inside his jacket and unzipped the pocket that held his gun. He removed the SIG and took up his position, ready to go high.

Fineas joined him, his gun drawn, hunched low. He nodded.

Though they'd seldom used the armed approach to breach a house, they had practiced it.

Wesley reached for the old knob and forced the door open.

It fell in with a shriek of hinges then Wesley entered, fast and high, bringing his gun to bear.

The foyer was largely empty but Wesley almost squeezed off a shot at a full length mirror on the opposite wall.

"Clear." he said catching himself and moving to the archway.

Inside it was surprisingly well lit, thanks to gaping holes in the roof and the mirrors.

There were mirrors on at least every wall.

Wesley remembered what Dillon had said about his grandfather.

Tricks with mirrors.

Wesley led the way deeper into the house, the floor creaking and groaning with each step.

At the edge of the hall Wesley called out since it was obvious they would not have the element of surprise.

"Loren!"

He waited.

The hallway looked easily defendable, if they met trouble it would be better faced here.

"Loren!" he yelled again.

The house was ominously quiet.

Deathly quiet.

There were stairs leading down in one corner.

"I'm going down." Wesley said and before Fineas could protest about splitting up he was heading down the stairs, pulling a flashlight from his pocket, one handed, SIG held firmly in the other.

Fineas continued with the upstairs.

He cleared three rooms. The house had been large and strangely laid out, with rooms leading into rooms haphazardly.

"Loren, sweetie?" he called. Still nothing.

His heart was constricting.

Behind him he heard the floor groan and he turned, expecting Wesley but keeping his gun at the ready in case it was not.

He made his way to the last room, trying to step lightly, only eliciting quiet protests from the floor.

At the doorway he paused, then entered the next room, leading with his gun.

The room was empty save for a single door.

It looked like a closet and the sight of it made Fineas' stomach twist anew.

With every increasing dread he crossed to it.

His left hand closed on the knob, right hand still holding the Glock at the ready, though the gun trembled noticeably.

He didn't know why he felt with such certainty that he was about to find a body, but he did.

Taking a breath he prayed that it wasn't Loren then opened the door.

The closet was empty.

Wesley descended the stairs carefully, hugging the wall as much as possible.

It was obvious this had been the cellar at one time and he didn't trust the stairs to have weathered time quite so well.

It was dark, but light still shone through the gaps in the upstairs floor boards.

He used his flashlight to sweep the base of the stairs, swinging his SIG with the beam.

The floor was stone at the bottom and it was possible to move without too much noise, aside from the rustle of detritus that had collected on the floor, leaves and other debris that had blown in through the gaping roof.

The cellar had been partitioned off into separate rooms, making the search more difficult.

He ran his flashlight along one wall and suddenly the whole room lit with a flash.

Startled, he looked for some enemy then he realized it was just another collection of mirrors.

Dillon hadn't been lying.

The rules told him to start with the first door he came to but instinct told him to skip it. The same with the next door.

The third door Wesley forced open and looked into a small room.

There were some crates stacked in the corner and on the rear wall there was another door. This one had a deadbolt on it.

In the flashlight beam it gleamed.

The lock was new.

"Loren!" Wesley yelled. "Loren, can you hear me!"

He thought he heard a muffled response but couldn't be sure, it could have been his imagination, and now his heart was hammering in his ears, drowning out most everything else.

"Stay back!" he yelled and lined up to ram the door.

The lock may have been new and the old door could have been reinforced but he planned on tearing the hasp from the wall.

He slammed into the door with his shoulder and decided this wall must have been anchored in stone.

"Get back and cover your eyes!" he ordered then placed the SIG over the hasp.

He looked away and squeezed the trigger.

The brick wall exploded.

The shot brought Fineas running.

In his panic to get downstairs he must have taken a wrong turn because he went from the old kitchen back to the entry foyer.

He ran down the short hallway back to where they found the stairs.

As he reached the stairs he though he heard the sound of an engine outside, and he hesitated, looking back toward the front door. He didn't want to get trapped in the basement of this place.

He took a breath and plunged down the stairs.

Loren was bound, gagged and blind folded.

It was all Wesley could do not to rush to her and free her immediately instead he forced himself to clear the small room.

She was lying on an old mattress, there was a broken wooden dining chair in one corner and three mirrors, one on each wall aside from the wall the door was on.

He noticed that they were angled strangely, almost as if designed not to catch the light. They were also polished, shining like new unlike the other mirrors in the house which had cracked and grimed over.

The room was clear and Wesley grabbed his pocket knife and crossed over to Loren, setting the SIG on the floor.

He pulled the blindfold first, then the gag.

Loren was stoically not crying but she collapsed into his arms as soon as he let her.

She put her still bound hands behind his head and he held her.

"Wes," she said, though clenched teeth.

They both fought tears as they clung to each other, reassurance that this was real.

Wesley forced himself to pull away from the embrace. "Do you know who took you?" He had to remain on topic.

"They jumped Dillon in an alley, I don't know exactly, they had masks. I knew it was… Dillon said… Is he alright?"

"He's fine," Wesley said coldly. "Just fine."

"I think they threatened him and they said something else, something I didn't get. They were going to kill me, weren't they?"

"You're safe now." he said and held her tight again, never wanting to let go. Just the thought of losing her forever was something he couldn't face.

"Is that all they said?" he asked.

This time it was Loren who pulled back. She studied him, "They…" she broke off. "They said something about you…" she said slowly, unsurely and Wesley feared he knew what it was.

He sawed through Loren's bonds and stood up slowly, snagging the SIG in his right hand.

"Wesley…" Loren said slowly, her expression slipping towards terrified.

Wesley brought the SIG up.

CHAPTER 30

Tully reached the bottom of the stairs and looking down the hallway.

He was momentarily paralyzed by what he saw.

Wesley was aiming his SIG at Loren.

The whole scene played out in slow motion.

Wesley brought the gun up, though the distance was great Fineas though he saw a bewildered expression on his daughters face.

Fineas brought his gun to bear on Wesley but he couldn't believe his eyes.

Then the gun fired three times.

Just like Missy he thought detachedly.

Fineas squeezed off two rounds, even as his conscious brain screamed at him not to.

But Wesley had just shot Loren!

Again, his world had been completely torn apart.

And then, Wesley shattered.

Even as he ran toward the end of the hall Fineas' brain finally gave him an explanation.

He'd shot a mirror.

When he realized that he stopped and whirled around, looking for Wesley.

The hallway was empty.

"Loren!" Fineas yelled, hearing his voice echo around him he realized it was more a scream of desperation.

He tried the door nearest to him and found it locked. He'd missed one door but ran down to the next.

It was open and this door lead into another, also open.

In that room there was a stained mattress and glass fragments.

"Loren!" he wailed.

He moved on down the hall at a run but that was the only door open.

He returned and crossed the small first room to the second room behind it.

Fineas didn't catch the details, just the stained mattress, darkly stained, and the shattered mirror.

Then he noticed the hole in the wall behind the mirror and crossed to it.

He pressed against the wall and the whole panel moved revealing a narrow passageway.

It was dark and dank, but then so was most of the basement.

It was the only option, the only way Wesley could have gone.

But where was Loren?

Fineas ran down the passage.

Wesley held the SIG out ahead of him as he rounded the right rear corner of the house.

He'd seen him come this way and knew his quarry was close.

He wondered how the standoff would go and he was relieved Loren wouldn't be there to see it. At least he hoped she wouldn't come back. The emotional toll would be too great and he couldn't honestly say he knew what her decision would be when faced with the two of them.

Then Wesley saw him, up a hill, heading for the trees.

Wesley gave chase and ran in an arc, bringing himself around in front of the fleeing form of Dillon Howard.

"Stop right there!" Wesley ordered and brought the SIG up, aiming for Dillon's chest.

The A.D.A. froze, but only for a split second before bringing his own pistol to bear.

Wesley stared down the barrel of the Beretta and tired not to swallow visibly.

"Drop it." Wesley ordered. "You can shoot me but you're not going to throw off my aim." He sounded convincing but he knew at this close range there would be no split second between trigger and impact and it was very unlikely Dillon would miss as he clutched his gun, two handed.

Wesley was willing to bet it was the same .45 that had been used on Missy and Lorenzo Washington. The gun that they were trying to pass off as his.

Wesley wanted to improve his stance but he was afraid moving might prompt Dillon to shoot.

"You can't get away with this," Dillon said, a savage look on his face. "You can't kill without impunity, there will be consequences."

"Why the act?" Wesley asked. "It's just the two of us and we both know I didn't kill them."

"Do you really expect me to believe that?" Dillon demanded. "You know, I could shoot you right now and walk away the hero?"

Wesley stayed quiet because Dillon might have been right. He'd noticed a subtle change in Fineas in the car. Maybe it was just fatigue, but there had been a shift in their relationship again.

In the back of his mind he wrestled with the thought.

Maybe this would be for the better?

Maybe giving up and letting Dillon take him down would solve everyone's problems. The catalyst would be gone. He hadn't chosen this life, these events, but the results were the same...

Wesley opened his mouth, but Fineas cut him off.

"Wesley, drop it!" both Wesley and Dillon turned to look at Fineas, his own gun drawn and aimed at Wesley.

"It's not me," Wesley said immediately. "It's him."

"I don't care who it is." Fineas said his voice cracking. "I want both of you to drop your guns!"

"I'm afraid that's not something I'm about to do Fineas." Dillon said. "I'm sure you could take this lying, murdering, crazed lunatic out, but not before I hit the ground."

"I didn't do it." Wesley said firmly then abruptly, "What are you doing here Dillon?"

"I'm looking for Loren, I got a phone call that said to meet the killer out here because he had Loren, and who do I find but you?"

"Wesley, drop the gun." Fineas said, Wesley recognized the scolding tone from his younger years and felt his heart clench.

"Fineas, it's not me!" Wesley said, sounding more like a child.

Fineas struggled to keep his hand steady, trying to process what he'd just seen. But he didn't trust his eyes.

Wesley couldn't have shot Loren!

"Where's Loren?" Dillon asked and Wesley thought he understood.

A few tricks, a lot to do with mirrors and deception...

Those words had proved to be a threat.

Thinking back to the cellar room, Wesley knew why Fineas was aiming at him.

It could be explained, that was easy enough, and yet it wasn't.

His vision began to cloud as tears formed in the corners of his eyes.

He knew where this was ending.

"Wesley. Please." It was Fineas, pleading with him.

Wesley wondered how he'd done it.

How he'd been set up. He saw his options.

Loren was alive, he knew that.

She loved Dillon, he'd watch out for her.

He'd killed for her after all.

Wesley shut his eyes and let out a final shuddering breath.

In those last seconds choosing to stop fighting, to give in; he was the outlier in a world seeking normality.

"One life owed," he whispered and turned his gun on Fineas.

As a police officer, Wesley knew that Fineas' reaction would be to shoot. It was all he could do.

Tully fired twice.

The shots closely spaced and reactionary. He gasped after the last shot had been squeezed off.

"What the hell were you thinking!" he yelled at Wesley, as the boy fell to the ground.

He rushed forwards.

"It would have been easier." Wesley said, shakily.

"Easier for who?" Fineas asked, biting back tears and bile. "Don't you think I would have eventually found out?"

Blood pooled around Wesley's hand as he tried to staunch the bleeding, past training kicking in.

Fineas breathed heavily.

His aim had fortunately been off and he hadn't meant to squeezed off two rounds. Only one had found its mark. But it only took one.

Silently he cursed himself.

He'd known it was coming and he thought he could have moved quick enough, but he hadn't.

He put his hand over Wesley's and applied pressure. He couldn't tell whose hand was shaking worse.

"You were going to let that happen to Loren?" Fineas asked, because he knew she wasn't dead; Wesley hadn't shot her.

His eyes had been wrong.

He'd come to realize that fully in these last horrible seconds. His mental lethargy had cleared with the shock, too late to steady his hand.

"I thought it would be over. I thought he was just after me." Wesley said sadly.

"Yeah, while murdering three people." Fineas said and grimaced as he examined the wound's location. "I don't want Loren seeing this."

He looked up at Wesley who was with him, crouched over the collapsed form of Dillon Howard.

"You take her to the car and call the paramedics." Fineas ordered.

Wesley nodded and slipped his hand out from under Fineas'. He looked at the blood and wished he could wipe them clean.

"He didn't shoot me." Wesley said as he stood. "He's involved in killing four people and then doesn't shoot me on sight?"

"Now? Really?" Fineas asked.

"He was the puppet. James was behind this, do you think he's here?" Wesley asked, still clutching the SIG.

Fineas really didn't want to think about anything at the moment. He was still having trouble wrapping his head around what had just played out.

He'd shot Dillon.

He'd gone with his heart and now he'd shot his daughter's fiancée.

"I don't know! Fineas said. "James wouldn't do it himself."

"No," Wesley agreed. "He probably had someone in the department." He tightened his grip on the gun and turned to head for the car.

The gunshot surprised both of them; Wesley, the more so as he staggered back under the force and sting of the round.

His chest burned.

Already he felt blood, hot and sticky on his skin.

He didn't make a sound; just slowly fell to his knees.

He thought of heroes of fiction taking a few in the chest, wincing, staggering on. But then, he'd never claimed to be a hero, he thought, as the world went black around the edges.

Tully grabbed up his gun and spun around to see the shooter.

It was Jake.

"Drop it!" he yelled at his deputy, who looked surprised and immediately lowered his sidearm and set it on the ground, he stood raising his hands.

"It's just me." he said. "You're safe now boss."

"Safe?" Tully asked incredulously.

"Let's get Howard to the hospital. Loren's at the car, she's already made the call." Tully forced himself to breathe. Wesley had thought Dillon had an accomplice, possibly in the department.

Jake would be perfect, possibly the only other person who hated Wesley as much as Dillon.

But that knowledge was offset by the few flashes of investigative integrity Jake had exhibited over the past few days.

He needed time to sort this out and now time was the one thing he did not have with two men bleeding out behind him.

He either had to cuff Barry, shoot him, or trust him.

"It wasn't Wesley, Jake, it was Howard!"

"What?" Jake asked, appearing genuinely surprised.

"Wesley was innocent."

"No, the evidence, he had a key to... No, no, no." Tully nodded and lowered his weapon. Jake was running a hand through his hair with an expression of shock and horror that couldn't be faked.

"Get over here and take care of Howard." Tully ordered. "Barry! Now!" he added when Jake didn't snap to. He hoped he got through but didn't have time to waste. He hurried over to Wesley and dropped to the ground. In doing so he felt a pang at abandoning Howard since he was the one who had pulled the trigger but he wasn't about to risk anything happening to Wesley, not after what they'd just been through.

It was another chest wound, fortunately Jake's aim hadn't been pinpoint accurate but that just meant Wesley's heart was continuing to pump blood outside his body.

They'd need a med-evac chopper, especially this far out in the woods.

He was debating what to do when he felt Wesley's hand grasp his. He looked down and saw Wesley's eyes open and focused on him.

"Does it hurt?" he asked.

"Yes..." Wesley said through clenched teeth.

"Good, good." Tully said. "Loren!"

Wesley tightened his grip and Tully knew he was trying to protest but this wasn't the time. Tully would have done anything to not have Loren see this, but it was life and death. He needed her.

"Why... didn't I... wear... a vest?" Wesley gasped. His grasp started to weaken and Fineas felt the tremor in his hand.

He was going into shock.

"Wes, hang on, we'll get you out of here in a minute. If I need to drive your car is there anything I should know?" he asked, trying to keep Wesley's mind active.

"Sure…" he winced. "Let… Loren drive."

Fineas almost smiled.

Wesley grimaced. "Tell… Loren… I…" Fineas smiled encouragingly.

"Tell her?" he prompted. Wesley's eyes were becoming unfocused.

"Tell her… I'm sorry." Wesley's eyelids fluttered shut.

Loren didn't know how long she lay on the stinking mattress. Hours to be sure, but hours felt like days.

Her memory was patchy but she remembered Dillon's pleading with her, the urgency to leave, her reluctance.

She remembered getting to the car, the drive across town, the alley and then the men…

After that her memory ceased, she knew they'd jumped Dillon and taken her to a van.

She'd been blind folded then they drove for a while.

She'd ended up locked in that room wondering who was after her and if she'd ever see her family again.

Then she'd heard Wesley, then her father, the sound of floor boards creaking above her, then Wesley closer and closer.

She realized then that she'd expected Wesley would be the one to find her, wanted him to be the one…

She'd strained against the gag trying to call out, to respond then she'd begun pounding the floor with her feet.

Wesley told her to stay back, then the sound of a single shot, deafening after so long with silence.

Then the hood came off and there he was.

She'd hugged him and he'd hugged her back and in his embrace she'd felt safe. It felt hauntingly right and she hadn't cared at that moment about anything outside of them.

He asked what had happened and she'd asked about Dillon.

His reply concerned her.

"He's fine, just fine." he'd said and there was a cold contempt in his words that mere jealousy couldn't have explained away.

She tried defending her fiancée. "I think they threatened him and they said something else, something I didn't get." She assumed the answer was in there, maybe Dillon hadn't said anything?

"They were going to kill me, weren't they?" she'd asked as emotions took over.

"You're safe now." Wesley had assured her. "Did they say anything else?"

His question prompted something, she remembered Wesley's name in the conversation.

"They said something about you..." she said and watched a subtle change of expression as Wesley sliced the bindings on her ankles, then wrists.

It was then she saw the face in the mirror.

It has a ghastly and contorted pale shape. Dark eyes stared down at them and she nearly froze.

"Wesley..." she managed.

Wesley saw the direction of her gaze and stood up, then turned, bringing his gun up.

"Cover your face!" Wesley hissed and unleashed three rounds into the glass.

The mirror shattered and most of the shards fell straight down.

Somewhere in the house two more shots sounded.

Wesley looked back through the doorway.

Then crossed over to the full length mirror he'd destroyed.

About head height there was a hole in the wall, letting someone see into the cellar room, beyond it was a dark tunnel.

Wesley kicked at the wall and immediately a panel, a door, opened.

"Come on!" he called to her and aimed his light down the narrow passage.

Something crashed down the passage way, it sounded like doors closing.

Wesley led the way at a run and Loren followed.

They reached the end of the corridor. Above them were two doors in the ceiling, steps led to them.

Wesley took a couple of steps and used his left hand to push open one of the doors, in his right he held the gun.

No menacing figure lurked and Wesley climbed up the last steps.

Loren followed.

"Go to the car and lock yourself in." Wesley told her and handed over the key fob. "Don't let anyone in except for me or your dad, understand?"

"But, Wes..."

"Just do it, okay?" Wesley pleaded, eyes looking away from the house.

"Dad or you." Loren said with a nod and took the keys.

"Loren, I..."

"Yeah, I know." Loren said, cutting him off, then she hurried around the side of the house and Wesley sprinted off.

Loren glanced over her shoulder as she neared the front corner of the house.

There was the black Mercedes, sinister and imposing, but behind it was her dad's Ford. Standing next to it was Jake Barry.

"Loren!" he said and started toward her.

Me or your Dad...

"Jake," she said and edged toward the Mercedes.

"You're alright?" he asked. His concern seemed genuine.

"More or less, I'll be fine."

"Where are they?" he asked.

"There's someone else, behind the house." she said.

"Stay here, call the station and get back up!" Barry ordered and drew his sidearm, then sprinted around the house toward the hill.

Loren opened the door and got into the driver's seat.

She pressed the lock button and then reached for her phone, which of course was still at the house.

She turned, studied the buttons on the steering wheel then the dash, she turned on the ignition and pressed the green phone button hoping that Wesley's phone was synced to the car.

A dial tone played over the speakers, she punched in the numbers to the station using the keypad.

The call was connected but the phone rang on and on.

Then she heard the gun shots.

One, two... silence, a terrifying silence.

She drummed her hands on the steering wheel.

Another pop of gunfire.

She opened the door and listened to the stillness.

And then she heard her father's voice calling to her.

Terrified, she rounded the house and ran up the hill.

Her imagination played out horrific scenes, but this time the truth was worse than her imagination could ever have summoned.

CHAPTER 31

When Wesley Cobin next opened his eyes he found himself staring up at Jake Barry.

It was not the greeting he had hoped for and for a moment wondered if hell was a real place.

Then he recognized the generic appearance of the room beyond his old tormenter as a room in the County General Hospital.

"You shot me." Wesley said slowly refocusing on the deputy.

"Yeah." Barry said sheepishly.

"It hurt."

"Again, sorry about that."

"Good thing… you can't shoot."

"Don't be mean about it."

Wesley grimaced as he tried to inch up straighter. Jake stepped forwards to help but Wesley shook his head. "Is Loren okay?" he asked after getting his thoughts in order.

"Yeah, she's fine, don't worry."

Wesley nodded.

"Good thing you weren't the guy," he said. "Or we'd all be dead." Barry didn't comment.

"Where is Loren?" Wesley asked.

Barry looked uncomfortable. "She's around." he said.

"Around here?" Wesley asked.

"Sure."

Wesley tried sitting up further but Jake stopped him.

"You still need to rest. You've got a lot of pain killers in you right now."

"I noticed." Wesley said. He was having a hard time focusing his vision and even to his own ears his speech was slow, his thoughts muddied. "So, she's around?"

"Yeah, around."

Wesley looked confused, then his features clarified and he leaned back against the pillow.

"Dillon."

Barry smiled sympathetically.

"Yeah."

"So, he's alright?"

"Worse than you but he's been conscious for about a day now, you've been in and out."

"Funny, I don't remember that." Wesley said and blinked his eyes. His eyelids were getting so heavy...

"Sheriff's getting everything clear with the Mayor and Briggs."

Wesley snorted.

"That'll take years. What are you for?" he asked.

"I'm here to protect you." Barry said with a grin. Wesley groaned.

"I'll ignore that." Jake said sportingly.

"You shot me, remember?"

"So imagine what I'd do to the other guy."

Wesley managed a weak smile. "I think I'd feel safer if..." Whatever he'd been planning on saying was lost, probably for the best, as sleep reclaimed him.

"I still don't know what the hell you were thinking." Fineas said, he sounded calm enough as he stood next to Wesley's bed later that day.

"I don't either," Wesley said groggily. "Stupid idea now. Guess I didn't think you'd do it. Really didn't think you'd shoot Howard."

Wesley seemed to be doing better at least he was sitting up. The events of... whenever it was he'd last been conscious swirled around his head.

"How long did you know it was Dillon?" Fineas asked.

Wesley shrugged, he noticed Fineas was on a first name basis with Howard and felt a small pang of jealousy. "I don't know. I always liked him for it but it took a while for me to realize it wasn't just wishful thinking."

"But you knew by the last crime scene."

"Why do you say that?" Wesley asked, trying to remember back.

His head was still puffy feeling and his thoughts felt like they had to strain through sand before coming to him.

"When you punched Dillon, that wasn't just because he said something to you, was it?"

"Oh, that." Wesley said. He could still see the shoe prints in the sand, left by a man with a habit of rocking on his heels when nervous.

"You contaminated the crime scene on purpose. You saw something there, something that could have dropped him in the suspect pool?"

"I didn't want Loren to go through that again, not if I could help it."

"So you were going to let a killer go free?"

"It wasn't him, least not then. Howard's deal wasn't about killing. That was always James. Speaking of James, what's going on with him?" he asked.

"It's being dealt with." Fineas said. He wanted Wesley recovered as soon as possible so he didn't want him fretting over the case.

"So what about your confrontation with Dillon, I'm assuming you knew by then?" Fineas asked rather dryly.

"I haven't done much in making your lives easier. I still owed you and I just figured I'd be the least missed. You'd been through it before…" he broke off with a shrug.

Fineas tried replying but found himself simultaneously choked with grief and filled with anger he finally settled on parental annoyance and growled. "Don't you ever do something like that again!" He took a calming breath. "Radburt found a botched fingerprint in Bell's Jeep. It would have exonerated you and would have placed suspicion on Dillon so it wouldn't have helped anyway."

"Radburt?"

"Apparently."

Wesley stared at Fineas for a moment. "Why..?" he stopped, afraid to go on, but nonetheless he did. "Why didn't you shoot me?"

"Because I couldn't!" he exclaimed. "Didn't you realize we've never gotten over you? I've missed you for three years, if I'd have shot you, if you'd died, do you have any idea what life would have been like? It wouldn't have been over for us and I don't want you to ever forget that!"

Wesley nodded. "You didn't shoot me, but you shot Dillon?"

"Because I know you. You've almost given up twice in the two decades I've known you. You weren't starting then. You were telling the truth, I knew that the whole time but I didn't want to tip off Dillon. I was hoping I could talk both of you down but just before you played that…" Fineas shook off the building anger. "Before you did what you did, I saw the look in his eyes. When you did that, he started to move. He was going to take you down and he was aiming for your head. I just meant to clip him, but I reacted too fast."

"Have you talked to him?" Wesley wondered.

"Yes." Fineas said simply.

"And?" Wesley asked.

"Not now. You need lots of rest still."

"I'm not going the break."

"Nonetheless…"

"Please?"

Fineas shrugged. "There's nothing to tell really, he won't talk and Bell won't deal."

Wesley nodded, he would expect nothing less.

"Where's Loren?"

Fineas frowned. "She's not here right now. She had to clear her head."

Wesley tried to hide his disappointment.

"But, she left this for you." Fineas said and handed Wesley a sealed envelope. Wesley took it, wondering if it would answer any of the questions he longed to ask but probably never would.

"Oh, she also borrowed your car."

Wesley smiled, after all she'd said about the automatic? He suspected she'd driven the Benz back home and in so doing had come to appreciate the merits he'd pointed out.

"The SL." Fineas added.

That changed things.

Wesley was even a touch annoyed although he did feel guilty for it. He was very possessive of the car that had been his mother's.

"Well, I'll let you get some rest." Fineas said, pulling Wesley away from his own musings. "I've got someone posted outside the door at all times, just in case."

"Would they happen to be any of the people I suspect still want me dead?"

Fineas just smiled. "I'll have the nurse lock your room. Good night." And with that Wesley was alone again.

Wesley looked at the letter in his hands and wondered what to do.

He was hurt that Loren hadn't seen him before she'd left. He didn't know entirely what she was going through but he thought he'd been through something similar.

To be fair he'd waited three years to talk about it.

He also knew that he loved her.

In his mind she'd always love him the most, more than Dillon and so now, she'd see the opportunity they had and act. Instead, she'd swindled the keys to his most valuable vehicle from his kind hearted guardian and left.

With uncharitable thoughts he opened the letter.

It wasn't a feeling he could sustain as the words began to blur through his tears.

He traced the salutation with his finger, and the signature.

"I love you." He whispered in the silence of his room.

CHAPTER 32

Two Months Later

Loren stood somberly at the gravesite.

She'd dressed in black, as was fitting, but she stoically avoided looking like the grieving fiancée.

She'd broken off their engagement after all.

She looked down at the simple tombstone, fitting for a civil servant of no great means, she looked at the letters but still found herself in shock. Too much had happened.

Dillon Howard was buried in ignominy. The whole town was in an uproar and for a time it had been liable to tear itself apart.

Dillon had never confessed to his role in the murders, but the case against him had been coming together. They said it was only a matter of time before they had him. All he needed to do was give up James Jefferson, but the D.A.'s office wasn't willing to lower the charges enough to coax Dillon into rolling on the ringleader. Maybe it had also been fear.

If so, it was well founded.

Dillon's murder had been very public, so while Loren hadn't been there to witness the horrible event, News 12's cameras had captured it and played it over and over and over.

Eventually she'd seen it.

Her father had been against the media presence, as Dillon was escorted out of the hospital, but it was the State Police who had the final say.

The Jefferson's used the crowd as cover.

Loren felt woozy again, standing next to the grave. She was used to the feeling. Her week long escape hadn't dispelled it and she still found herself at times on the edge of losing control.

But at least it was a feeling her family understood.

One of them very intimately.

She looked over her shoulder at the lone figure, hanging back, away from the group of mourners.

Wesley Cobin wore black as well, but he kept his distance out of respect to the man that had hated him. He felt many things, but not guilt, at least not for the things he'd had no part of.

Perhaps, if he'd tried harder three years ago, five people would still be alive. Dillon Howard wouldn't have stooped to collude with James Jefferson to plan murder, or at least cover it up.

But he had done nothing more than set the stage, he hadn't written the script. They each had delivered their own lines.

"I don't know how you managed to pull this one off."

Wesley didn't turn, he recognized the voice of Commander Briggs and he had no desire for a confrontation. Not now.

"I have to give you credit, you managed to get the only two people who could prove your guilt to turn on each other a whole month after your little 'tell all'. That took planning."

Wesley wanted to sigh, but he was too tired.

"There's nothing I can say that will change your mind so please forgive me for not trying." he said wearily.

"James is still out there, we can still get the truth. Just when you think you got away with it, when this whole thing has blown over, I'll be there."

Wesley turned to face Briggs, against his better instincts.

"It never blows over." he said. "It never goes away. Life goes on but it's never the same."

"No, but it looks an awful lot like you're getting everything you want."

Wesley wanted to say something, to make Briggs understand that he would never have put Loren through something like this, but there was no point.

"Well I hope you find time to carry on the man hunt after your disciplinary hearing." Wesley said, forcing himself to smile smugly, but it wasn't an action he enjoyed as much as he used to.

He hadn't won.

He'd survived.

But to someone like Briggs, they were one and the same.

EPILOGUE

Fineas walked from his office to the squad room, espresso in hand.

He looked over the scattered desks and then checked his watch.

Jake Barry and Timothy Langston, one of the new kids, were the only two there.

It was five after.

"Where's your partner?" he asked Barry.

Barry shrugged, about to give a reply when the phone on his desk rang. Fineas nodded for him to answer it.

"Deputy Jake Barry." Barry answered.

Fineas headed toward the front desk, half listening to Jake's phone conversation.

"What? Of course. Where? Did you say swamp?"

Tully tried puzzling out what swamp in question the call was about.

Outside he saw the Jeep whip into the parking lot and aim for its designated parking space. He was surprised that Radburt allowed the Jeep out of the garage as mud clung to the wheel wells and coated the burgundy paint work in a fine brown haze.

Speaking of swamps. He thought and wondered just where his soon-to-be son-in-law had been.

Outside Wesley hurried toward the station.

It was rare for him to be late.

But, the kid did have a lot on his mind, not that the wedding hadn't been in the works long enough. It was past four years since his first proposal.

Barry interrupted Fineas' thoughts.

"Sheriff," Tully turned to his deputy, who had the telephone receiver pressed to his ear. His expression was grim. "I'm on with a Sheriff's office in South Carolina. They just pulled a body out of a swamp."

Tully's grip tightened on his mug. "What?" he asked distantly, déjà vu raising the hair on his neck.

His deputy sighed before delivering the news.

"They think they found James Jefferson."

Made in the USA
Charleston, SC
06 September 2012